# DEAD LIKE ME

## KELLY MILLER

Black Rose Writing

www.blackrosewriting.com

ISBN: 978-1-61296-150-7

PUBLISHED BY BLACK ROSE WRITING

www.blackrosewriting.com

Printed in the United States of America

*Dead Like Me* is printed in Garamond

*Dedicated to my family
for their never-ending support.*

# Acknowledgments

Publishing my first novel is a dream come true. I couldn't have done it without the help of a long list of people. Please indulge me while I take a moment to especially thank:

God. Thank you for this amazing ride.

My most precious family members: Winston, Emily, Andrew, and Daniel. Thank you for sharing me with my characters. I couldn't have done this without your love and support. Even though three of you are too young to read my novel, you'll always be my biggest fans.

My mom, Cindy Bass. We've lived a lot of life together and there's no one I would have rather had by my side.

The dynamic duo of Danny and Tracy DeGrace. Danny is my go-to guy for all things police related. Any procedural mistakes are mine and mine alone. His wife Tracy is an ER nurse who's always there to help me answer the tough medical questions.

My critique group: Jessica Ruth, Chris Coad Taylor, Lisa Vogt, and Skip Warren. Thank you for critiquing my work. My words are better for it, and the body shots were worth it.

My readers: Julie Ard, Dave Miller, Kristine Mylroie, Fran Orenstein, Patricia Reeb, and Lisa Vogt.

Officer Roy Paz and all the men and women who work for the Tampa Police Department.

Reagan Rothe at Black Rose Writing for taking a shot on an unknown author.

M.G. for letting me use his poetic words written a lifetime ago on a Dairy Queen order form.

Vince and Ruth Kegel for using their superb photographic skills to make me look beautiful.

The Florida Writers Association and all of its members.

My blog readers whose encouragement sustained me on this very long journey.

We did it!

# DEAD
# LIKE
# ME

# TUESDAY

# CHAPTER 1

Taking a deep breath, I ducked under the yellow crime scene tape strung between two ancient oaks. Early this morning a call came in from Thonotosassa, a small city bordering Tampa on the northeast side. Just on the fringe of our jurisdiction. Apparently, a neighbor walking his dog had discovered the body of a young Caucasian female.

Following the dirt driveway, I arrived at a vacant, single-story house. Scratch that. Make that a rotting, vacant house. The weather's so different in Florida compared to where I grew up in the suburbs of Chicago. Up north the drastic temperature changes make paint peel away from the houses. Down here, the paint stays intact, but left unchecked a black mold can devour a home. The end result was a place looking like the one in front of me—as if some disease ate away at it from the inside out. I estimated the house stood on two acres of land. Although there were neighbors on either side of the property, the trees surrounding it gave it a secluded feel.

"Welcome back, Detective Springer," a chipper voice called from behind me.

Looking over my shoulder, I saw my partner of two years, jogging to catch up.

"Yeah. Great welcome present. You really shouldn't have." Snapping on my latex gloves, I wondered how much worse this day could get.

"Glad to see the shrink cleared you for duty."

"Finished my last session this morning." I assumed Dr. Grace would authorize my return to work today, but I'd stormed out of her office before I could work out the details. "A case is just what I need. Maybe I'll finally be able to work the smell of bleach off my hands. I don't think my bathtub can survive my staying home one more day."

Detective Patrick Jessup chuckled and flashed a boyish grin. *Probably trying to envision a domestic Kate Springer.*

I hit the lottery in partner assignments. When I moved to Tampa, it took seven years of busting my ass before I saw a promotion. There were plenty of detectives who didn't want a woman watching their back. Patrick wasn't one of them. He had six sisters and often joked he was most comfortable in a room full of estrogen.

At thirty-five, Patrick still had that "all-American" boy next door look. His unassuming presence lent itself well to his profession. On more than one occasion, perps had underestimated Detective Jessup only to find themselves caged behind two-inch steel bars. With his good looks and chiseled physique, I used to tease he was probably the high school quarterback who married the prom queen. Got it half right. He was a star ball player at the University of South Florida until a defensive end cut his career short with a blitz that shattered his right kneecap.

It sounded like all the action was at the back of the property. Patrick and I walked around the house to the rear tree line where crime scene tech Lucy James was hunched over photographing a small mound. It was partially covered with sticks, brush, and decomposing leaves.

"A neighbor found the body before work this morning," Lucy said. "Actually, his dog is the one who found it."

Lucy stepped back and lowered her camera. I squatted to get a closer look. The leaves surrounding the girl's right arm had been trampled. Her right hand lay exposed, palm side up. Her wrist revealed a jagged double heart-shaped birthmark. Teeth marks surrounded her thumb, likely made by the dog who found her. With all the barking I'd heard since I arrived, I was surprised a whole pack of mutts hadn't sniffed the body out.

The stench of death smacked me full in the face as the wind suddenly shifted. After all these years, I still hadn't become accustomed to the smell. It was like taking a whiff from a partially sealed milk jug, one sitting outside in the direct sunlight for two weeks.

Lucy knelt beside me, bagging debris that would later be tested for trace evidence. Most of the leaves on and surrounding the face had been scattered from either the wind or the dog. I could tell the victim was female, but I waited for Lucy to finish gathering the last few stray pieces before the girl's features could be seen.

Stifling a quick gasp with a fake cough, I lurched up and stepped away. "Sorry . . . I don't want to contaminate . . . the evidence." It was a weak excuse but all I could come up with.

After steadying myself, I glanced over my shoulder to make sure I'd seen correctly. Lying on the ground, face towards the sky was me at the age of thirteen.

## CHAPTER 2

Okay, so it wasn't *really* me, but the child on the ground was definitely a dead ringer for the young girl I used to be—except the hair. More than two decades later, I'd expect better taste than what we had in the '80s. I tried to make light of the situation, anything to get my mind off what I'd seen. But my vision blurred. I leaned against a nearby tree, praying no one noticed it was the only thing keeping me upright.

Patrick appeared at my side and in a hushed tone asked, "Are you alright, Kate?"

No way in hell was I going to tell my partner this small discarded child was the spitting image of me at that age. At least not until I got a handle on what it all meant.

"I'm fine," I said, avoiding those concerned eyes that could read me all too easily. "I think I just swallowed a damn lovebug."

I lead the way back to the body, feeling Patrick's questioning stare burn into my back. Harry Ellis, the medical examiner, was checking the victim's internal temperature to estimate time of death.

Lucy looked up at me and mouthed, "Are you okay?"

*What was I, an open book today?* To be fair though, Lucy was my best friend and could read me pretty well. Although, if I were being painfully honest, she was my only female friend. I've never been much into bff's, sleepovers, and painting each other's toenails.

Lucy James was one of the first people I met after moving to Tampa. We had a case where some truly ingenious thinking on her part turned up a knitting needle during a search of a townhouse. The discovery of the murder weapon led me directly to the killer. Since then, we've been pretty tight.

I gave a slight nod to my friend and looked down at the girl lying on the ground. She wore all black—shirt, jeans, and tennis shoes. Her only jewelry was cheap tarnished hoops in her ears. Lucy carefully removed the long strands of jet-black hair that had become tangled on the victim's forehead.

I turned my attention back to the medical examiner, kneeling over the body. "Figured out time of death yet?" I noticed the gruffness in my voice and reminded myself to play nice.

"As you know," Harry Ellis said, "estimating the time of death is not an exact science. This extended period of extreme heat we've been experiencing definitely speeds up the rate of decomposition. She's in full rigor and has a body temp of 82 degrees. Taking the variables into consideration, I'd estimate she's been dead between ten and fourteen hours. That puts time of death Monday evening somewhere between 7 – 11 p.m."

Ellis collected some of the insects feasting on the body then gently lifted the victim's shoulder off the ground. "From the purplish bruising on her backside, it looks like she was left in that position after being strangled. I'm not sure if the perp killed her at this location or somewhere else before dumping her body here."

"Strangled?"

"Yes. The bruising on her neck is consistent with manual strangulation. And her eyes show petechial hemorrhaging. Of course, I can't say for certain until I open her up, but that's the preliminary cause of death. It should get you started anyway."

I looked closer at the bruising on the victim's neck. "Do you know what she was strangled with?"

"Good old fashioned hands. The deep purple discoloration and outline of thumbs on either side of the wind pipe indicates the killer was facing the victim while strangling her."

"So she saw it coming," Patrick said. "There's a good chance the victim fought back against her attacker. Maybe we'll find some skin cells underneath her fingernails."

"One can only hope," Ellis agreed. "I'll bag her hands to make sure any evidence isn't contaminated."

"Can you estimate her age?" I asked. *Focus, Springer. Focus.*

"Gauging from her bone structure, I'd guess somewhere in the range of eleven to fourteen."

"What about identification on the body?"

"Nope. Nothing in her pockets—no ID, keys, or cell."

"Any sign of sexual trauma?" Patrick made no effort to mask the disgust in his voice.

"No immediate signs. However, the button from her jeans is missing," Ellis said, pointing just above the zipper of his own pants.

"How soon can you autopsy the body?" Patrick asked.

"Not until tomorrow. I'll try and get you my final report by Friday."

"Friday?" I threw up my hands. "Are you serious?"

Patrick grabbed my elbow and pulled me aside. "What's wrong with you, Kate? Are you intentionally trying to piss Ellis off? You know these things take time. It's not like ours is the only body in the morgue. Keep dishing out this attitude and our Jane Doe will end up last on his list."

"It's just . . ." I jerked my arm away from him. "Fine. You're right."

"Now if you think you can stay out of trouble, I'm going next door to interview Eric Steele, the dog owner. Maybe he can give me some information about this house and who owns it. I also want to get a timeline on his whereabouts last night."

"Fine. I'm going to head out to the street. Take a fresh look around." I was in no mood to talk to anyone right now anyway. Thoughts were all jumbled in my head, swirling as if on a Tilt-A-Whirl at the county fair.

Realizing my fists were clinched so tightly they ached, I took a few deep breaths and slowly opened my fingers. First my counseling session with Dr. Grace, now a look-alike murder victim. The hits just kept coming.

As I saw it, there were two ways this could play out. First, my resemblance to the dead girl was a coincidence. Maybe my imagination was running in overdrive. The other option—the victim was somehow linked to me. I know I'd never seen her before, so until we could identify the body, I'd have to put that supposition on hold. If I let myself, I could go round and round until I drove myself crazy.

*Get it together, Springer. There's a little girl counting on you to bring her killer to justice.* Couldn't do that if my own problems were taking center stage. After a few more deep breaths, I did what came naturally. I pictured myself stuffing my emotions into a box and shoving it high on a shelf. I'd get back to them later. I knew from experience, they wouldn't be ignored for long. For now, I needed to calmly and objectively look at the scene before me.

Once I reached the street, I felt steadier. I looked around to get a feel for the area. Why this piece of property? What made the killer pick this house? I already knew the person who murdered the victim cared about her because he, or I guess she, took the time to cover the body. It showed remorse. In most cases, I'd find a blanket covering the victim. But with the dogs barking, the killer might have been worried about detection. Instead, he covered the girl with whatever was lying around. I still wondered why the killer dumped the body where it was relatively easy to find. Why not bury her at a quieter location?

The main road was well-traveled, at least during rush hour. Many commuters tried to bypass the gridlock on I-75 by taking the more scenic route of Morris Bridge Road. Across the street was wooded. On this side of the road, the overgrowth of trees camouflaged the houses. Even the black mailboxes seemed to blend into their surroundings.

The neighbor who'd discovered the body, Eric Steele, lived on the left side of the crime scene's property. A dark colored wooden fence obstructed the view of his driveway. Stenciled across the middle was a crude skull and crossbones, turned a dingy white color. *Lovely.* I'm sure Patrick was enjoying his interview with the dog owner.

This property had no gate covering it. Instead a rusted sign stood sentry at the front of the driveway. It dangled on one hook and looked as if it were about to be devoured by the trees. I yanked off the leaves obscuring the words and realized it was an advertisement for the sale of the property. I jotted down the bank's name and contact information, and punched their number into my phone. We needed their permission to search the house. We couldn't prove a crime had been committed inside, so we had no probable cause for a search.

After numerous transfers and waiting on hold listening to mind numbing Muzak, I rethought my decision on getting a warrant. Might have been quicker after all. Finally, I got clearance from all the necessary parties and a promise they'd send me the names of the previous owners. I headed back towards the house, walking in the grass parallel to the dirt driveway.

"Hey, Russo." I gestured over to the newest crime scene tech in the division. "Come here for a minute. Looks like we've got tire treads from a single vehicle. Can you take some photos?" The faint marks were scattered along the entire length of the driveway.

Russo removed the lens cap from his camera. "They don't look composed enough to get a decent cast impression."

"I'm thankful we haven't had rain these past two days. Pretty unheard of during rainy season. Our crime scene could have been a complete washout."

At the end of the driveway, there were foot impressions, but again too wind scattered. Drag marks began where the tire treads stopped. *Definite dump job.*

Before going to examine the inside of the house, I coordinated with the technicians intending to search the surrounding wooded area for evidence. We decided a grid search would be the best option. I didn't envy them the task at hand. Oak and pine trees jostled for position making a very dense search area. Avoiding all the prickly plants no matter how careful they were looked impossible. The techs would be picking tiny thorns out of their clothes for a week.

After Russo finished cataloging the tracks, I dragged him into the house to begin our search. If the place chose today to crumble to the ground, at least I wouldn't be alone.

# **CHAPTER 3**

Finally finished searching the house, I stood on its dilapidated porch while the sweat beading up on my neck poured down my back. My short sleeved blouse clung to my skin. A tickle on my forearm caught my attention, and I grabbed a rogue lovebug, throwing him to the ground. Lovebugs were lightning bugs minus the light. The damn things were attracted to the hottest thing they could find. Unfortunately now, that was me.

I looked up and saw Patrick squeeze through the trees that acted as a natural boundary line between this property and Steele's. Patrick's lips were pursed, and I doubted his red face had anything to do with the heat as he swiped at the pine needles sticking to his khakis. Wrinkles, stains—it was enough to ruin his whole day. Odd how it contradicted his easy-going personality. Though not vain, Patrick had some serious pet peeves. His clothes were one of them.

Unlike Patrick, I accepted the fact when I worked an outdoor crime scene, I'd be a crumpled mess. Later, I'd grab some extra clothes from my trunk and change back at the precinct. For now, I reached up and pulled out the simple ponytail holder working overtime to keep my hair together. I put the band around my wrist and used my fingers to smooth out my straight hair. The Florida sunshine had brought out the blond highlights in my normally light brown hair. Unfortunately, the sun also made freckles pop out on and around my nose. Cute as a button was not a description any detective liked to hear. At least I'd been able to keep the crow's feet away. I'd just turned thirty-seven, but my friends said I could easily pass for ten years younger. Then again, all my friends were cops, and they're notorious liars.

"I've got a new one for you, Patrick." I grinned, looking down at the cuticle I'd been picking at since I discarded my latex gloves. "What's the name of the newspaper where Peter Parker got a job in the comic book *Spider-man*?"

Sometime during the past couple of years, Patrick and I had started asking each other trivia questions. Who knew how it started? We'd shoot them back and forth when there was a lag in the investigation or the tension needed cut. We each tried to come up with some forgotten little fact to stump one another. Although by unspoken agreement, it couldn't be too archaic a question. Patrick asked more television and movie related questions, while I quizzed him on history and other boy topics.

"That's the best you've got?" he shot back.

"Quit stalling." I walked down the porch steps, joining him near the dirt driveway.

"*The Daily Bugle.*" A smile spread across his face.

An easy one, I'll admit, but at least I got his mind off his pants.

"Did you find anything useful in the house?" Patrick asked.

"Not unless you call crushed beer cans and roaches the size of your fist useful. From the amount of cobwebs hanging in the house, it looks like it's been empty for years. Russo is processing a few things inside, but I think it's a dead end. I doubt the killer even went in the house. Smart move," I said, looking back at the place. "The bank gave us permission to search the house. They took it over in March 2009 and have yet to unload it. When I get back to the precinct, I'm hoping I'll have the names of the previous owners waiting for me. Did you have fun with Steele?"

Patrick groaned. "Loads. Besides working for one of those home helper companies doing repair jobs for little old ladies, Steele's a dog breeder." Patrick looked down at his pants again, angrily brushing at the black hairs clinging to the material. "He reported last night around 1 a.m. his Labradors were causing a commotion. I could tell Steele felt bad that he didn't go check it out, but in the past, he'd drag himself out of bed only to find a raccoon or armadillo scurrying past the pens."

"Let's look at the timeline. The victim could have been killed as early as 7 p.m. on Monday night. Then dumped here around 1 a.m. this morning and discovered later at 7:30 a.m. Where was Steele last night?"

"He looks solid. Monday he was at the lanes with his bowling league. He's divorced so he usually stays late hanging out with his buddies at the bar. Steele didn't get home until approximately 12:30 a.m., and he'd just hit the sack when he heard the dogs. That's why he didn't want to get up again. I'll check his story out later, but I think we can cross him off our list."

"Does he know who used to own this house?" I asked.

"No. Steele's only lived next door for the past year. He bought the place right after he married wife number two. She's not in the picture anymore, but Steele said the house next door was vacant when they moved in. I'm going to talk to the responding officer who canvassed the neighborhood and see if I can find out anything else."

"I'll go back to the precinct and start checking missing persons. Try to get an ID on our girl. Then I'll follow the paper trail on the house."

"Good. You're so much better at all that computer stuff." Patrick batted his eyelashes. Definitely not pulling off sweet and demure.

"Are you trying to butter me up, Detective Jessup?" I played along even though I knew better. Once upon a time Patrick had considered getting an undergraduate degree in computer science. He's a real whiz with a keyboard. He changed his mind because he couldn't stand being cooped up all day. Whenever the option presented itself, he chose interviewing witnesses or searching for suspects.

Walking towards us, Lucy James interjected. "Most people think because the saying 'butter up' means to thickly lay on the flattery it comes from how smoothly butter spreads on bread. Not true. There's an ancient custom where Indians would throw butterballs of ghee at the statues of the gods to seek favor."

When Patrick raised his eyebrows, Lucy added, "Ghee is clarified butter Indians commonly used in their cooking."

"Oh, of course . . . ghee." Patrick tried to remain straight-faced.

I just made a big show of rolling my eyes and told Lucy I'd call her later. Too bad I didn't have some ghee and a statue. I could use some favor about now.

Patrick walked me back to my car. "You sure you're okay?" he asked. "I mean the inquiry cleared you of any wrong doing in the shooting. I know it was only the second time you've ever had to pull your gun, but you have to remember, it was self-defense."

Patrick thought my moodiness was due to the officer-involved shooting investigation. If only. "Really. I'm fine, Patrick."

Patrick looked down at the ground, knocking a few pebbles into the grass. "Sorry I only called once while you were on leave. It's been a hell of a time for me too. Alina and I finally put her mother into a residential care facility. Her Alzheimer's has progressed too rapidly. She can't stay at home by herself anymore."

I placed my hand lightly on Patrick's forearm. "I am so sorry, Patrick. Make sure you tell your wife my thoughts are with her." He said he would and turned to leave.

Back in my car, I rested my forehead against the steering wheel. Strands of hair fell forward fanning around the wheel. I was being a self-centered bitch not offering Patrick more than a lame *I'm sorry,* but right now I couldn't handle anyone else's problems. I could barely deal with my own.

What the hell was I doing keeping vital information from my partner? If Patrick held back a detail on a case, no matter how insignificant, I'd never forgive him. Not disclosing the fact I resembled our Jane Doe, whether it was important or not, could forever damage our relationship.

What would Dr. Grace think of this new development? Finally alone, I couldn't help but replay the last fifteen minutes of my counseling session. It was like a movie seared into my brain. One that couldn't be turned off with a flick of a remote.

I could hear Dr. Nina Grace asking me, "Why didn't you share this when we first met after the shooting?"

"Don't take this personally, Doc," I said avoiding her intense gaze, "but I don't make a habit of getting all gushy with complete strangers."

"What made you decide to tell me today? There has to be some serious stressors in your life to make you open up now, thirty years after it all started." Dr. Grace sat with her hands folded together, resting underneath her chin as if in prayer.

When I didn't answer, she added, "Most victims don't disclose about their abuse until they're in crisis. What's going on with you, Kate?"

Fidgeting in my chair, my body instantly stilled when I heard the word *victim*. "First of all Dr. Grace, I am nobody's victim. I haven't been that frightened little girl in a long time." Once I got the words out, I unclenched my jaw, took a calming breath, and tried to get more comfortable in my overstuffed seat. Impossible. "And secondly, you're not the only person I've talked to about this. It's just . . ."

What was I doing? Only a few minutes left on the clock, and here I was baring my soul. All I had to do was get through this last session, and I could be done with these weekly heart-to-hearts. The department had put me on paid leave and forced me to visit the good doctor's office after shooting a suspect in a kidnapping case gone bad. Well, gone bad for the kidnapper that was for sure, since he was now six feet under in a long wooden box. I'd put him there, which landed me in this damned uncomfortable chair.

Finishing my thought, I repeated, "It's just talking to you about this case these past couple of weeks . . . I guess it hit too close to home. The kidnapper was the little girl's grandfather. He'd molested her for years before he snatched and murdered her. There were too many similarities to my own story. Why? Are you surprised I was molested as a child?" I scanned Dr. Grace's face, looking for signs of disgust or even worse, pity.

"No. From what you've said in previous sessions, I suspected there may have been some sexual trauma in your past."

"*Some* sexual trauma," I smirked. "That's a nice way to put it, Doc. But how about we call it what it really was. Six years of living hell! Six years of weekends and summer vacations at the mercy of a sick bastard who liked to touch little girls." During my tirade, I realized I'd wrapped my hands so tightly around the ends of the chair my knuckles were turning white. Slowly, I unpeeled each finger, allowing blood to flow back into them.

Dr. Grace sat across from me in her high-backed chair staring, willing me with those big brown all-seeing eyes to go on. She must have understood the need to purge the toxic thoughts running through my head.

"And do you know who it was pretending to care so much about me during the day but whose mask came off at night to reveal the real monster? Robert White."

One second fuming and full of anger, now I could barely say his name above a whisper. "Robert White. My babysitter. The man my mother had entrusted to take care of me. I was only seven. He was old enough to be my grandfather. He always . . . no . . . I can't."

Abruptly I stood, knocking over the vase of flowers sitting on the table next to my chair. I barely registered the water tumbling out onto the floor as I ran from the room.

I heard a distant honking of a car horn. I raised my head up off the steering wheel, looking blankly out the dusty windshield. Was I really so overwhelmed with my memories of abuse that I was projecting the face of my thirteen-year-old self onto this unknown victim? *Dammit! Why couldn't I put the past behind me?* I'd seen the shrinks, talked until I had no words left. But every few years, the emotions rolled over me like a tidal wave.

Before I could talk myself out of it, I grabbed my phone and punched in Dr. Grace's number. My shaky fingers kept hitting an 8 instead of a 9, forcing me to redial twice. I had to leave a message.

"Dr. Grace, this is Kate Springer. Can we talk . . . soon? I know today was supposed to be our last session but something happened at my crime scene this morning, and well . . . I'm going to be swamped these next few days with the investigation, but I'm sure I can get away for a few minutes later today or this evening. Just call me . . . and thanks."

# CHAPTER 4

Back at the precinct, I rolled my chair up to the desk and pulled out my notebook. I wanted to jot down my impressions of the crime scene in the hopes of organizing my thoughts. For a visual, I grabbed my cell phone and brought up a picture of the young victim. I wondered if right now some mother was frantically searching for her daughter, her little girl who never made it home last night. I placed my thumb just above the victim's hairline and studied her facial features. The resemblance was uncanny. Thirteen. An extremely challenging age, but for me a liberating one.

I heard coughing and lifted my head off my palms. Should have kept it down. Detective Donald Wozniack glared at me with his usual contemptible sneer. He was a lifer in the department. The one always passed up for promotions, but with a case clearance rate high enough to keep him on the force. Over time the chip on his shoulder had grown so large even if someone wanted to pat him on the back, they'd need a ladder. Seemed like that chip grew every time I was around.

"What's wrong, Springer? You on the rag?"

"Yeah. Thanks for the tampon I lifted from your desk this morning." I could see the color rush up his neck towards his cheeks. He looked like a teapot ready to whistle. Smart ass remarks wouldn't win me any points, but to hell with it. I didn't have to take shit from older men anymore.

When he marched off, I turned my attention back to the list I'd compiled. White preteen/teen female, strangled Monday between 7-11 p.m., body left behind vacant house approximately 1 a.m. Tuesday, body left exposed yet covered up indicating sign of remorse, killer knew victim?

I needed to find out if anyone matching the physical description of our victim had been reported missing so I entered the girl's pertinent information into the NCIC—National Crime Information Center—the nationwide database for missing persons. I included eye and hair color; sex; race; approximate height, weight, and age. The double heart-shaped birthmark on her right wrist would help reduce the number of bogus matches.

As usual, the system moved at a snail's pace. Absently, I thought back to when I was thirteen and the event that had finally pushed me into divulging the secret of my abuse.

I'd been staying the weekend at Robert White's house and hadn't been feeling well. I walked into the kitchen, hoping to find some acetaminophen in one of the drawers. Robert rushed up behind me. I jumped when he grabbed my arm.

"Katie! You're bleeding. What's wrong?"

"What do you mean?"

Robert pointed to the back of my shorts. I twisted my head to see what he was looking at. Then it dawned on me. Horrible cramps had wracked my abdomen for the last couple of days. In fifth grade, I'd learned about the menstruation cycle, so I knew its biology. But to start my period here, in front of Robert, was beyond mortifying.

When I finally managed to stammer out that I'd started menstruating, I had to repeat myself twice. I could barely find the words much less say them out loud. I summoned the courage to meet Robert's eyes and saw a murderous look of hate radiating from them. My skin crawled with the heat of his stare. Robert stepped closer to me, his face looking down at mine. I felt the warmth of his breath when he exhaled, the stench of stale cigarettes lingered.

"What good are you now?" The way he uttered those few words, in a cold measured tone, was scarier than if he'd yelled them with seething rage. He stormed out of the house, slamming the door so hard it actually cracked the frame. I fell to the floor and pulled my knees up to my chest. I rocked back and forth, bleeding into my underwear terrified of what he would do to me later that night.

A beeping noise broke my reverie, and I glanced over at my computer.

If there was a hit, I'd have a name to go with my victim. *Nothing yet.* The ping must have originated from Jones' desk as he was the only other detective in the homicide room.

One large common space on the eighth floor housed us all. There were seven desks, actually just six plus one dry docked boat. Staring over at Detective Jones' corner, I couldn't help but smile. Jones, an avid fisherman, was only half a year shy of his retirement. Pranks ran rampant in the department, and last month a couple of the guys got him good. They'd rigged his desk to look like a boat. White PVC piping sat on top of his desk about two feet high, imitating a bimini. The opposite side of the desk had a ship's wheel bolted to the side panel. It even turned. The finishing touch was a metal cleat nailed to the middle of his desk. How he worked around the huge hunk of steel I'll never know? But Jones loved it and laughed harder than anyone.

A message popped up on my computer screen—No Match Found. Guess my victim didn't have family searching for her yet. Nobody had reported her missing. My Jane Doe may have had no one caring for her when she was alive, but I was in her corner now, and I'd be damned if I let her down.

I jerked open my desk drawer, hoping to find something to tide me over until I could pick up a late lunch. My lucky streak was still intact—I found nothing. Tuning out my growling stomach, I turned my attention towards the email I'd received from the bank. Time to start hunting down the previous owners of the Thonotosassa house.

<>

A little before 2 p.m., I turned away from my desk, my nose involuntarily sniffing at the air. A wonderful greasy smell taunted my belly. Before I could seek out the culprit, Patrick showed up with my favorite burger from Five Guys.

"If you weren't married, I'd kiss you."

That big sheepish smile I'd come to love, spread over his face. Of course, Patrick was more like the little brother I never had, but I still liked to poke fun at him.

"Though rarely seen, what was the name of Norm's wife on *Cheers?*" Patrick asked, plucking a fry out of his own greasy lunch bag.

"Are you kidding me? I've seen every episode of *Cheers.* Twice. That's an easy one. Vera."

Last Christmas, I bought two copies of the same trivia book. I gave one to Patrick, the other I'd been slowly memorizing. Since receiving the gift, he'd yet to stump me, and I could tell it frustrated the hell out of him. For a detective, he sure was a little slow on the uptake. Then again, it could just be a guy thing.

Patrick rebounded from his stinging defeat, all business. He scooted his chair over to my desk to deliver his report, unpacking his lunch while he spoke. I already had half my burger eaten.

"Eric Steele's alibi for the night of the murder holds up. The owner of Royal Lanes confirmed Steele showed up shortly after 5 p.m. to bowl on his league. He stayed late, closing the place down. In fact, once midnight rolled around, the owner had a hard time getting rid of Steele and his drinking buddies. I talked to the other neighbors. Of course, they were all hear no evil, see no evil, and shocked tragedy struck right next door."

"Typical. I couldn't find a missing person's report on our Jane Doe. There's no listing that fits her description. Pitiful a girl so young hasn't been missed yet."

Patrick visibly cringed. My heart went out to him. These cases were especially hard on him considering he had three young daughters.

"Got luckier on the house where we found the body," I said, munching on a fry. "The last owners, actually the only owners, were a Mr. and Mrs. Lynch. A computer search confirmed they're still together. They have adjoining plots over at Oak View Cemetery. Evelyn Lynch died three years ago of pancreatic cancer. Everett died a year later from a heart attack. The good news," I said, rubbing my hands together, "is they're survived by one son. Tommy Lynch."

"Keep it coming." Patrick put down his sandwich. He could probably smell the trail beginning to heat up, like a bloodhound ready to follow a fresh scent.

I looked down at a copy of Lynch's driver's license. "Says here, he was born in 1968 which makes him forty-two now. He's 5'9", 240 pounds. Which means—"

"He's shorter and fatter."

"Right. Who doesn't lie on their driver's license? He's got a chubby face but still has all of his hair."

Patrick craned his neck to get a better look at Lynch's picture. "Maybe our Jane Doe somehow stumbled into Tommy Lynch's cross hairs. He strangles her and dumps the body behind his parent's old house."

"Didn't you say Eric Steele has only lived next door for a year? If you do the math, Lynch would never have known a whole pack of barking dogs moved in next door."

"We need to get Lynch in here for questioning."

"Good luck with that."

The phone on Patrick's desk rang. He turned around to answer it, and I snagged a handful of his fries.

"Detective Jessup."

Patrick listened to the caller for a moment and pushed a button on the phone so I could listen in.

"Harry, I put you on speaker so Detective Springer could listen in. Can you repeat what you said? We didn't catch it all."

"If you haven't put a name to your Jane Doe yet, I might be able to help identify her."

"Did you find some ID on the body after all?" Patrick asked the medical examiner.

"In a manner of speaking. My assistant Joel was prepping the body for autopsy. Looks like my schedule's freer than I thought. I'll be able to get to it later this afternoon. Anyway, the victim's shoe fell off when Joel removed the body bag. He happened to see some writing in the heel. It wasn't legible in the right shoe, but when he checked the left one it had the name Kimberly Callahan scrawled in black marker."

"That's great, Harry. You've been a big help."

"I'll call if something else jumps out at me. Oh, and hey Jessup, thanks again for those Lightning tickets. I can't believe you got rink side seats to the home opener next month. My son's a huge hockey fan."

"Not a problem. Enjoy." Patrick disconnected the call.

"Suddenly found room in his schedule? Yeah, right."

Patrick gave me a wink. "By the way, I got a call from Lucy on the way upstairs. The search of the surrounding wooded area was a bust. They sent everything over to FDLE but doubt any of it belongs to our murder scene." The Florida Department of Law Enforcement was responsible for analyzing trace evidence. Our lab only processed latent prints.

"Lookie here," Wozniack interrupted. I'd failed to notice his return to the homicide room. "If it isn't Malibu Barbie and Ken."

Patrick and I looked at each other as if asking *did he really just say that*. Patrick shrugged off the insult, but my cheeks reddened. I couldn't believe I let that horse's ass get under my skin. Jones and a couple of the other detectives in the room were laughing along. That's all we needed, a new in-house nickname. Before I could fire back a retort, Wozniack lumbered off to answer his ringing phone.

To divert my attention, Patrick reminded me, "We need to find an address for Kimberly Callahan and go give her parents the bad news. Before a reporter does it for us."

Patrick hated this part of the job even more than I did. He still hadn't gotten the knack of detaching from the moment like I had. Years of practice proved I could be present in the here and now yet far removed from the emotions it created.

"But first," he said, cleaning up the mess from his lunch, "we need to update Sergeant Kray on what we've discovered so far."

"I can tell you what he'll say." I dropped my voice to a deep base. "Jessup, Springer, you better watch your asses on this one. Young, white female found murdered. I don't have to tell you what a media nightmare this is going to be. You'd better find this asshole and fast. And whatever you do, keep your faces out of the paper!"

# <u>CHAPTER 5</u>

After the short but not so sweet meeting with Sergeant Kray, Patrick and I took separate cars to Kimberly Callahan's house located south of Bearss Avenue on Wedgewood Drive. Kimberly's neighborhood was only thirteen miles from the crime scene but at least a twenty-five minute drive in Tampa traffic. More during rush hour.

I pulled up in front of the house and noticed a beat up Chevrolet Caprice in the driveway. Though Kimberly lived in a densely populated neighborhood, the area didn't look very neighborly. The houses were in various states of disrepair with more dirt than grass in the tiny rectangles posing as front yards.

Tampa's a patchwork quilt kind of town. You had the poor neighborhoods like the Callahan's where kids grew up too fast, became parents too early, and stayed within a ten-block radius their entire lives. Then you had the yuppies that lived in Hyde Park and the United Nations over in the heart of New Tampa—folks from Haiti, Turkey, India, New Jersey.

The Callahan's house sagged under its own weight. The front screen door barely hung on, attached only at the top bracket. Patrick used a light touch to get it open or the door would have fallen on top of him. The block house looked as if it was originally painted yellow but after a long battle lost to the elements, the only hint of color peeked through near the roof. Mold had crept up the walls. Now they were mostly brownish green.

Patrick knocked on the front door for almost a minute. Finally, we heard a woman holler for us to come in. Since mom couldn't be bothered to make it to the door and gave a shout out instead, she was either expecting someone or not concerned about the security of her neighborhood. Patrick entered the house first, surveying the room before stepping aside so I could enter. I had to fight the urge to push him out of the way.

We found Cheryl Callahan sitting on her couch taking a drag off a cigarette. Her hands were shaking as she put a lighter on the coffee table in front of her. With her ragged appearance and the stench of whiskey wafting off her, it looked like she needed a little hair of the dog. Since it was late afternoon, she'd either passed out from an early day of drinking, or had been sleeping off a late night.

Cheryl didn't seem too surprised to see cops at her door. After we showed her our badges, she tried unsuccessfully to flatten her teased out bushy brown hair. It would be easier to teach my cat to fetch than tame the wild beast on her head.

"Sorry officers, I was just layin' down for a minute," Cheryl said, slurring her words. "Not feelin' too great. I've gotta poundin' headache." Patrick and I gave each other a knowing smile.

"Sorry to wake you Mrs. Callahan—"

"Ms. It's Ms. Callahan. I haven't been a Mrs. in a long time." Having looked into the Callahan family before driving out, we knew Ms. Callahan's husband had died in a car accident four years earlier.

Patrick gave me a slight nod. It was our signal. A lone female parent meant I would do the interview. If there was a dad involved, and the more vocal of the two, Patrick would ask the questions. It was more for the comfort level of the parent than any real difference in our interviewing styles. Since I was doing the talking, Patrick would focus on Cheryl's reactions, evaluating her potential involvement in the crime.

"Ms. Callahan," I corrected. "I'm Detective Kate Springer, and this is my partner Detective Patrick Jessup. Can we speak to your daughter, Kimberly?"

Nervous, Cheryl stood. "Can I get ya some coffee?"

"No thank you." Patrick also shook his head no. Ten to one the coffee cup she came back with was filled with Jim or Johnny and not a fine French roast.

"Kimberly's not here," Cheryl said, raising her voice from the kitchen.

"Is she in some kinda trouble?"

"No. We'd just like to speak to her. Can you tell me when you last saw your daughter?"

Cheryl weaved back into the living room, sipping from her coffee cup. *Stalling tactic.* Right about now she was probably deciding whether to lie or play it straight, confirming the fact she wasn't going to be awarded Mother of the Year.

"I guess it was yesterday. Monday. I heard her leave for school in the mornin.'" It sounded like the truth. She must be worried.

"Do you have a recent picture of Kimberly?"

"Over on the wall." Cheryl pointed across the room with one hand while taking a drag off the cigarette in the other. A lifetime of smoking had etched deep wrinkles into her face, leaving her with a look of someone who's known too many hard times. "It's this year's school picture."

When I walked closer to inspect the photograph, I saw Kimberly and this morning's Jane Doe were one and the same. Again, I noticed the resemblance to my younger self. It was the bone structure. We both had narrow, oval-shaped faces with high cheek bones. Kimberly's skin was milky white. Clearer than mine at that age, but the coloring was the same.

The only real difference was the hair. Kimberly's—jet black—looked dyed. In the photographer's light, it had a bluish sheen to it. She wore it shoulder length with bangs covering her forehead. Of course in 1987, when I was in middle school, I had the cliff. It was the term the girls used back then to describe the Aqua Net sprayed bangs that looked and felt as hard as a cliff. That's the year everyone bought Michael Jackson's album, *Bad.* Me in my leg warmers, I preferred George Michael's, *Faith.* There were similarities between Kimberly and me, but again, I had to wonder if I only saw what I wanted to see. I'd dredged up a lot of old feelings at the shrink's office this morning. Was it skewing my sense of reality?

"Can we borrow Kimberly's picture for our files?" I asked. Cheryl nodded, and I took the frame off the wall handing it to Patrick. He was removing some clothes from a chair so he could sit.

"Ms. Callahan, how old is Kimberly?"

"Thirteen, but she'll be fourteen in less than two months. Now, you gonna tell me what this is all about?" A hysterical note crept into her voice, and I knew she'd shut down unless I told her the truth.

I steeled myself for the words I knew would tear this mother's world apart. Best to get it over with. I took a seat next to her on the couch. "I'm sorry to have to tell you, but we found your daughter, Kimberly Callahan, dead this morning." I knew I had to follow-up with another question quickly, or she'd want the details of the death. And as uncaring as it sounded, I needed Kimberly's mom as lucid as possible if I hoped to get anything out of her before she crawled back into a bottle.

"Ms. Callahan, can you tell me why you didn't file a missing persons report on Kimberly?"

"My baby . . . she's . . . she's dead?" The tears hadn't started yet. Cheryl was still in shock. Ignoring my question she asked, "How do ya know it's her? There are plenty of girls who look like my Kimberly."

"Of course you'll have to identify the body to make a positive ID, but I'm sorry to say it's only a formality. The deceased girl is the one in that photograph." I pointed over to the 8x10 in Patrick's lap. "She had a double heart-shaped birthmark on her right wrist and her name written in the heel of both shoes."

A gasp of recognition escaped through the hands Cheryl had so tightly fisted to her mouth. "Her beauty mark . . . when she was a little girl, I'd trace around its edges over and over." Cheryl sat silent for a few moments, obviously lost in a memory. After I coughed, she went on. "And Kimberly . . . she was so mad at me when I wrote in her new shoes. She complained she wasn't in kindergarten no more, but I told her those shoes were expensive. I didn't want no one takin' them."

"Ms. Callahan, can you tell me why you didn't call the police when Kimberly failed to come home last night?"

Cheryl bolted up so quickly, I was unsure of her intent. She looked around the room bewildered then began straightening the coffee table. Hearing this kind of news brought out a variety of emotions. Some moms would completely break down, often times needing sedation. Others would sit and calmly answer questions until the realization finally hit them.

Then they were inconsolable. Still others like Cheryl felt the need to stay busy. I guess they thought if they could focus on the mundane tasks of life, they wouldn't have to think about the child who was never coming home again.

"It's not the only time Kimberly's done this, been out all night. The first time it happened, I looked like an idiot callin' the cops. She came home the next mornin' acting like it was no big deal. And after that, well . . . she always came home before."

"What grade was Kimberly in?"

"Eighth grade. Buchanan Middle School's only down a ways." Cheryl pointed towards the east and continued the hopeless task of cleaning the front room.

Clothes covered most of the furniture and half empty take out boxes littered every flat surface. Not only cluttered, the small space also had a layer of grime coating the floors, furniture, even the walls. If I sat on this couch much longer, I might need to be dusted myself.

Cigarette hanging out of her mouth, Cheryl kept her hands busy by collecting all the ash trays and dumping the butts into one of the larger rounded bowls. It looked like something a five-year-old would make. Maybe little Kimberly had come home one day after art class with a present for her mommy.

"How'd Kimberly get hurt? Was it an accident?"

"No, I'm sorry. Kimberly was strangled."

At the word strangled, Cheryl sharply inhaled and instinctively brought a hand to her neck.

Do you know anyone who would want to hurt your daughter?" I watched Cheryl intensely, looking for any signs she may be the killer.

"No, never. I mean she wasn't no angel, but she sure as hell wasn't into drugs or nothin' like that. I made sure she stayed away from all that stuff."

"Is there someone we can contact for you? Maybe a friend who can come over?"

"No. There's no one."

I didn't push the subject. Later I would call a friend of mine who was a grief counselor. She worked well with parents whose children had been murdered.

I handed my notebook and pen to Cheryl. "Can you give me a list of the people in Kimberly's life? Aunts, uncles, best friends, anyone she babysat for?"

"No, it's only me and Kimberly. I'll give you her friend's names, but she didn't babysit. She did clean house for an older neighbor on the next street over." After she wrote down everyone's name and all the contact information, I changed tactics.

"I'm sorry to have to ask this question Ms. Callahan, but can you recount your whereabouts on Monday?"

"Why are you askin' . . . oh, is that when Kimberly . . . ?" When she couldn't finish the sentence, I nodded.

"I've been lookin' for jobs. My unemployment checks ran out last week. Had an interview on Monday mornin'. What a joke. I sat in a big room with about a hundred and fifty other people all fightin' for the same job. Obviously, I didn't get it. So I went down to the lounge on the corner. When I got tired, I came home and went to bed."

After I wrote down the name of the bar and the company she interviewed with, I asked Cheryl what time she got home.

"Wasn't checkin' the clock. All I remember is it was still light out when my head hit the pillow." In late September, the sun usually set a little after 7 p.m.

"And you said the last time you saw Kimberly was yesterday morning before school?" Cheryl nodded the coffee cup half raised to her lips.

"Can you tell me if your daughter had a boyfriend?"

"What, Kimberly?" Cheryl snorted. "She was way too young. Anyway, she wasn't interested in boys yet. Good thing too. I don't want her makin' the same mistakes as me. Didn't . . . didn't want her makin' the same mistakes, I mean."

At this last statement, it finally hit Cheryl the dial on her rough life just got turned up a notch. She hung her head and tears started to fall. The coffee cup in Cheryl's lap collected the salty drops.

"Ms. Callahan, can we search Kimberly's room? We might find a clue as to who she was with Monday evening."

A quick nod was all she could manage.

Patrick motioned for me to follow him to the front door. "Middle school lets out at 4:15 p.m. I need to hurry and get over there so I can talk to Kimberly's teachers and classmates."

"I'll stay here and get started on Kimberly's bedroom."

I turned to ask Ms. Callahan where I could find Kimberly's room, but she'd already left. Through the kitchen doorway, I could see Cheryl stretched up high on the tips of her toes, grabbing a fifth of whiskey from a top shelf. I decided to find her daughter's room on my own. Time to leave Cheryl to the oblivion I knew she craved. I more than anyone could appreciate the need to deaden painful feelings.

## CHAPTER 6

With a house this small, I had no problem locating Kimberly's bedroom. Of course, finding her name decorated in bubble letters across the door didn't hurt. It struck me how immaculate her room appeared. A stark contrast to the rest of the house. It was probably Kimberly's way of exerting control over the chaos in her life.

I pulled out my cell phone and dialed the crime lab, requesting a technician to the Callahan residence to dust for prints. It didn't look like a murder had taken place in this room, but I still needed to know who'd been hanging out here. I also placed a call to the grief counselor. Gayle wouldn't arrive until later this evening due to a prior commitment with another family. I warned her that Cheryl would probably be drunk but Gayle told me not to worry, it wasn't her first rodeo.

I pulled on my latex gloves and turned my attention back to Kimberly's bedroom. The space seemed absent of the many electronic gadgets found in kid's rooms these days. No game consoles, computer, or television. Probably spoke to the level of poverty she lived in, not the lack of desire to have those things. I'd check with her mom to see if she owned a cell phone. Although a couple of hours from now, it would be easier to check with the phone company than try to roust Cheryl from the stupor she'd be in.

The latest flavor of the month decorated Kimberly's walls. Hannah Montana and Justin Bieber were the only two I recognized. They hid the cracks in the walls. Somewhat. Even without a head or foot board attached to her twin bed, a yellow and white polka-dotted bedspread cheered the room. Nothing under the bed, not even a lone dust bunny. I started searching her drawers and nightstand. Nothing out of the ordinary. I opened the folding closet doors and found a stack of blue plastic tubs. A few well-worn dresses dangled on hangers opposite the boxes. A poster of Strawberry Shortcake was discarded in the corner.

Throwing my blazer on the bed, I sat Indian style on the thinning beige carpet. I mean crisscross applesauce according to Patrick's youngest daughter. What was this world coming to that we had to be politically correct even in kindergarten? Crisscross applesauce. What the hell did that even mean anyway?

I decided to tackle the contents of the tubs and hit pay dirt on the third. A paper envelope held a few dozen pictures with Kimberly front and center at various ages—smiling a toothless grin on the lap of a man who could be her father, Kimberly building sandcastles at the beach with her mom in what looked like better times, holding up rabbit ears behind a friend sitting at a picnic table.

I found it disheartening to view photographs of people who'd recently been murdered. Life captured in the split second before the flash showed most victims wearing a smile unaware of the future hurtling towards them.

These pictures of Kimberly looked different from her school picture. Here her hair was a light brown color similar to her mother's. I made a mental note to find out when the change in color occurred. And since the backs of the pictures were blank, I'd have to get names to go with the faces.

After searching the tubs, I stood and listened to my spine pop with every move. Like Garth Brooks said *I'm much too young to feel this damn old*. In the far corner beside Kimberly's bed, I noticed some black shiny fabric peeking over her comforter. Her backpack. Looks as if she'd made it home on Monday after all. Assuming she didn't skip school. Another thing to check.

Rummaging through each page in Kimberly's purple binder, I found one photograph—strike that, actually half a photograph—stuck to some algebra homework. I didn't even want to know what the gooey brown substance was causing it to stick. The picture had been torn down the middle. This half showed a grinning Kimberly Callahan and the other, well who knows? Hadn't found a camera yet. Maybe one of her friends snapped the shot. I'd keep the photo and ask around.

The only other picture in the room sat in a frame on the nightstand near Kimberly's bed. Your basic family shot with mom, dad, and daughter dressed in matching blue jeans and white shirts. The father was an older version of the man in the candid shot holding Kimberly on his knee.

Not much else in the room. No hidden journal taped under a dresser drawer. No map with a red circle and a meeting time jotted down. As with Kimberly's name written in her shoes, sometimes it was just that easy. I worked a case last year where it looked like a sixteen-year-old girl had committed suicide, until I found her online journal. It outlined plans to run away from her overly possessive father. There was a strange dynamic between the two of them and after I interrogated the father for nine hours, he finally broke, admitting to having staged the scene.

Once I'd finished searching Kimberly's room, I closed my eyes. I wanted to clear my head. That way when I opened my eyes, I could quickly glance around to see if I'd missed the forest for the trees. Sometimes the most telling item was the one in plain sight or something that should be there but wasn't.

Turning slowly, I faced Kimberly's marred dresser. Something nagged at me. A detail flirting with my subconscious. Bracelets. She had eight thin rubber bracelets in a variety of colors lying on top of the dresser. They were the jelly bracelets made popular in the '80s. Normally I'd chalk this up to poor fashion choice, but last fall I learned middle schoolers wore them for a different reason, and it had nothing to do with picking the perfect accessory. They were considered sex bracelets and had recently made a resurgence. Each colored bracelet signified what intimate act the wearer was willing to perform. The sexually active kids in school wore them, and when one got snapped off, they were expected to initiate that act on the one who snapped it.

From what I could remember, some of the colors were pretty innocent like orange meant kissing and yellow meant hugging. But then you had others like blue and black which meant participating in oral sex and intercourse. Kimberly had every color of the rainbow. Now I had to find out if she wore them to school. If so, which colors did she wear? Were the bracelets only for show, or was she an active participant in these trendy new sex games? I might find Kimberly wasn't as innocent as her mom claimed.

Emotionally spent and not wanting to deal with the drunken, grieving mother in the living room, I waited on Kimberly's bed for Lucy James, the tech assigned to this print job.

Who killed Kimberly Callahan—jealous boyfriend, mother's boyfriend, stranger? Could the mother have committed this heinous crime? What did it take to become a killer? The subject of profiling towered high on my nightstand. Studies of men suggested an extra "Y" chromosome in a male's genetic material as the culprit. Another hypothesis pointed to an inherited gene. Still other so called experts alleged pornography, violence in the media, childhood abuse, and poverty could mold a would be murderer. Hell, even premenstrual syndrome had been used as an excuse. Some lady attacked a state police officer after he stopped her for a DWI. She was found not guilty due to temporary insanity caused by PMS. That's one monthly friend a girl could do without.

Looking at my own tragic past, I wondered sometimes why I hadn't become a killer. I had fantasized about it enough. In my young mind, I thought Robert White's death was the only way to break free from the abuse. That's how twisted my thought process had become. Exposing him wasn't an option, but murder was.

Poisoning. That was my favorite fantasy method and the only logical choice. Simply sprinkle a little rat poison on top of Robert's cereal. Only one thing kept me from following through. It wasn't the frightening notion the retaliation would be epic if the poison didn't kill him. No. The main reason, ironically enough, was jail. Guess I'd watched too many women's prison movies. Late night HBO flicks always had the innocent female prisoner falling prey to physical and sexual abuse from multiple sadistic prison guards. That didn't sound like an escape.

Somewhere deep inside me, I knew the abuse would eventually end. I was smart and one day I'd leave for college. I always had my eye on the prize, and I didn't want to do anything that would hinder my future plans. I was intelligent enough to know I couldn't poison Robert and get away with it. Strychnine would show up in his system.

Still, I envisioned what it would be like to tell the police my sob story after I'd killed the man who'd been molesting me. Would they let me walk? Would it be deemed justifiable homicide? Looking back now, I'm sure I would have gotten a free pass. This was a time before the Menendez brothers took out their parents, an age before it was common place to have eight-year-olds shoot their fellow classmates.

So what did it take to become a killer? Who knew? It wasn't my job to determine how the psyche of a homicidal maniac was formed, just hunt him down and get him into a lineup once the deed was done.

My phone beeped, indicating an incoming text message. Lucy had arrived. When I opened the front door, I saw her walking across the lawn one hand on a metal suitcase, the other yanking on her glasses that had become entangled in her reddish-brown hair. *Lucy and her hair.* She was always complaining it went limp too quickly in the near tropical humidity. Add that to glasses that were too large for her oval-shaped face and Lucy would be considered a plain Jane in the high standards of today's society. She knew this, and it made her terribly self-conscious. But I really loved Lucy's belly laugh. It sounded like a pig getting stepped on with a six-inch stiletto heel. She soaked in about a half second of enjoyment before her embarrassment caused her to cover her mouth. I told her to embrace her little quirks. They were eccentricities, not faults.

<>

"Once we process the rest of the house, do you want to grab a quick bite?" Lucy asked. We were finished with Kimberly's room, heading towards the kitchen.

"Sure." I tried to muster some enthusiasm but failed miserably.

"Kate, what's wrong? You haven't been yourself today. Obviously, the psychologist cleared you for duty. You should be elated."

"Elated. Right." What *was* wrong with me? From the age of seven, I'd learned how to bury every miserable feeling and show the world a happy face. Why couldn't I paste a smile on today?

I tried again. "Sure, Lucy. Let's pick up some subs. I'll get crazy and add some lettuce. Haven't had anything green in a week."

Cheryl Callahan sat at the table with a pack of Marlboros, a half empty whiskey bottle, and a full tumbler of amber liquid.

"Excuse us, Ms. Callahan," I said through the haze of smoke. "We need to search the kitchen next."

Drunk and belligerent, Cheryl slurred. "Why?"

"Kimberly was killed at a different location from where her body was eventually found," I answered. "We need to check your house for evidence to see if she died here."

"NO! Get the hell outta my house."

I needed to persuade Cheryl to change her mind. If she didn't voluntarily allow us to search the rest of the house, I'd have to go through the trouble of getting a warrant and come all the way back out here tomorrow. In a murder investigation, time was of the essence.

"Ms. Callahan—"

"I said get out! I wanna be left alone." Then as if she were a full balloon whose knot had been untied, Cheryl's entire body sagged, all the air escaping. Anger turned into anguish. "Leave me alone . . . please."

I ushered Lucy out of the kitchen. Cheryl had earned the right to her request. We let ourselves out, and once at our cars, I got a call from Patrick.

"Springer," I answered.

"Kate, how soon can you get back to the precinct?" Patrick sounded out of breath. "I've got Tommy Lynch coming in to answer some questions about his possible involvement in Kimberly Callahan's murder. Remember, his parents owned the house where we found Kimberly's body."

"Just a sec." I turned to Lucy and begged off dinner. Doomed to another meal of Fritos and Coke from the vending machine.

"What's going on?" I asked Patrick.

"When I got to Buchanan Middle School, I talked to the ladies in the front office. They gave me a list of Kimberly's teachers. One printed off the list, then she—. You know . . . never mind. The point is our Tommy Lynch has been subbing Kimberly's math class since the beginning of the school year."

"What?" I jogged the rest of the way to my car. "Wait a minute. I looked into this guy's background. He has an accounting degree."

"Well now he's a substitute teacher. Kimberly's regular math teacher is on maternity leave, and Lynch took over the class. I also confirmed he subbed some of Kimberly's classes last year."

"So Kimberly didn't just stumble into Lynch's cross hairs, she was sitting front and center in his classroom."

"This could be our link."

"Could be," I agreed. "But I'm still confused. Why is Lynch coming downtown? I thought you were going to interview all of Kimberly's teachers at school today. Didn't you already sit down with him?"

"No. Lynch called in sick today."

"How interesting. Maybe he was out too late dumping a body."

"Murder can be exhausting."

"How'd you convince him to come in?"

"My natural charm of course."

I laughed. "Great job, Patrick. I'm headed back now. I searched Kimberly's room, but Cheryl won't give us permission to search the rest of the house."

"I'll start working on a warrant."

"Thanks, but what about Kimberly's autopsy scheduled for this afternoon?" Both of us hated being in the morgue so Patrick and I took turns attending autopsies. He was up next.

"Apparently someone more important jumped in line. Kimberly got bumped to tomorrow morning. Guess free tickets only go so far."

I looked down at the weakly lit numbers on the dashboard clock and realized I'd hit the height of rush hour. "Make sure you wait and eat breakfast after the autopsy."

Patrick groaned. "Really? You bring that up now? I'm trying to finish my burrito."

"Bastard. At least you get dinner." I was so hungry, I could almost smell the melting cheese from here. Then again, it could be the stale odor of Mexican takeout emanating from the back seat. Looking over my shoulder, I could barely make out the black leather it was so littered with crumpled take out bags. I really should clean it up. *Maybe tomorrow.*

"How do you know there's not a burrito sitting on your desk this very minute?"

"Two meals in one day? Now I suppose you'll want me to name my first-born after you."

"No, that's okay. If it's a girl, you can name her Patty. Patrick would be cruel."

"Smart ass. Now astound me with your keen detective skills. Tell me what you learned about our victim."

Patrick gave a warmhearted laugh. "The consensus is that Kimberly Callahan was an exemplary student back in the sixth grade. Then in seventh, her grades started to slip. But her teachers said with a little hard work, she'd rebound."

"Let me guess, she fouled out?"

"No, but if we're going to run these basketball analogies into the ground, I'd say she completely quit the team. This year she totally fell apart. Kimberly was already failing most of her subjects and had started cutting classes."

"I wonder if the timing of her downslide had to do with mom's drinking," I said.

"Sounds plausible. The principal let me talk with some of Kimberly's friends. One girl in particular, Junie Foster, informed me she used to be her best friend. She's pretty shook up over the murder. The girls were inseparable throughout sixth grade. Kimberly would always sleep over at Junie's house; more and more that next year. Junie knew Kimberly's mom drank too much, and Kimberly wanted to spend as little time at home as possible. When eighth grade started, Kimberly began hanging out with a new crowd, a rougher group of kids. Junie calls them the Buchanan Boneheads. She said Kimberly even dyed her hair from brown to black and started dressing differently. Junie still seems pissed about being tossed aside."

"Yeah, I found a bunch of black clothing in Kimberly's dressers and figured it was an early teenage rebellion thing. Did you get to talk to the

Boneheads?"

"Kind of. I talked, they stared. I've had it up to here with crappy teenage attitudes." I envisioned Patrick raising his hand to his brow demonstrating just how much he'd "had it".

"Up to where?" I goaded him. Hand signals weren't real useful on the phone.

"Shut it, Springer. Anyway, all the names Cheryl gave us were friends from sixth and seventh grade. There wasn't a single Bonehead on the list."

"I wonder what else Kimberly kept from her mom?"

Coming up on "Malfunction Junction", the fondly nicknamed section of Interstate 275, traffic completely halted in front of me. *Great, a complete parking lot.*

"Patrick, do you remember the case where we discovered the new fad for those jelly bracelets?"

"The Lopez case, right?"

"Yeah." I leaned over, searching the glove compartment for some long forgotten stashed snack. "I remember how you freaked when you found them in your oldest daughter's bedroom. You went a little overboard considering she'd just turned eight and to her it was only a fashion statement." I slammed the glove box in frustration. "Anyway, guess who had a colorful little stack on her dresser?"

"Looks like mom was clueless on so many levels. We didn't find any bracelets on the body."

"No, but I found Kimberly's backpack in her bedroom. She could have taken them off after school."

"I confirmed Kimberly attended all of her classes on Monday."

"Good." I could delete that mental note. "Did you see any of the kids at Buchanan Middle School wearing the bracelets?"

"Now that you mention it, Junie wasn't, but all of the Boneheads had them on. I guess Kimberly picked up a new hobby."

"I don't know if Kimberly sported all of the colors, but she owned them. She most likely engaged in some kind of sexual activity. Did you hear anything about a boyfriend?"

"Junie and the other girls didn't know of any," Patrick said. "But admittedly they weren't real interested in keeping up with Kimberly's social life."

"Interestingly enough, I found a torn picture in Kimberly's bedroom. She's in half of it, but I don't know who's torn out. You can just make out a hand gripping her shoulder. Having had experience at being a teenage girl once—"

"A long, long time ago," Patrick interjected.

"Ha, ha. Anyway, I figure an old boyfriend's been torn out. It has bad breakup written all over it. In the picture, Kimberly has jet black hair, so it must be recent. We need to find this boy."

"I cleaned out Kimberly's school locker," Patrick said. "But I'll wait until tomorrow to go through it since Tommy Lynch is next on our list. What's taking you so long anyway? Don't think I can keep Wozniack away from your burrito much longer. He's like a bloodhound when it comes to fattening food. He sure as hell didn't get that gut from eating his veggies."

Patrick disliked Detective Wozniack almost as much as I did. Almost. They'd been partners for three years before I transferred to the department. So Patrick was the only one in the division not sweating getting stuck with the new chic.

"If you could do something about this damn traffic, I'd be there sooner. What's your feeling on the mom?" I wanted to hear Patrick's opinion since I wasn't sure I could trust my own instincts lately.

"Do I think she did it? My gut says no, but I'm not going to close the door on the possibility."

"I agree." I slammed on my car horn. *Damn traffic.* "Hey, I've finally got a trivia question that's going to stump you."

"You think? Why don't you put your money where your mouth is, Springer? If I get it wrong, I'll buy your lunch for the rest of the week but when I'm right, you're picking up the tab. Deal?"

"Deal." I'd been saving this juicy question for just the right time. Free food seemed as good a reason as any. "Who was the youngest man ever to be elected president?"

"Pay up, Springer. It's Theodore Roosevelt. He was forty-two."

"Sorry. I said 'elected president'. Theodore Roosevelt was never elected. He assumed office in 1901 after the assassination of President William McKinley. The answer is John F. Kennedy. He was elected into office at the age of forty-three." I could hear Patrick gasp as he realized his mistake. I only wished I could see his expression.

Unfortunately, I couldn't rub it in since my phone started beeping. "Patrick, I've got another call coming in. Gotta go."

I breathed a sigh of relief at the name popping up on the caller ID. "Hello, Dr. Grace. Thanks for getting back to me."

"Not a problem, Kate. I'm glad you feel comfortable enough to call me. The last thing you need is to suffer in silence."

It's a good thing she couldn't see my eyes rolling. "Right. Well things have changed since I left you that message. It looks like my case is really heating up. I won't be able to meet tonight. Can you fit me in tomorrow morning?"

"I'm sorry, my schedule's full from 8 a.m. on. How about I get into the office early? Does 7 a.m. work for you? I'll bring the lattes."

Quickly calculating the drive time to Dr. Grace's office, I realized I'd have to get up before the rays even made an appearance on the sunshine state. I decided if I ate breakfast in my car, I could get in an extra fifteen winks.

"Sounds good. And thanks for thinking of me, but it's B.Y.O.P." Smiling at her silence, I explained, "Bring Your Own Pop. I'm a Coke drinker. No coffee for me. Can't even stand the smell of it."

# CHAPTER 7

Walking into the cramped windowless confines of our interrogation room, the first thing I smelled was sweat. Tommy Lynch was about as nervous as Detective Wozniack in a room full of angry feminists. Lynch shifted his eyes back and forth between me and Patrick.

Sizing each other up, I noticed Lynch was one of those rapid blinkers. Very distracting. I wanted to smack him upside the head to make him stop. How was I supposed to concentrate on the questions I wanted to ask if I was busy counting how many times he blinked?

I extended my hand in introduction, hoping it wouldn't come back moist. "Hello, Mr. Lynch. I'm Detective Springer and you already know Detective Jessup. I want to thank you for coming downtown to answer some questions. Especially since you're not feeling well. You called in sick to work today, right?"

"What? So. Why am I here?" I could hear Lynch's outrage with every overly enunciated word. He tried to back up his chair from the table, probably to make room for his massive gut, but the wall stopped him. Next to me Patrick smiled and gave the slightest shoulder shrug.

"Mr. Lynch," I continued, "we're interviewing anyone who's had direct contact with Kimberly Callahan."

"Who is Kimberly Callahan?" It was like he was blinking out an S.O.S.

"Kimberly Callahan is the eighth grader at Buchanan Middle School found murdered this morning. She was a student in your math class."

"Oh, that's what this is all about." The blinking stopped. "I sub for a lot of brats in Hillsborough County. So do a bunch of other teachers. Why would you think I had anything to do with her murder?"

"I didn't say you did. I only said we're talking to folks who've had regular contact with her." I still couldn't get over the fact Lynch instantly relaxed the moment I told him he was here because of a murder investigation. *If he wasn't guilty of murder, what was he guilty of?*

"Do you deny having substituted at Buchanan Middle School?"

"No, but I have no idea who this Kimmie person . . ."

"Kimberly. Kimberly Callahan." Patrick slammed down a picture of Kimberly lying on the morgue examination table. "Do you recognize her now?"

"No! Damn!" Lynch jerked his head to the side clearly repulsed.

"If you don't know this girl, Tommy, then why is it we found her dead on the property your family used to own?"

"What . . . What do you mean? The place on Morris Bridge Road?" I could almost see the wheels in his head turning realizing this connection tied him to a murder. I was afraid he would lawyer up, but like most of the idiots who'd sat in that seat before him, Lynch kept talking.

"When my dad died, the bank took that house back. Would have been nice to keep it in the family. You know for when I eventually get married, but I couldn't afford the payments. The economy went sour, and I'd lost my job. Damn politicians screwing up this country. Eventually, I took a substitute teaching position. It's only temporary, until I can find something in my field. Those idiot school kids. They don't give a shit about what I'm trying to teach them."

"Tommy, you forget. We've been to your property. All the overgrown brush out there, the average bystander wouldn't even know the house was there. The killer had to have some connection to it."

"My parents owned the house, not me. And quit calling me Tommy. It's Tom." Lynch was pissed, almost spitting out his words.

"You know what I think, Tommy?" Patrick went on as if he hadn't heard a thing Lynch said. "I think you were sitting in your little teacher's chair one afternoon, furious you were stuck in some meaningless, insignificant job, when Kimberly Callahan landed in your sights. What'd she do Tommy, make fun of you? Did she crack a joke at your expense in front of the entire class?"

Blinking was back. Score one for Patrick.

"What'd she do, make fun of that bulging gut of yours or maybe the nose hairs you haven't trimmed in a decade?"

Lynch folded his arms across his broad chest, shutting us down.

My turn. "No, Detective Jessup. Mr. Lynch was doing the best he could. He had to make a living, didn't he? Only a matter of time before some other firm snatched him up. Then he'd quit that crappy teaching job. They didn't understand him there. Those middle school kids were punks. Kimberly Callahan got what she deserved. If it wasn't Mr. Lynch teaching her a lesson, she would have eventually provoked someone else, right?"

"Right. No. I mean no. I had nothing to do with her murder. And I know my rights. Either charge me or let me go because I'm done talking."

"You're right, Mr. Lynch, you've been Mirandized. You're free to leave at any time. But if you go now, without answering any more questions, it only makes you look guilty."

When uncertainty crossed his face, I kept going. "Where were you Monday evening?"

"An alibi. Are you asking me for an alibi?" Lynch's blinking accelerated.

I had to close my mouth before the word *duh* escaped. Instead, I politely nodded.

Silence.

"Would you like us to ask a little slower?" Patrick prodded. "Can you account for your whereabouts yesterday?"

Lynch let out a sound somewhere between a sigh and a growl. "I got to Buchanan a little before 9 a.m. Taught all day, then came straight home afterwards."

"Were you home all night? Can anyone vouch for you?" Patrick asked.

"Yes, I stayed in all night . . . alone. Oh hey, I ordered pizza around 6 p.m." Lynch perked up, thinking he was off the hook.

"Sounds like a pretty pathetic evening. Is that the norm, Tommy?"

A vein in Lynch's neck started to bulge. It looked like he might stroke right there in his seat. Hope not, the paperwork would be a bitch.

"Why did you call in sick today, Tommy? You look fine to me."

"I woke up with a migraine, okay. It eased up after lunch, but I think it's starting to come back. You know, I came here voluntarily, and this is how I'm treated. Like some suspect?"

"No, Mr. Lynch. You're not a suspect. I apologize for Detective Jessup. He gets cranky when he has to work late. If you don't mind, please write down the name of the pizza joint you ordered dinner from last night. I'll go verify the information as quickly as possible and if everything checks out, I'll have you on your way." I handed him a pen and notepad.

As if invisible strings were tightly fastened to all of the muscles in Lynch's body, he sat rigidly in place. When he heard the magic word *go*, it was like an invisible pair of scissors cut those strings. His cheeks went slack. His fists loosened. I could see his entire body instantly relax.

"Would you like something while you wait?" I asked. "A coffee or soda?"

"Sure. A coffee, black." Lynch threw Patrick a snide look. Unfazed, Patrick flashed his silly, little boy grin. After countless hours spent by my partner's side, I could read the words his body language spoke. *Well played, Kate.*

I didn't have much time before Lynch started getting antsy. I stopped a fellow officer passing in the hall and asked him to do me a favor—pour some end of the day sludge for my suspect and get him a newspaper. Time would drag less if Lynch had something to read. He wouldn't feel so insecure with Patrick staring at him while the minutes ticked by. I hoped the two boys could play nice while I was gone.

Now I had to convince the ASA we needed a warrant. Tough fight though. Patrick had run a background check earlier and Lynch didn't have a record. I'd have to play up the fact Lynch not only taught at the victim's school, his parents used to own the property where Kimberly's body was found. Add a sympathetic judge into the mixture, and it might be enough. The last thing I wanted was for Lynch to go home and destroy evidence linking him to Kimberly Callahan's murder. The bastard reeked of guilt. Who knows what we'd find inside his house?

# CHAPTER 8

I stood on the cracked stoop of Tommy Lynch's flea bag apartment. The sound of a baby wailing streamed out of an open window above me. Somewhere else in the building, I could hear the raised voices of a man and woman arguing. What language they spoke, I didn't know, but the curse words were easily detectable.

The ASA had pulled through in record time. Back at the precinct, Patrick and I served Lynch with a search warrant for his place and told him he was free to go—for now. Hope he enjoyed riding the bus. Lynch would have a rough time getting to class with his car impounded. When I informed Tommy of the impending search, his face dropped. Based on his reaction, we could bank on finding something incriminating.

After my partner, a crime scene tech, and I entered Lynch's apartment, I thanked Patrick again for the burrito I'd wolfed down on the way over. "Here's to a fabulous week of free lunches. Mexican was definitely a good start."

Patrick ignored me.

Looking around the living room, I had to laugh at the stereotypical decorating style of a single, white, middle-aged man. Definite man-cave motif. Most of the room was taken up by a lazy boy recliner which sat across from a 65" plasma TV.

Patrick let out a soft whistle. "Top of the line. That flat screen had to set him back more than a few grand."

"What is it with boys and their expensive toys?" I asked.

In front of the recliner sat a TV tray with the remains of that night's dinner. A roach scurried through the crumbs littering the inside of a pizza box, causing Patrick to flinch. He looked my way, checking to see if I'd noticed his reaction. I quickly turned my head. Sometimes Patrick was more woman than I was.

When I turned back around, Patrick was in the kitchen, flipping through mail haphazardly strewn across the counter. I headed deeper into the apartment, wanting to take a quick survey before I tore the place apart. Three closed doors stood in front of me. Eenie, meenie, minie, moe. Door on the right, you are a winner. Not much to see. Just a bathroom about the size of a janitor's closet. Hell, my food pantry was larger. A quick look through the medicine cabinet and drawers. No prescription or recreational drugs. Door number two held Lynch's bedroom. Big surprise, bed wasn't made. And judging by the odor, the sheets hadn't been washed since he'd moved in. After a poke here and there, I decided to let Patrick have this room. I moved onto the third door.

"Holy . . ."

Studio quality lighting straddled each side of a massive sleigh bed. A camera sat on top of a tripod pointed at the mattress. I walked into the room carefully navigating around the filming equipment and stood near the edge of the bed. The top sheet was rumpled, half of it lying over the side touching the floor. Black satin sheets. I rubbed the slippery material in between my fingers. I knew the feel of the material even with latex gloves on. They were the same type Robert White had on his bed. I'd always hated the feel of satin. Cold and slick. Like a hundred snakes slithering along my body.

A memory, almost two decades old, flashed and unfolded in front of me as if on a movie screen. Little Kate sat on Robert's bed, propped up on her knees, the sheet gathered around her body, trying to maintain some semblance of dignity. Robert's weapon of choice—a Polaroid camera. She posed as instructed, a fake smile glued to her face. If she could pretend hard enough, the photo shoot would be short. Robert would gather up the pictures, sitting on the dresser in various stages of exposure, and add them to his collection. If Kate couldn't portray the emotion Robert asked for—.

"Kate, what do you . . ." Patrick stopped midsentence as he walked into the bedroom. "Holy shit!"

I shook my head trying to push back the memory that had gripped me. "Mr. Lynch has been a very naughty boy," I finally managed.

After Russo photographed the room, Patrick checked the video camera. Digital. Unfortunately, there was no tape to confiscate. After pushing a few buttons, Patrick confirmed the camera was clean. All the memory had been erased.

Still unable to shake the memory, I thought about what life would have been like if Robert White had access to the Internet. In my day, the invention of the Polaroid camera was a pedophile's dream. No nosey store clerks asking questions, no need for a dark room. Now the Internet offered pedophiles a whole new level of interaction with each other. Trading kiddie porn pictures like baseball cards, streaming live video, exchanging grooming techniques.

"Have you discovered a computer anywhere in this dump?" Patrick asked.

"Not yet. Maybe it's in Lynch's Acura. I'll call the garage and see if the techs found one." I was glad to have an excuse to leave the room so I could collect myself. Walking down the hall, I chastised myself. *Stop obsessing over your own problems, Springer. This is about Kimberly, not you.* I pushed Robert out of my mind and told myself to focus on uncovering evidence to put Lynch behind bars. Technicians were searching Lynch's car hoping to find proof he'd transported Kimberly's body in the trunk of his Acura. A computer would be a bonus.

I finished up my phone call and went to tell Patrick the techs at the garage had indeed found a laptop. He pumped his right arm back in victory.

"Don't celebrate yet. There's some serious encryption software loaded on Lynch's machine. It's already been sent over to the lab to see if one of their guys can crack the code. Our case has priority, but it could still take awhile."

Patrick grumbled under his breath.

"Yeah, I know. I wanted to find some kind of hard evidence tonight. A picture or video of Kimberly, so Lynch's ass would be sitting on a cold metal bunk this time tomorrow."

The only other incriminating evidence found in Lynch's house was a wardrobe of kinky costumes. They were in a variety of adolescent girls' sizes. Looks like Tommy liked to play dress up. Hopefully, their fashion sense didn't trump their common sense, and they kept the tacky outfits on during filming.

"I bet Tommy sells images of preteen girls on the Internet," Patrick said. "Look around. He has every gaming system ever made. No way can he afford all these high-priced toys on a substitute teacher's salary. He has to be supplementing his income somehow."

"I can't wait to dig into Lynch's financial records." The man was guilty of something, but I had no hard evidence and didn't know which crimes to charge him with.

Patrick called Sergeant Kray to request round the clock surveillance on Lynch. We didn't want this scumbag skipping town. Who knows how much cash he had stuffed away? At least Lynch would be coming home to an emptier apartment tonight. The technician had bagged all of the filming equipment and costumes as evidence. I was only sorry I couldn't find a valid reason to confiscate his TV.

"Why don't we call it a day?" Patrick said. "I'm sure my wife would appreciate having a warm body next to her tonight. And the kids will already be in bed." He gave me a wink.

"Thanks for sharing. Really appreciate it. Especially since the only thing I have waiting for me at home is a resentful calico sitting in front of an empty dinner bowl."

When we were searching Lynch's apartment, I'd thought about telling Patrick of Kimberly's resemblance to my thirteen-year-old self. But once we found so much incriminating evidence against Lynch, I figured it would only muddy the waters. Telling Patrick about this link didn't automatically mean I'd have to tell him about my abusive past, but Patrick was a good detective. He cared. He'd eventually get it out of me. Nobody I worked with knew about the sexual abuse I'd endured as a child, and I wanted to keep it that way.

I looked down at my watch, wondering if the cat could wait another hour. After a day like today, I could use a shot of tequila. Or two. Then I remembered my appointment with Dr. Grace scheduled for the crack of dawn. Probably best to head home and crash for as little time as I had left.

# WEDNESDAY

# CHAPTER 9

"It makes me sick to see people who've been abused turn around and hurt a child," I blurted at Wednesday morning's session with Dr. Grace. "More than anyone, they should know how devastating it is to be raped."

Dr. Grace raised her infamous right eyebrow in concern. Probably because of my avoidance of what was really bothering me than what I actually said. The problem was I still hadn't sorted out what my resemblance to the dead girl meant. I really didn't know how to approach Dr. Grace with it.

"If a victim doesn't work through his feelings about the abuse he's endured," Dr. Grace said, "it's very likely he'll take it out on someone else. He'll bottle up all that rage and self-hatred and turn it out towards the world. He'll want another person to hurt as badly as he does."

"That's psychobabble bullshit!" I said, sitting up straighter. "For years, I was raped. While my classmates enjoyed their summer vacation swimming at the community pool, I was trapped inside Robert's house. Never knowing what was coming next—in a state of perpetual fear. Just a sadistic monster's plaything. Yet after all that, I didn't turn into a pedophile. Hell, I'm the poster child for overcoming an abusive past. I never turned to drugs or alcohol to drown my sorrows."

"I would agree you've excelled in your professional life. You're a decorated detective in the Tampa Police Department. But are you happy?"

That was the zinger. When I wasn't looking, the doc went straight for the jugular. I grabbed my Coke from the end table and traced my finger along the can's top. "Rarely have I ever met a genuinely happy person. And I wonder . . . of those who seem so joyful, what percentage is simply masking their true feelings? Are they using every ounce of strength to paste a smile across their face? Does the effort it takes physically exhaust them?" I sat back and stared at Dr. Grace, waiting for a response.

"Is that what you do? Do you show the world one Kate Springer, but on the inside, you're someone completely different? Have you ever let anyone see the real you?"

*How to play this?* I knew I was damn tired of pretending, so I decided to try on the truth for once and see how it felt. "I'm a detective, and I'm very good at my job. I know how to read people, to find out what they like and dislike. I find out what qualities a person is attracted to, and show them that girl. I guess it's the same in my personal relationships. You know what? The effort it takes is exhausting."

"So maybe the Kate you parade in front of the world belongs on a poster for *How to Overcome Child Abuse,* but the real Kate is just as screwed up as the rest of us."

Dr. Grace adjusted her glasses, letting me take a minute to absorb what she said. I averted my eyes from her intense stare, acting like I found something interesting outside the window.

"You're very busy at work," she continued, "and I know we won't be able to see each other regularly. I think you should start journaling again. That way when you're feeling overwhelmed, or you have a thought you'd like to discuss with me, you can write it down. You also need to explore who you really are. Take time to analyze *your* likes and *your* dislikes? Once you know that, then you can work on being your authentic self. Kate, do you have a lot of self-talk?"

"What do you mean 'self-talk'? I'm not crazy, Doc."

"I'm wondering if you're constantly talking to yourself. Is an internal soundtrack always playing inside your head?"

"Yeah," I said in a hushed tone. "It drives me crazy. Sometimes it's so overwhelming. I can't make the ugly thoughts go away."

"Many times simply getting those vile words out of your head and down on paper helps take away the hold they have over you."

When she asked me what some of the thoughts on that loop were, I rattled off an abridged version. "I'm not good enough. I should be over my past by now. I'm weak."

"That's why I think starting up your journal again will help. If you write down that internal soundtrack, you can slowly begin to quiet the thoughts. Then we can work on stopping them altogether." Dr. Grace gave me a smile of encouragement. She almost made me believe she could help. Almost.

"I'll try it," I conceded.

"Kate, what are some of your triggers?"

"Triggers? The only trigger I know is the one attached to my Smith and Wesson. Pretend I'm not a shrink, would you?"

"Sorry." Dr. Grace smiled sheepishly, tucking a strand of dark hair behind her ear. "I simply meant, what triggers your childhood abuse memories? For example, will a certain song take you back?"

"Yeah, it's odd." I scooted forward in my chair. "For me, smells are the strongest trigger. I won't date a guy who washes with Irish Spring soap. The smell makes me want to gag. Baby Powder is another. Robert White always smelled of Irish Spring soap, Baby Powder, and stale cigarette smoke. Lovely combination." Nervous energy caused my legs to bounce, looking as if I had tremors. I replaced my can of pop on the table so I wouldn't spill any.

"Sure. The sense of smell is our most powerful sense, and it can bring back a memory just like that," Dr. Grace explained with a snap of her fingers. "What else triggers your abuse memories?"

"The way certain things feel. For example, if a man's hands are too cracked and hard, I can't be with him either." I stared down at my fingertips. I remembered how Robert's fingers would trace the curvature of my spine and the feel of his rough skin would make me want to jump out of mine.

"You've mentioned more than once being with a man. Have you had many sexual partners?" Dr. Grace tugged at her right earlobe, and I could see the holes in each ear where earrings should have gone.

"Sure, I've had my fair share. But sorry, I don't kiss and tell." I tried to lighten the mood in the room, but Dr. Grace threw me a silent stare, letting me know I wasn't getting off that easy.

"What do you expect, Doc? At an early age, I was trained sex equaled love. Let a man have sex with you, and he'll tell you he loves you. It's what we all want to hear, right?" I knew all the psycho bull behind it. Daddy left to start a new family, leaving little Kate behind looking for a male figure to step into that fatherly role.

Quietly I added, "I guess I've been using sex to find someone to love me."

"Has it worked?"

"No." I laid my hands on my legs trying to calm them.

"The problem is one of respect. When you introduce sex too early into a relationship, your partner doesn't respect you."

"Respect is a two-way street. Once I have sex with a man, I no longer respect him either."

"What's the longest relationship you've had with a man, Kate?"

"Not long. I mean if something more than a physical relationship develops, I usually cheat on him."

"Sounds like a good way to sabotage a relationship. Break it off before he has the chance to hurt you."

I nodded.

"You like to be in control, don't you?" Dr. Grace's right eyebrow slowly crept upward. I noticed that always happened after she asked a question taking us into uncharted territory.

"It doesn't take a genius to figure that out." My voice was so thick with sarcasm, even I cringed. I know I'd had a rough couple of weeks, but I shouldn't take it out on the one person who was trying to help me. I started again. "Yeah, it's probably one of the reasons I became a cop. When I'm wearing my shield, and feel the weight of my gun against my hip—I'm invincible."

"What would happen if you weren't in control?"

I thought carefully about Dr. Grace's question. I'd worked hard to inject as much control into my life as humanly possible. I didn't even want to think what would happen if . . . *No. Don't go there.* Grabbing a tissue from the decorative box sitting near me, I started to shred the paper into tiny strips. I didn't like where this line of questioning was going. Should have been warier of her right eyebrow. "Losing control? Won't happen."

"Where was your mother in all of this?"

"Sorry to disappoint you, Doc. You want to hear how mom was a drug addict or maybe knocked me around when she had one too many?" I added my own eyebrow shrug. "No, she was just a stupid, young kid who wasn't ready to have a baby. She wanted to go out and party, have fun. So mom thought the heavens had opened up and dropped down an angel when Robert White volunteered to babysit for free."

Looking back on it now with cop's eyes, I could see how easily Robert had manipulated her. She worked a low paying factory job, doing her best to get by. Robert befriended her and eventually earned her trust.

"She was totally clueless about it all," I continued. "I found out later my aunt asked my mom if she thought anything inappropriate was going on. Of course mom said no. But get real. When a mother comes to pick up her eleven-year-old daughter, and the girl is walking around wearing just the guy's t-shirt and her underwear, what would you think? It doesn't take a detective to figure out there's sex involved."

Dr. Grace took off her glasses, folded them together, and placed them on the desk in front of her. "Though purely supposition, I would say your mother had an inkling abuse was happening, but her mind couldn't process the fact. She didn't want to believe it could be true. Unfortunately, it sounds like she turned a blind eye. I'm sorry she wasn't there for you."

I quickly swiped a traitorous tear that had escaped down my cheek. "Yeah well, I made my peace with her years ago. It was only as an adult I could appreciate how hard she had it. As a single mom, she made the best choices she could. My mom's a really sweet woman. She made some mistakes, hell some real doozies, but without her support afterwards, I wouldn't have made it. I only wish . . ."

Dr. Grace turned her hands palms up, trying to reach out to me. Instinctively, I placed mine under my legs. The shredded tissue lay in a haphazard crisscross pattern across my lap.

"You wish what?"

"When I finally broke down and told my mother about the abuse, I wish she would have insisted I go to the cops and prosecute the son of a bitch. I was a kid, only thirteen. What the hell did I know? I was more worried about the kids at school finding out than him getting away with it. The thought of going through a trial horrified me. So I begged her to let it be. My mother didn't turn Robert in, instead she confronted him. Told him she knew about the abuse, and he'd better leave town, or she'd tell the police."

"Where did Robert go after your mother confronted him with the allegations?"

Confused, I shook my head. I tried to shake free the fuzziness that suddenly overcame me. My head felt like it was full. Like a strong external pressure squeezed it.

"Away."

"What do you mean, away?"

A hysterical tone crept into my voice. I recognized it, realized it wasn't like me, but still couldn't control it. "I don't know! At the time I didn't care, just away from me . . . I guess I never really thought about it. It's like . . . I finally told my mother. She made him go away. And I closed the door to the abuse. At the time, I pushed all those feelings down and didn't think about them again for years. Then in college, everything started resurfacing. But even then, I only focused on the actual abusive acts and not him." Again I shook my head trying to clear it. "I know I'm not making any sense. It's hard to explain and . . . I'm feeling . . . heavy."

I blinked slowly, trying to focus on Dr. Grace. "Anyway, Robert moved away, and I haven't heard from him since. I guess that's why I became a cop. I'm trying to do penance. Make up for not putting away my own pedophile."

"Kate, do you think Robert is still abusing little girls?"

My breath hitched and I pulled my fingers to my parted lips. From the look on Dr. Grace's face, I could tell she was worried for me. I doubled over, putting my head in my lap. My entire rock solid facade began to crumble as I realized at this very moment another little girl might be terrified Robert would come into her room tonight.

Dr. Grace stood, walked around the desk, and kneeled before me. She knew I didn't like to be touched or coddled, but she must have hated to see me tormented. This time I didn't resist. She took me into her arms and held me while I sobbed.

Two separate soundtracks played in my head at once. Dr. Grace's voice whispering words of comfort like, "It's not your fault . . . you repressed it in order to cope . . . more than your mind could handle . . . you had to find a way to go on with your life." At the same time she spoke, my own inner voice argued *my silence put other girls in danger. How could I let that happen? Where do I go from here?*

A plan began to formulate. I would find Robert White. I would put every resource I had into tracking him down. I would find out if he'd abused other girls and whether he was still abusing them. Repeating this over and over in my head, I began to feel more in control. I wasn't that same scared little girl. I had the power now, the law on my side.

It suddenly felt as if a shot of ice water had been injected directly into my veins. Every muscle in my body stiffened. I abruptly pulled away from Dr. Grace, leaving her sitting back on her heels. I ignored her concerned look and told her I would take care of everything. As I stood to leave, the white strips of tissue fell from my lap floating to the floor like a cold winter snowfall.

# CHAPTER 10

Empty squad room, prayer answered. Though not unusual before 9 a.m. I hadn't allowed myself to shed another tear and definitely wasn't in the mood for chit chat. After I left Dr. Grace's office, I realized I'd never gotten around to telling her about my resemblance to Kimberly Callahan, the whole reason I made the appointment. It would have to wait. Right now I was a woman on a mission. If Robert was out there, I'd find him.

I sat down in front of my computer and opened the LexisNexis link on my desktop. This program's used by law enforcement to quickly locate people, discover connections between suspects, and a host of other useful things. These days every move we make leaves an electronic fingerprint. From our purchases at Starbucks to paying property taxes, it's difficult not to leave a trail.

I typed in Robert's name, birth date, and location of birth. I quickly discovered he was born to Jacquelyn and Thomas White. The baby of the family, Robert had two siblings—an older sister and brother. The brother died in an accident in 1943 after Robert turned eight. Robert lived in Newton, Illinois until he joined the Navy at age eighteen. Looks like he missed the Korean War by only a few months. He was dishonorably discharged two years into his service. Not having access to his military records, I didn't know the reason for his discharge. But knowing Robert, it probably had something to do with his inability to take orders.

Robert always told stories of his Navy days. He traveled all over the world, a story for every port. Funny how he left out the juiciest detail of all —the military kicking him to the curb. After the Navy, Robert moved to Elgin, Illinois where he resided up until the time he met me. A few more key strokes, and I found that after his confrontation with my mother, he moved only forty-five miles south to Joliet, Illinois. Not far. Looks like Robert lived there for less than a year. After that, I couldn't find any trace of him. No activity after 1987. His credit cards stayed open but inactive. He completely fell off the grid.

Then a thought came to me. Could Robert White be dead? Seventy-five was getting up there. Maybe he keeled over after enduring an extremely painful bout with cancer, or electrocuted in a freak home renovation accident. Probably should have checked that possibility out first. But no, a death certificate had ever been issued in his name.

Next I ran his name through AFIS, the national database containing the fingerprints of felons. It also lists people who've applied for jobs requiring background checks. If Robert had ever applied to work for a government agency or even a daycare, his name would pop up in the system. Nope. Not listed. No felonies. If Robert ever committed a misdemeanor, I'd never know it. It'd be too hard to track down since minor crimes are only listed in the county where charged.

Most likely Robert changed his name to avoid future detection. I decided to check if he'd legitimately switched it. No record. If he'd changed his name, it wasn't legal. Robert could have easily assumed a new fraudulent identity. Find a child who'd died, and take over his social security number. If Robert had acquired a dormant number and the child's date of birth, he'd be able to open lines of credit, apply for a driver's license, everything needed to start a new life.

It still felt like ice water ran through my veins. The goose bumps popping up on my forearms cemented the fact. For the moment, I'd exhausted every possibility. I had to accept it would take more time than I had right now to chase down that abusive bastard. It wasn't fair to Kimberly to split my focus. She deserved one hundred percent of my attention. After I solved the Callahan case, I would take vacation days, personal leave, whatever it took to finish the hunt.

*Focus, Springer. Focus on Kimberly Callahan.* To do that, I did what came naturally. I opened the mental box caging my emotions, took all of the rage and self-loathing that threatened to overflow, and slammed them inside.

Deep breaths.

Now, what were the facts of the case? What other information did I still need? And what were my next steps? Kimberly came home from school Monday afternoon and sometime that evening between 7 – 11 p.m., she was strangled. The killer dumped her body in the early morning hours of Tuesday, September 28 at the house Tommy Lynch's parents used to own. Later that morning at 7:30 a.m., a neighbor's dog discovered Kimberly's lifeless body. Tommy Lynch worked as a substitute teacher and had known interactions with Kimberly during class at Buchanan Middle School. A search of Lynch's current residence uncovered filming equipment and adolescent sized costumes. His car revealed a laptop containing heavy duty encryption software.

Damn. My pen ran out of ink. *Get a grip, Springer.* If a simple problem like this raised the blood pressure, it wasn't a good sign for the rest of the day. I scavenged around on top of my desk looking for something to write with. It's a wonder I could find anything with all this mess. I yanked open my bottom desk drawer and instead of another pen, found Malibu Barbie staring up at me.

Wozniack! That bastard. Still in its box, Barbie wore a skimpy purple bikini with sunglasses perched atop her head. A homemade badge was glued to her chest and a paper gun affixed to her hip. I wondered if Patrick would find Ken in his desk. I seriously had to start plotting my revenge.

Finally locating something to write with, I slammed the drawer closed and started jotting down the list of information I still needed to find out. I didn't know if Lynch's laptop had incriminating photos or video of our victim, if his vehicle had evidence that could be traced back to Kimberly, or financial records that could provide any clues. I also needed to find out more about Kimberly. Interview people who were close to her and check out her social networking sites. I had a full day's work ahead of me.

I was about to search for Kimberly's online presence when Patrick appeared at my desk. A grim twist to his usual smile told me all I needed to know about the autopsy.

"The highlights?"

"Sure." Patrick drew his answer out in more of a breath than an actual word. "As Ellis suspected, Kimberly died of asphyxiation due to manual strangulation. She also had a hematoma on the back of her head and extensive bruising on her hip region."

"Was the hip bruising from a beating or from being restrained?"

"It was consistent with the perp straddling Kimberly's hips while strangling her. She most likely received the hematoma when her head hit the ground. Thankfully, there was no sign of sexual trauma, but Ellis said she was menstruating at the time of her death. Her hymen was torn. She wasn't a virgin. A minute semen stain was also found on the outside of her jeans. It looks like the killer may have ejaculated through his pants, leaving a transfer. Ellis doubts there's enough of a sample to test for DNA, but he sent it over to the lab. It'll be a few weeks before we get the results. A sample of skin cells found underneath Kimberly's fingernails was also sent out."

"When will we get Ellis' final report?"

"Friday. Hopefully. But we won't see the toxicology screen for at least three weeks. FDLE is also analyzing the trace evidence found on the body. There were four hairs found on Kimberly's sleeve and multiple synthetic fibers along her backside and in her right front jean pocket."

"That's all we've got to work with? A few fibers and some hairs? Hairs probably left from the dog who found her."

"You know the stats as well as I do. Eighty percent of trace evidence disappears after the first four hours, and with an outside crime scene . . . well, all bets are off. We're lucky we got what we did."

I threw my pen across the desk. Patrick grabbed it before it fell, setting it down in front of me.

"Fine," I conceded. "What do we have on our killer so far?"

"There's no sexual assault. Maybe our guy just gets off on strangling young girls or . . ."

"He was going to rape her," I said, finishing Patrick's sentence. "But something went wrong, and he strangled her first. Maybe Kimberly pissed him off. He chokes her thinking he's only going to scare her but doesn't know his own strength. Kills her. As he chokes her, she instinctively fights back, getting some of his skin underneath her nails. He gets off on the struggle and ejaculates, leaving a sample for us to find on her jeans."

"It seems so sloppy. It has all the earmarks of an unorganized killer. Leaving trace evidence of semen and skin. Dumping the body instead of burying it."

"Definitely not premeditated. Probably a first timer. We should look for reports of peeping toms, indecent exposure, stalking, and other related crimes in the area. Maybe he's escalating. At this very moment, the killer could be looking for another girl wanting to get right what he screwed up Monday night."

It sounded plausible, but how did the victim looking like me factor into the equation. Or did it?

"After the autopsy, I got a call from Brian Porter," Patrick said, rubbing his temples with the pads of his thumbs. "He's had his computer working overnight trying to hack Tommy Lynch's software encryption program. He finally cracked it a few minutes ago. Porter said there were hundreds of images as well as a handful of video files. We need to check them out. See if Kimberly made her debut in any of them."

When the case involved children, normally I would be the reluctant volunteer sitting in the tiny 5x5 windowless room scouring the faces. It was a special spot set aside specifically for looking at explicit images. The department wanted to show respect for the victims, therefore we didn't view photos and video in public areas. At some point, a sign that read *Purgatory* had been affixed to the door. I'd always been better at distancing myself from the impact of the depraved acts being perpetrated upon these kids. This time though, I couldn't spare Patrick.

"I hate to do this to you partner, especially after the morning you've had, but I think it's important you look through the images on Lynch's computer. You visited Kimberly's school. The videos could contain other Buchanan students." Patrick knew I spoke the truth, but he still didn't like it. Once you've seen photographic documentation of children being abused, those images permanently seared themselves into your brain.

After Patrick left to begin his daunting task, my cell phone rang. I'd always wanted to set my ringtone to the COPS opening theme song but worried it was too unprofessional. *Bad boys, bad boys*—that song always got my pulse racing. Instead, I suffered through this piercing, shrill ring. I could have changed it to a more pleasant jingle but on the up side, even in a crowd of ringing phones, I could always pick mine out.

It was the crime lab. "We finished processing Tommy Lynch's Acura, Detective Springer. There's no sign of blood or other fluids on the interior of the car or in the trunk. It doesn't look like he transported a body in this vehicle. And don't worry, it doesn't look like it's been cleaned either. Maybe not ever."

That was important. A criminal, trying to cover up a crime, would use bleach and other cleaning agents under the misconception it would remove all traces of blood from an enclosed space like a car trunk.

"Thanks." Discouraged, I disconnected the call and turned my attention towards the large envelope laid on my desk during my computer search for Robert White. It was a copy of Lynch's financial records. I decided to tackle the numbers next. It was least I could do. Sticking Patrick with three crappy jobs in one day was cruel. But first, this mountain of paperwork called for a Coke.

Some people had a weakness for coffee. They loved the aroma, the warmth on their fingers as the heat radiated through the cup, the exquisite near scalding taste of that first sip. Not me. I like my first jolt of caffeine to come from a Coke. And from a can, not a two liter bottle or fountain drink. There's a giddy pleasure in popping the top and hearing the fizzing sound. And that initial bite of caffeine from the morning's first swallow. For me, that's heaven.

I stood, stretched my legs, and headed towards the vending machine. On the way there, I texted Patrick the bad news about Lynch's car. I was looking down at the cell phone's screen and failed to notice Detective Wozniack turn the corner. Barreling straight into his massive gut, I heard him exhale "oomph". Though he tried to hide it, I could tell I got in a good shot. *That's for the Malibu Barbie you jackass.*

"Watch where the hell you're goin', Springer."

"Watch what you're eating, Wozniack. Then maybe you wouldn't be leading with that big 'ol pork belly of yours." I briskly walked off before he could return fire. Damned if I'd mention the doll and give him the satisfaction of knowing I'd already found it.

# CHAPTER 11

Patrick emerged from Purgatory a few minutes after I'd finished reviewing Lynch's financial records. He looked as if his soul had been ripped from his body with a wire hanger.

"If Tommy Lynch was strung up by his balls, covered in sugar water, and dipped in a hill of fire ants, it still wouldn't be punishment enough. Anyone who takes advantage of young girls like that . . ." Patrick sunk into his chair and shook his head.

I sat quietly, waiting for him to pull himself together. He finally started speaking, though his eyes remained closed. Probably still seeing an endless parade of faces. "It looked like all the girls were somewhere between eleven and fourteen. Middle school age. I didn't find any photos or video of Kimberly Callahan. But there was a video with a date stamp of September 27. Tommy started filming at 8:17 p.m. Looks like he didn't want to give us an alibi for Monday because he was busy shooting porn of an underage girl." Patrick opened his bleary eyes. "So even though Tommy's a sick bastard, he's not our sick bastard."

"That bites. I really thought we had our guy." I shook my head in disbelief.

"Looks like Tommy's using Buchanan and other middle schools to troll for girls. I recognized one of the Boneheads, sorry, I mean one of the young ladies I tried to interview yesterday. Man, yesterday. Seems like a week ago."

"Well for what it's worth, I looked through Lynch's financials. His story's pretty consistent with what we already knew about him. He put himself through night school, earning an accounting degree. Did well for himself until the economy went south, and he got fired. Lynch quickly ran through his savings and eventually took a substitute teaching job. He barely subsisted on his meager earnings. Until six months ago. Then a large influx of deposits showed up in his bank account transferred from an online PayPal account. Looks like Lynch pulled in close to ten grand a month from a subscriber website where he posted his own sick kiddie porn."

Patrick rubbed a hand over his baby smooth face. "Kate, I really need some air."

"Want some company?"

"Thanks but no. I need to be alone right now."

"I hate to ask but when you get back, can you write up your report on the images? I'll put it with the rest of the evidence we have against Lynch and hand it over to the Cybercrimes Division. We can't charge this sleazebag with murder, but they can still put him away."

"Sure. Later I plan on tracking down the neighbor Kimberly cleaned house for. I want to find out what kind of relationship they had and see if he can shed some light on her last few days. Check out his alibi, too."

"Since we're a bust on Lynch, I'm going to keep sniffing around the ex-boyfriend angle."

After Patrick dragged himself out the door, I decided to push off lunch. It was already half past noon, but I could hold my stomach off a little longer. I still had no idea who Kimberly was—her hopes, her dreams. None of her friends were willing to talk to us. In a way though, Kimberly could speak for herself. Speak from the grave by way of her social networking sites. These days, teens happily opened their lives up to complete strangers tweeting what they had for breakfast, blogging about their new hairdo, complaining about their classmates on Facebook.

So far, none of the social networking sites had gotten back to me about my warrant. The passwords they could provide would make the search much easier, but even without them, most teens were loose with their privacy settings. Kimberly didn't have a computer at home, but she could have updated her account at school or even the library.

I checked out Twitter first, searching for the name Kimberly Callahan. I got three choices and easily narrowed down the list from the attached photos. When I clicked on Kimberly's name, the pop up box showed she hadn't tweeted in over a week. However, the last two tweets were listed. "Can't wait to get a license so I can get the hell out of this house!" and "Can you believe the nerve of him? Blowing me off like that. I won't be ignored!" Unfortunately, Kimberly never named "him".

Next, I logged onto my own Facebook page and searched for Kimberly. She had an account but surprisingly, her privacy settings only allowed approved friends to view her page. The juiciest details were usually the ones kids tried to hide. Guess they'd just have to marinate until my warrant came through.

From there, I navigated to the online website YouTube. This popular site contained everything from videos of squirrel's waterskiing to dads taking one in the family jewels from junior's baseball bat. Because YouTube had made overnight successes of more than one singing teen, kids hungry for fame regularly uploaded their own performances hoping to go viral.

Kimberly posted six videos under her own channel, each only a few minutes long. The first clip was shot in a girl's bedroom. It had a date stamp of late August of this year. School had already begun. It showed Kimberly with a group of girls singing into hairbrushes. At the end of the song, they all collapsed into a heap on the bed with peals of laughter ringing out. Kimberly wore pigtails and pajamas too large for her frame. She looked much younger than her thirteen years.

"It's not right," I mumbled to the computer screen. "I promise you Kimberly, I'll find your killer. Someone will pay."

It all seemed so unfair. Not only had Kimberly been dealt a crappy hand in life, but that life had been extinguished much too early. I wanted justice. Maybe no one fought for her when she was alive, but I'd be damned if I let it play out that way in her death.

I tried to focus on the joy she'd found hanging out with her friends. The same girls starred in four of the other videos, though this time they were dressed in all black. Most likely the Buchanan Boneheads.

The last clip looked to be shot using a low resolution cell phone camera. It was difficult to make out anyone in the video because of the dark grainy quality, but I could hear loud rap music and multiple voices laughing. After a moment, the camera operator went in for a close up.

Kimberly's face appeared on the screen. Her head was on a boy's chest, a dreamy smile on her face. The difference in height told me he was much older. When the picture zoomed out, I saw Kimberly spill something out of a red plastic cup as she swayed slower than the music demanded. The boy's face was turned away from the camera, but I could see one of his hands resting on her butt. If this video was posted on Kimberly's channel, she probably cared for the boy she was with. I'd have to find out the name of her dance partner.

Now it was time to tackle Kimberly's locker contents. I'd retrieved the evidence from lockup while Patrick was in Purgatory. I bent over to pick the box up from the floor but stopped, grabbing my head instead. I was lightheaded from skipping lunch. My eyes ached from looking at a computer screen and rows of numbers all morning. I rubbed my temples, trying to fend off the headache I felt rushing at me like an express train.

I grabbed a couple of Tylenol from my desk drawer and washed them down with my last swallow of warm Coke. After giving my stomach a pep talk, I heaved the box onto the extra chair sitting beside my desk. Before I opened the lid, I paused, slowly cocking my head to the side. I'm sure it looked as if I were listening to something inside the box, but no, I was breathing in a familiar aroma emanating from within. I'd know that perfume scent anywhere. Secret No. 7.

With just one whiff, instantly my mind's eye saw a nine-year-old Kate Springer emerge from the bathtub. Robert White stood naked, dripping wet, holding a thick white towel towards the little girl. But the rich lushness of the fabric could do nothing to warm her. After painstakingly removing every droplet of water, Robert pulled out a bottle of Secret No. 7 from the medicine cabinet. It sat between his aspirin and tube of hair cream. He would always squirt the perfume bottle three times, spraying tiny droplets of liquid directly onto the girl's naked skin. In the cramped bathroom, the fresh air quickly disappeared, replaced with a heavy cloying mist. With the towel recklessly discarded in the corner, Robert lifted the motionless child like a groom carrying his bride—.

*Nope.* I quickly shook my head to clear the memories that gripped me like a vice. Even though I'd stamped them out long ago, it seemed, lately they were all jostling in line waiting for their chance to be remembered. I'd always hated the smell of Secret No. 7. Created in the early 1940's, I'd once heard it referred to as "a frigid fragrance; like a marble statue, lovely but lifeless." That's exactly how I felt about the scent. I always wondered why liked it. The cop in me figured the perfume had been worn by someone prominent in his life, maybe even his own abuser. Maybe defiling me while I wore the scent was a way to get back at that person who had hurt him. Of course, I was only assuming he was sexually abused. But then, most child molesters were only continuing the cycle of violence that began with them.

Finally lifting the box's lid, I found the .25 oz bottle of Secret No. 7. A little had leaked and darkened a patch of the brown cardboard. This was the real thing, not the eau de parfume knock off. It had to have cost at least a hundred bucks. No way could Kimberly have afforded this fragrance. First the resemblance and now the same perfume. Could I be going crazy? It felt like I was spiraling, my body turning faster and faster, stuck in a tornado. The detective in me said it was crazy to take these two events and blow them out of proportion, connecting the dots and making a line where one wasn't. After all, wasn't Secret No. 7 considered the world's most legendary fragrance?

Trying to put my personal feelings aside, I readjusted my detective's hat and kept searching through the box. I painstakingly read through each paper in Kimberly's five subject notebook and even leafed through her two textbooks, looking for any notes tucked inside. Nothing. I shuffled through pens, pencils, and other odds and ends, stopping when I came to a small case. Almost like an eyeglass case but square shaped. A small digital camera sat inside. Bingo! It was an Olympus Stylus. Pretty pricey model. I knew from my own recent buying trip it cost almost $300. Obviously, I opted for a cheaper brand, but I wondered how Kimberly got her hands on this little toy.

After turning the camera's power on, I began advancing through each picture. I stopped when I came across the one found in Kimberly's closet, the ripped photograph. This time I could see who was in the missing half. A young man, definitely older than Kimberly. Looked about sixteen, probably in high school. Tall and gangly but not freakishly so. It just looked like he'd recently sprouted and the rest of his body hadn't quite caught up. I wondered if it was the same mystery man from the video. At one time, Kimberly had obviously cared for this boy but something had to have happened for her to want to rip him out of the picture.

I studied the photograph closer. The boy was cute, had brown hair that parted on the left and angled over across his right eye. I could imagine he was the sort to constantly flip his head trying to clear his vision. A pair of sharp scissors would take care of that problem. But when I saw his jeans riding below his boxers, I knew it meant only one thing. He was a punk.

Unfortunately during my search, I didn't find any boys' names covered in hearts. I guess I had to go old school. Or should I say high school to find a name to match the guy in the picture. Super. I loathed every minute of it the first time around. That's why I happily passed off the school interviews to Patrick yesterday. The one bright side—lunch. I'd perfected eating pizza by the slice in the car.

# CHAPTER 12

After marking off two high schools from my list, I hit pay dirt. I felt like a kid again standing in Chamberlain High's administrative office waiting for the principal to meet with me. Luckily, I had my black blazer on over my white tee. It would have been extremely embarrassing sporting underarm sweat marks. I don't know why I was intimidated. Kate "Goody Two Shoes" Springer could have been my nickname in high school. I never spent one afternoon in detention, much less sent to the office for bad behavior.

A well-endowed woman strode towards me with her hand extended. I bet the high school boys really "stood" at attention in her presence. "Hello. I'm Vice Principal Saunders. I'm sorry but Principal Beckham can't leave her meeting with the superintendent. She asked me to join you. If you could please follow me back to my office, I'd be happy to help with whatever you need."

After I introduced myself, I removed the photograph of Kimberly Callahan, a new untorn copy I'd printed, and put it on Ms. Saunders' desk. I pointed to the young man in the photo. "According to the secretary in the front office, this boy, Jason Reeves, is a junior here at Chamberlain High School. Is that correct?"

Looking closer at the picture, Ms. Saunders shook her head, a weary look crossing her face. "Yes. One of our more challenging students. Is Mr. Reeves in some sort of trouble?"

Now the tricky part. I didn't want Ms. Saunders to clam up, so I needed to do a little creative storytelling in order to get her to answer my questions. I added a concerned tone of my own. "No but through the course of an ongoing investigation, something's come up. Frankly, I'm worried about Jason. Is he at school today?"

Kelly Miller

Ms. Saunders consulted her computer. "No. It looks like he has an unexcused absence for today . . . and yesterday. No parent called in on his behalf. But that's not unusual. Jason Reeves is truant quite often. Do you think something has happened to him?"

"That's what I'm trying to find out. Do you know any details of his home life?"

"Jason Reeves entered Chamberlain High School as a freshman two years ago. I believe he's lived in Tampa all his life. As I understand, it's just him and his dad. Jason's mom left when the boy was very young. The senior Mr. Reeves works long hours and rarely shows up for parent-teacher conferences. I know Jason has a job after school. He's been sent to my office for falling asleep in class."

"And Jason's how old?"

Ms. Saunders glanced at her computer screen. "Seventeen."

"Do you know where he works?"

"At one of the local grocery stores. I forget exactly where." Ms. Saunders unnecessarily smoothed down the sides of her perfectly styled hair. "It looks like the late hours are impacting his grades. The school year has just begun, but three of his teachers have already informed me of his failing grades. It's a no-win situation. These days, many families need everyone in the household to contribute financially to keep their heads above water."

"Has Jason ever been in trouble for fighting?"

Ms. Saunders flashed a dimpled smile and shook her head no. She pointed at the picture. "He's no bully. If anything, he's been at the mercy of some of the other boys. A few of the athletes have a tendency to take it too far with the less popular boys."

I raised my eyebrows, ready to follow up with another question, but Ms. Saunders quickly interjected.

"No, no. I didn't mean to imply . . . Chamberlain High School has a zero tolerance for bullying. I can assure you Jason's never been involved in a fight on school grounds."

For now, I let it go. "So what crowd does Jason hang with?"

When Ms. Saunders answered me with a frown, I asked, "You just indicated he doesn't hang with the popular crowd. How would you categorize him? Nerd, skater, teacher's pet, hippie, preppy, loner, druggie, or band member." Although band member and nerd were usually synonymous, at least back in my day.

"We don't label children at this school, Detective Springer."

"With all due respect Vice Principal Saunders, nothing has changed in the past twenty years. When I was in high school, you had the jocks and the geeks, and today you still have your jocks and geeks."

Ms. Saunders' pinched up face looked like she smelled a foul odor. It was probably all the bullshit she was shoveling.

"I really have no idea where you would pigeon hole Jason Reeves. I need to finish up here. It you'd like to speak to Jason's teachers or friends, I can arrange that."

Guess I hit a nerve. Brown noser. I would definitely peg her as having been the school brown noser. I added my own wide, fake smile, minus the dimples. "I would really appreciate that. And thank you so much for taking time out of your busy schedule to meet with me."

<>

I chatted with all five of Jason's teachers, then waited in an empty classroom for Kyle Winters and Justin Jenkins. The consensus held that along with Jason, they were the three musketeers. I didn't get much more intel from the teachers than I had from the vice principal. However, Jason's teachers didn't have a problem "pigeon holing" him. They said he was a punk wannabe. Okay, so maybe I'm paraphrasing. Basically, Jason was all trash talk in a crowd but didn't have the stones to back it up when confronted by an authority figure. Throughout his illustrious high school career, Jason had been the target of some bullying but nothing over the top. Nothing every skinny boy going through high school hadn't endured.

When Jason's friends walked through the door and saw me sitting on top of a student desk, one of them added a little swagger to his walk. I almost laughed out loud.

"Hey there, sweet thing." That from the lanky blond one. I could see why they were nicknamed the three musketeers. The boys looked so similar, they could have been brothers. The only difference was the hair color—blond, brown, and black.

"It's Detective Kate Springer of the Tampa Police Department," I corrected curtly. "When is the last time either of you saw Jason Reeves?"

"Yo, yo, yo. I don't wanna talk about my brother JR. Let's talk about you and me," Blondie said readjusting himself.

Idiot. I always hated it when white boys thought they were some gang banging bad ass. "And you are?"

"I'm JJ, baby."

"Well JJ baby, be a good little boy, and get your ass back to class." I bolted up, getting right in his face. "You and I are done talking."

"Damn, sister. Just trying to be friendly. Shit, check ya' later K." As Justin Jenkins left the room, he looked over his shoulder one more time. He opened his mouth to add what I'm sure was another not so pleasant innuendo. Seeing the look on my face changed his mind. Instead he left, softly closing the door leaving me with Kyle Winters, the black-haired musketeer.

"Sorry about Justin. He can be a real jerk sometimes, but he's an okay guy."

"If you say so." I motioned for Kyle to take a seat.

"We've been friends since fifth grade. Same with Jason. Why ya checking up on him anyway?"

"He hasn't been to school in two days. Do you know where he is?"

"Dude, it's not like cutting class is against the law."

"Actually it is, but that's not why I'm here. Have you seen him?"

"Nope. Been trying to track him down myself. Is he in trouble?"

"I've heard he misses school on a regular basis."

"So. We all do. But he never ditches me and Justin. We've been calling and texting him for two days. He's giving us the brush off."

"When did you last speak to Jason?"

"Monday after school. I asked him if he had to work. When he told me he didn't, I asked if he wanted to catch the Bucs game with Justin and me over at my house. Bucs were playing prime time. Monday night football, baby. Man, the refs really screwed us out of a win. Dude, if Freeman hadn't—"

"Kyle," I said, interrupting his post-game analysis. "So the three of you watched the game together?"

Kyle Winters shook his head. "No. Jason said he had to finish his English Lit paper. It was already late, and if he didn't turn it in on Tuesday, Mr. Grady would blow a gasket." Mr. Grady would have to take a number.

"That was the last time you two talked?"

"No."

Talking in circles with this kid gave me a Slurpee headache. I spoke very slowly, trying to remain calm. "Please tell me when you talked to Jason again."

"He texted me at . . ." Kyle grabbed his backpack and dug around inside for his cell phone. "At 5:56 p.m. He wrote KC AT IT AGAIN FREAKS TEXTNG ALL DAY HAD ENOUGH—"

Kyle stopped midsentence. His face grew pale. He pursed his lips and snapped his phone shut. Abruptly, he jumped off the top of the desk. I grabbed the loose backpack strap that dangled down his back to stop him from leaving the room.

"KC. That stands for Kimberly Callahan, right? Kyle, what was Jason going to do?" The boy shook his head, and I thought I'd lost him. Eventually he muttered, "All this . . . these questions, it's because of Kimberly's death isn't it?"

I nodded.

"It's all anyone's talking about this morning."

"Kyle, I need to know what Jason said in his text."

"No way."

"If you don't tell me right now, then in accordance with statute 387.42, I have the right to seize your phone as potential evidence in a homicide. I'll get what I need when the crime lab prints out a history of all your past texts." Kyle's face morphed from anger into concern once he'd digested the bullshit I'd served up. "I'll make sure you get the phone back after we've made our court case in, oh I don't know, maybe five months from now."

"What! You're going to keep my phone for five months. That's so not fair."

I held out my hand, waiting for Kyle's cell. He finally conceded, sighing in disgust. "Fine," he growled.

I grabbed the phone and scrolled down to the message. The rest of it read GONNA SHUT THAT BITCH UP ONCE AND FOR ALL.

Kyle ran his hand through his hair and sighed again. "Kimberly was a freakin' psycho, dude. But that doesn't mean Jason was gonna hurt her. If anything, she'd have been the one to go off on him. Whoa, if she's dead, do you think he is too?"

"It's a possibility." I doubted it, but I wanted to give Kyle a little scare so he'd keep answering my questions. "Help me out here. Maybe I can find Jason that much faster."

Kyle nodded and sat after I motioned to the desk in front of me. I quickly scanned his phone's log and confirmed he hadn't received a call or text from Jason since 6 p.m. Monday night.

"When did Jason start dating Kimberly?" I asked, handing Kyle his phone back.

"Yeah, right." Kyle chuckled. "Good one."

"Would you like to let me in on the joke?"

"It's just . . . dude, they weren't boyfriend, girlfriend. At least not in Jason's mind. He met her at some party at Justin Jenkins' house. She was only like fourteen or some shit. When Justin and I saw Jason hitting on Kimberly, we were totally giving him grief. Serious jail bait. Jason told me it was his new plan for scoring with the babes. He said Kimberly was easy picking. Over the next few days Jason played her, and she finally put out. But it totally backfired. She hadn't been plucked yet."

At my questioning look, he added, "Kimberly was still a virgin. After that, she turned into a real leach. Jason stopped calling her, and she totally freaked. Kimberly kept calling and texting him, even showing up at his job. Dude, that's so not cool."

"When was this?" If Kimberly was texting, she had to have a cell phone somewhere. Maybe the killer took it.

"I don't know. Jason and Kimberly met at the beginning of school.

Dude, there was this righteous party. All these girls fr—"

I waved my hand, cutting Kyle off. I couldn't handle another tangent. *Dude, really!* "So they'd only known each other for a few weeks?"

"Guess so."

"Do you know if Jason's ever been to Kimberly's house?"

"Sure. What does it matter? I mean, he told me Kimberly's mom was a lush. Jason would go over to her house, and they'd do it right under her mom's nose." For as much as Kyle feigned disgust at the thought of Jason and Kimberly together, a note of awe crept into his last statement. I guess Kyle hadn't had the balls to sneak a quickie in his parent's house yet.

"Was Jason upset Kimberly wouldn't leave him alone?"

"You bet he was pissed. Dumb ass. Jason should have known better. But don't go thinking you're going to pin Kimberly's murder on him. She may have annoyed the hell out of him, but Jason would never kill her. He's not a psycho."

"You sure about that? You don't think maybe Jason got fed up, went over to Kimberly's house, fought over her being a 'leach', and when she still wouldn't back off, lost his temper and strangled her to finally shut her up?"

Kyle's backpack slipped of his shoulder, but he didn't register the bang when it hit the floor. He just sat there, mouth open, probably imagining the picture I'd painted.

"Why don't you give me Jason's home and work address? I'll find him, don't you worry." Hell, why waste time looking up the information when big mouth could give it to me.

Kyle returned my notebook, and I got up to leave. "Detective? You know what I told you earlier? The whole jail bait thing. You're not going to hold that against Jason, are you? I mean, Kimberly's dead, right? You can't hang some trumped up statutory rape charge on Jason now that she's dead. Right?"

I just smiled, kept my mouth shut, and turned towards the door. The thought of letting him sweat over it made my day.

When I tracked down Vice Principal Saunders, I guess she was still feeling pissy because she refused to let me search Jason's school locker. Told me I could come back when I got permission from Mr. Reeves or a warrant.

I decided to call the Publix on Dale Mabry Highway where Jason worked. Once I finally got through to the store manager and explained the situation, he was more than happy to talk. Sometimes having all the TV cop shows worked to my advantage. Guys like this so badly wanted to be a part of a real life investigation, they'd tell me anything I wanted to hear. The down side—wading through the bullshit. Embellishments were par for the course.

"Mr. Haney, can you tell me if Jason Reeves was on the schedule two days ago? On Monday?"

"No. He has Monday's and Friday's off. He works Tuesday through Thursday 6 - 11 p.m., and Saturday and Sunday 11 a.m. - 7 p.m."

After a quick calculation, I realized Jason put in over thirty hours of work a week. That added to a full workload at school, if nothing else, I could tell Jason was one hardworking kid. "Can you tell me about Jason's work performance?"

"Sure. I hired Jason when he was sixteen. I remember he came in for an interview on his birthday. It sounded like his family could really use the money. So I gave him a chance. Haven't regretted it . . . until a week ago."

"What happened?"

"I heard a commotion over on aisle five where Jason was restocking shelves. When I went to check it out, I saw a girl yelling at him."

I described Kimberly Callahan and asked if that sounded like the same person.

"Sorry. After twelve years on the job, all the faces seem to blur together. I did hear some of the exchange between the two kids, if that would be helpful."

When he didn't continue, I knew the store manager was looking for a pat on the back for being so instrumental with my investigation. "Yes, that would be a great help. Thank you."

"As I rounded the corner, I heard Jason say, 'You have to leave right now, or I'm going to get fired.' Then the girl said something like 'Good. After the way you treated me, you deserve everything you get. This isn't over. Not by a long shot.' Then she knocked a bottle of olive oil out of

Jason's hand, shattering it all over the floor. The girl ran out before I could get to them. Do you have any idea how hard it is to clean up an oil spill? It's unbel—"

"I'll bet. Mr. Haney, can you tell me if you've had any other problems with Jason?"

"After I told the boy he'd be let go if anything like that happened again, he seemed to get back on track. Well . . . until last night."

"What happened last night?"

"Jason didn't work his Tuesday night shift, didn't even call in. It's the first time he's ever pulled a no show. I haven't seen him since he left work Sunday evening."

"Thank you for your time, Mr. Haney. I really appreciate it."

"No problem. Glad I could help. If you need anything else, be sure to give me a call. And when you find Jason tell him if he doesn't show up for work tonight, not to bother coming back."

That was the least of Jason's worries. He wasn't at work on Monday or Tuesday. Looked like Jason wouldn't be using his job as an alibi. The picture Kyle Winters and the store manager painted made it sound like Kimberly was pissed Jason broke up with her. She became obsessed. Kyle said Kimberly practically stalked Jason.

Motive? From the sound of Jason Reeves' text, it sounded like he'd had enough of Kimberly. Jason may have met up with her on Monday night, and when she wouldn't agree to leave him alone, lost his temper, and killed her. I'd seen it before. Strangulation suggested intimacy and covering up the body showed remorse. Add that to the fact no one had seen Jason, and it looked like I had a new suspect to add to my list. Time to talk to Jason's dad.

But first, Patrick. Having spent countless hours in Purgatory myself, I knew what looking at all those faces on the computer could do to a person. Click through enough of the pasted on smiles, and eventually all you could see were the pleading eyes of each child begging to be saved. I knew those girls would be haunting my partner's dreams for many nights to come.

Patrick's voice mail picked up. "Jessup. This is Springer. How you doing, buddy? Did the air help? Probably not enough. Do what I do. Take a couple of shots at the firing range. Great aggression releaser. Anyway, got a name on the possible ex-boyfriend in the torn picture with Kimberly Callahan. Jason Reeves. He's a junior at Chamberlain High School. Just got done interviewing his teachers, friends, and boss. I'll give you an update later after I talk to his dad. If you need me, you know my number."

<>

Driving to Al's Auto Body, I realized I'd been trying to make myself as busy as possible so I could think more and feel less. Now stuck in the car, I had too much free time. I tried to keep my mind on the case, reviewing the facts, figuring out my next steps, but my mind kept wandering.

I sat at a red light waiting to turn into the repair shop. An exasperated mother stood on the corner, trying her best to wrangle her two kids. She waited at the busy intersection for the crosswalk sign to change. Her oldest child, who looked no more than four, wanted to dart into oncoming traffic. She had one hand on a baby stroller and the other a death grip on the squirming boy's wrist. The mom looked at the end of her rope.

*How do women do it?* I don't kid myself. I know I'm not cut out to be someone's mother. It doesn't seem fair bringing a child into this world. A place with so much unhappiness, so much ugliness.

There's peril around every corner. If you're lucky enough to be born with all your limbs and faculties, then you have to trudge through fluorescent lit hallways for thirteen years, maneuvering around bullies, school shootings, drugs, and gangs. You couldn't pay me enough to be a kid again. Children have zero control over their lives. They're told what to eat, when to sleep, how to act. As a child, I felt powerless. As an adult, at least I have the illusion of control.

A blasting car horn startled me, and I realized the stoplight had turned green. I jammed on the accelerator, pulling my car into an empty spot in front of Al's sure the mechanics were seeing dollar signs. They could look all they wanted, but they weren't getting their greedy little hands under my hood. The old girl might be hard and crusty on the outside, but it was what was on the inside that counted. And oh, did she purr.

I asked the bubble gum popping counter girl if I could talk to Mr. Reeves. Too busy to look up from her *Seventeen* magazine, she motioned with her head towards the door to her right. The garage housed three mechanics, all working on the undercarriages of vehicles. I had to raise my voice to be heard over the deafening noise of some whirring mechanical tool.

Harold Reeves, according to the name sewn onto his uniform, answered my shout and waved a beefy hand towards an outer door. I led the way to what looked like a small employee lunch room. Reeves had a nice smile. That changed after I introduced myself and asked where I could find his son.

"What do you want with Jason?" Reeves pulled out an already stained cloth from his back pocket and worked at rubbing the fresh oil off his hands. I doubted it would have any effect. They looked permanently stained.

"I'm worried about him, Mr. Reeves. Yesterday he missed school as well as his shift at Publix."

Harold Reeves smirked. "There's not enough crime in Tampa, the police department has to send out detectives to track down truant high school kids?"

"Well, there is the small detail that Jason's girlfriend, Kimberly Callahan, was found murdered yesterday."

*Not such a smartass now.*

Reeves hesitated for a split second. "Jason doesn't have a girlfriend."

I pulled out the picture of Jason holding Kimberly around the shoulder and challenged him. "You mean this isn't his girlfriend?"

"No. I've never seen her before. Anyway, that girl's way too young for my Jason."

"I agree. She's only thirteen. But none the less, I've confirmed she and your son were having an intimate relationship. So I'll ask again. Where is your son?"

A light sheen of sweat broke out across Harold Reeves' forehead. You could smell the worry seeping from his pores. "I haven't seen him in a couple of days. Monday he called me at work. Told me he planned on staying the night with Kyle Winters. They had to cram for a biology test. Kyle's good with his studies and helps Jason out a lot."

That might have been the story Jason fed his father, but I knew from Kyle he and Jason weren't together Monday night.

"When is the last time you actually saw your son?"

"Monday morning before school. I'm already at work when he gets home in the afternoon. But that doesn't mean shit. Jason wouldn't hurt no one."

"That's great to hear, but I really need to hear it from Jason. Here's my card. Call me once you track your son down. Since Jason's underage, you need to be present during questioning. I want you both at One Police Center by the end of today." I could almost guarantee it wouldn't happen, but I added the last part so Mr. Reeves would know the importance of finding Jason.

I headed back to my car and spotted an oasis in the desert. My favorite green and white sign blinked the words "Hot Now" in red neon. I was running late, but what the hell, there's always time to drive through for my favorite sweet treat.

# CHAPTER 13

Licking the last traces of a Krispy Kreme doughnut off my fingers, I fumbled to answer a call from Patrick. Jack Monroe, the neighbor Kimberly Callahan cleaned house for, was coming into the precinct for an interview. I told him to start without me that I'd watch when I got back. Probably wouldn't get much from the old guy anyway. So once again, I found myself navigating the Tampa gridlock. Stuck in traffic too long and Patrick's doughnut wouldn't make it back.

When I finally reached the eighth floor, empty handed, I hurried down the hall towards the interrogation viewing room. I didn't want to interrupt Patrick's flow, so I decided to watch behind the two-way mirror and jump in later if he needed me. As I drew nearer to the door, I slowed my pace. An odd combination of smells grabbed my attention. Usually the building had a clean yet nondescript smell. That is unless you were on the fourth floor where the seized marijuana plants were drying out. Now the hallway reeked of cigarette smoke with an undercurrent of something else. I couldn't quite put my finger on it.

I stepped inside the viewing room and stopped dead in my tracks. The smell—Irish Spring soap, Baby Powder, and cigarette smoke. I seized forward as if punched in the stomach. I couldn't catch my breath. Facing the darkened glass, I grabbed hold of the window's ledge to keep from collapsing to the floor. I could hear my heart galloping in my ears. Somehow my hands shook even though they had a tight grip on the cement windowsill. Staring into the room, my mind couldn't comprehend what my eyes were seeing. Patrick was supposed to be interviewing Jack Monroe. Then why the hell was he sitting across from Robert White. The man who'd molested me as a child?

Time slowed. I could hear the clock counting off the seconds, but they were somehow delayed. It was as if the ticking noise came from inside a deep tunnel instead of three feet to the right of me. I suddenly shrunk a foot and reverted back into the timid, little girl I used to be. I imagined the clothes I wore hung loose on my now smaller frame.

The combination of smells instantly took me back to the age of eleven. By this time, I was old enough to realize what was happening to me was wrong but still too young to figure out how to stop it. Hoping to ward off Robert's night time advances, I would stay up as late as physically possible. But never late enough. Eventually my eyes would betray me and close. Like clockwork, around 3:30 a.m., Robert would come turn off the TV, lift me from the couch, and carry me to his bedroom. Like a limp doll, I laid in his arms as he walked down the hall. The trip was never long enough. At some point I would awaken, but because I knew what was coming, I pretended to stay asleep. Robert always saw through the act.

Movement in the interview room snapped me back. I couldn't believe it. After all these years, Robert White sitting in my interrogation room. He must have changed his name to Jack Monroe shortly after he moved to Joliet. That's why the bastard didn't pop up during the computer search this morning. He was living under this new alias.

It had been twenty-four years since I'd last seen Robert, but I'd know that beastly wrinkled face anywhere. Even though his hair had turned completely gray, he still styled it the same slimy way—greased back with that damn V05 gel. I could see the striated marks where he pulled the comb through his hair. His eyes were still the same cold bluish-gray color. The color of glinting steel bars and just as hard. How could Patrick sit only a few feet away with just a table separating them? Couldn't he feel the evil emanating from this man?

Robert White—my tormentor, my boogeyman. The butterflies in my stomach felt like they'd sprouted hooked barbs and were trying to claw their way out of my abdomen. My mind forced my shaking hand to rise to turn the speaker's knob so the voices would carry through the little black box.

". . . yes, I've lived in Tampa, for oh, I guess nine years now. Lovely city, don't you think?" Robert White answered the question I hadn't heard Patrick ask.

"Yes. It's a great place to raise a family. Are *you* married?"

"Me? No. Once long ago, but sadly it fell apart all too soon. Wonderful lady though. I don't know how she put up with me as long as she did. But Lacy did have two beautiful little girls. Unfortunately, when the marriage ended, my relationship with them did as well. Pity. Anyway, I'm sure you didn't ask me here to find out my life story. You were saying about my poor little Kimberly."

I saw the slightest flinch of Patrick's back. He had caught the "my" as well.

"Yes, like I said on the phone earlier, Kimberly Callahan was murdered Monday evening. Her body dumped at a house on Morris Bridge Road in the early hours of Tuesday morning. Any information you could provide would really help our investigation."

Patrick was doing a great job putting Robert at ease, but I knew in my heart Robert wouldn't be easily fooled. He was putting on his own show. A master manipulator. Robert only showed the world exactly what he wanted it to see.

"Not a problem, Detective. Anything I can do to help. It just breaks my heart what happened to Kimberly. As you probably already know, she lives one street over from mine. I don't remember ever seeing her around the neighborhood until about a year ago. Guess she was almost twelve then. Anyway, I was in my yard raking up all those oak leaves that are always scattered about in the fall, when she came around the corner on her bicycle. I tripped over one of my own tree roots. She was such a dear, coming over to ask if I was alright and helping me up."

*Bullshit.* I bet he creamed his pants when he saw Kimberly. When he saw that little girl riding by, he probably saw my face. Bastard probably thought it was divine intervention, that he had a second chance. I'm sure he tripped on purpose, falling in order to arrange an "accidental" meeting.

"We struck up a friendship," Robert continued. "She was going through a rough patch and needed a friend. It was only her and her mother.

No other family in the area."

"Do you know Kimberly's mom? Cheryl Callahan?"

"Sure. I drop by every now and again, see if she needs help. I know my way around an engine, so I give Cheryl's car oil changes and what not. Kimberly told me after her dad died, her mom started drinking. As the years went on, Cheryl dove deeper into the bottle. By the time I entered Kimberly's life, her mom had pretty much checked out.

"Kimberly took care of everything at home—grocery shopping, cooking, housework. Plus she had her studies to contend with. I would give her a few dollars here and there, but I'm retired now and living off social security and my pension. Kimberly, God bless her soul, it was hard on her accepting handouts. When I fell and hurt my back last spring, she offered to clean my house. I think that helped her justify taking money from me."

"How often did Kimberly come by?"

"Always once a week to clean. But she was such a good girl. Since I'm not getting around as easily these days, she'd stopped by to check in on me every now and then. Guess she came to think of me as the grandfather she never had."

*Once upon a time, I had too.* I gave Robert credit, he was good. While he weaved his little yarn about poor Kimberly's home life, he looked directly into Patrick's eyes. He used all the right facial expressions at all the right times. He showed empathy and concern. There was no sign, no little mannerism indicating he was lying like the dog I knew he was.

"Mr. Monroe, how would you describe Kimberly's personality?"

"Until recently, she'd always been a hard working, caring young girl. Like I said, she had her hands full at home, trying to make the best out of a bad situation."

"You said, 'until recently'. What do you mean?"

"Things started to get worse between Kimberly and Cheryl. They had some horrible screaming matches. Kimberly told me her mom had gone into a rage one night and hit her. The next morning when Cheryl inquired about the bruise on Kimberly's cheek, her mom didn't even remember doing it. I . . ." Robert shifted in his seat, a pained look marred his features.

"I don't know if Kimberly had finally had enough of her mother's drinking or what, but once school started last month Kimberly started to change—her style of dress, her whole demeanor. I tried to get Kimberly to talk to me, to open up about her problems, but she wouldn't let me in. Then she began visiting less often, only came by to clean and pick up her check. I can't fault her though. She had too much on her plate. If anything, I blame myself. I should have done more, should have intervened with her mom. I really do miss Kimberly, Detective. The world is worse off for having lost her."

*Give me a break.*

"When did you last see Kimberly?"

Eyes averted up and to the left, Robert seemed to be searching his memory. His nonverbal cues read as truthful. Perhaps he wasn't consciously lying. Maybe he truly was a psychopath.

"On Sunday, Kimberly came over to clean. She wouldn't even talk to me. She had those little ear bud thingies in. You know the ones the kids always have stuck in their ears these days. Wish I'd known it was going to be the last time I'd ever see her. Maybe . . . maybe if I'd made more of an effort, Kimberly would have opened up to me."

"I'm sorry to have to ask this Mr. Monroe, but can you tell me where you were Monday night?"

"You don't think I had anything to do with poor Kimberly's death, do you?"

"I just have to confirm your alibi so I can cross your name off my list."

"I'm afraid that won't be possible young man. At my age, I'm no longer partying at the clubs until dawn. I hate to admit it, but I stayed home and watched my favorite recorded show, *Dancing with the Stars,* then headed to bed. I can't believe Florence Henderson is on this season. She's great. I tape all my night time shows, or I'd miss them. Of course then on Tuesday morning, I got up at the crack of dawn. But then, I really am a morning person. Went down to Denny's for my usual Grand Slam and later in the day—"

Patrick waved his hand back and forth to halt Robert's story. "Thank you, Mr. Monroe. That's fine."

I rested my forehead against the smoky glass. My skin soaked up the coolness, helping the perspiration that had beaded up dissipate. I started to doubt myself. Had Robert White really turned into a tottering old man? Or was it an act for Patrick?

I knew the signs of grooming. Pedophiles are smart. They often seek out low-income single moms who work one or two jobs outside the home. They look for broken homes where a young girl has low self-esteem and is in need of a father figure. The pedophile spends time and money trying to ingratiate himself into the family or into a relationship with the girl. After he becomes a trusted friend, he starts to test the boundaries of the relationship by pushing its limits. First, the pedophile might "innocently" brush up against the child's clothes to see what reaction he gets. From there he'll move on to hugging, tickling, kissing and more until he feels comfortable enough the child won't tell if he makes sexual advances. It's always hard for the child to break away once small acts of contact have been made because the predator makes the child feel guilty for not telling when it first happened. The abuse escalates because the child feels trapped in their shame.

I made a mental note to call the medical examiner to see . . . see what? I already knew Kimberly Callahan was sexually active. Ellis wouldn't be able to tell me if she was being sexually abused. *Get it together, Springer.*

"Detective Jessup, do you know any of the details of Kimberly's funeral?" Robert asked.

"No sir. You'll have to check with Ms. Callahan." Patrick stood, indicating the interview was over.

"I'll stop by then and see if there's anything I can do for the poor lady. I'm sure she's having a hard time right now."

"Yes. I'm sure she could use a friend."

Robert put both palms on the table, grunting as he lifted himself from the metal chair. His jaw was clenched. I could read the pain in each line of his scrunched up face. My hatred of the man had so clouded my judgment, I hadn't even noticed the cane propped against his chair. Then I remembered he'd mentioned hurting his back. I shook my head trying to clear the old memories jockeying into position waiting for their turn. I really needed to concentrate and study Robert with an objective eye. His skin looked pasty, a little too white to be healthy, and his hands showed the slightest of tremors. Robert's sport coat hung loosely around his frame. He'd probably lost a significant amount of weight recently. I even detected a slight dragging of his right leg as he exited the interrogation room.

A war raged inside me. I fought to hold onto the anger that had been my constant companion for over two decades. I simply couldn't reconcile the fact that this feeble old man was the monster of my youth. But I guess even evil isn't immune to aging.

All these years, I'd completely pushed Robert White out of my mind, just to get through each day. Seeing him now, being this close, I couldn't handle the emotions welling up inside. A cauldron of boiling liquid rolled in my stomach, threatening to bubble over. I brushed my hand against my cheek. It came away wet. I barely registered the fact tears had been streaming down my face the entire interview. I was breathing too hard. I told myself to calm down before I hyperventilated.

Patrick left the interrogation room, and I knew mere seconds separated him from the door to the viewing room. I had to get hold of myself, or he'd insist on knowing why I was upset. I couldn't tell him about Robert. Not yet. Especially not in this condition.

*Too late.* Patrick opened the door. I pushed past him, lowering my head to keep my face averted. I rushed to the ladies room down the hall.

Patrick hurried behind me, whispering as loudly as he dared. "Kate! Kate!"

I tried to ignore the concern in his voice. Fortunately, the bathroom stood empty. I rushed to the sink and splashed water on my face. I looked up at the reflection in the mirror afraid I'd see my thirteen-year-old self staring back. *No, not thirteen anymore. Thirty-seven. Not a victim anymore. A survivor. No one had control over me. I was in control.* Right now I had to decide. Would I crumble or would I overcome? I had to shore up all my reserves and once again paste a smile on my face. I could do it. I had years of practice. It was as natural as breathing.

I didn't want to confess my secret about Robert. Not yet. No one I worked with knew about my past, and I wanted to keep it that way. I refused to walk down the hall catching pitying glances shot my way, hearing whispers behind my back. But I had to decide once and for all if Robert was capable of killing Kimberly. If so, I had to come clean to Patrick right now. No matter the consequences.

I felt sure Robert had been grooming Kimberly, maybe even made an inappropriate move. The man I knew was capable of murder but the man who stood before me today was physically incapable. No way could he have lifted the dead weight of Kimberly's body moving her in and out of a trunk. Not to mention dragging her to the dumpsite. Robert could barely stand up from the table.

If divine intervention brought Kimberly and Robert together, it had also dropped him off right on my doorstep. Twenty-four years ago, Robert got away scot-free. He wouldn't be so lucky this time. I would make damn sure he'd go down for something. The statute of limitations had expired on my rape, but once a pedophile, always a pedophile. I'd bet my last breath Robert continued to abuse after he left Elgin. Hell, he'd practically said as much when he spoke of his stepdaughters.

I finished wiping the water from my hands and patted my face dry. Decision made. I wouldn't reveal what I knew about Robert, but I couldn't delay the inevitable. Patrick stood on the other side of the door waiting for me. Maybe I couldn't tell him the truth, but I could at least throw him a bone. It was the lesser of two evils.

When I pushed the bathroom door open, Patrick sprang away from the wall. "Kate, what's wrong?"

I took his elbow, and we walked farther down the hall to a more secluded corner.

"What's going on? I've never seen you like this."

"I need to tell you something, Patrick. Something I've kept from you. I feel so guilty for not having told you earlier. As your partner, as your friend, you always deserve the truth." I stopped talking and looked down at a crack in the linoleum floor.

"Okay, now you're freaking me out."

I milked the silence, hoping he would buy my explanation for my earlier display. Finally I said, "Yesterday at Kimberly Callahan's crime scene, do you remember when I got upset after I saw the victim's face? I moved away using the excuse I'd swallowed a lovebug. That wasn't the truth. When I saw Kimberly, I kind of freaked out myself. She looked like me . . . when I was thirteen."

"Uh-huh." Patrick spoke slowly, creases etched into his brow. Obviously, he didn't know what to make of my confession.

"Except for the hair, she was the spitting image of me at that age. I didn't say anything at first because I was confused. Then when we thought Lynch was our perp, I figured the whole look-alike thing was a coincidence. Now I'm not sure what to think." I looked over my shoulder to make sure no passerby had heard my admission.

"That's it? I mean don't get me wrong, I'm disappointed you didn't confide in me, but your attitude in the viewing room seemed a little over the top."

I nodded my head in agreement. "Seeing Kimberly's face . . . well this one's hit real close to home. I'm so frustrated we've hit a wall, and I feel guilty for keeping a detail like this from you. I'm sorry."

Patrick still looked skeptical but none the less, trusting. "You know Sergeant Kray is all over us to get this case solved."

"I know. I'm sorry. Where do we go from here?"

"It looks like we only have two options. Like you said, the resemblance could be a coincidence. The second option is you and Kimberly have some connection to the killer. Are you related to the Callahan's in any way?"

"No, I'm sure of it." At least that wasn't a lie.

"I need a little time to get my head around all this." Patrick rubbed the back of his neck and let out a sigh of frustration. "I still have to meet with the ASA later to prep for the Johnson case. I haven't had the luxury of being off for two weeks. Other cases need my attention. You're on your own for the rest of the night."

Patrick couldn't hide the unhappiness he felt. I understood. It would take time to heal the rift I'd created. Hopefully the Jack Monroe/Robert

White secret wouldn't tear us apart further. But with the emotional quagmire I was hip deep in, I was thankful I'd be flying solo tonight.

With another sigh, Patrick shoved his hands in his pockets. "When I meet with the ASA, I'll make sure to give her the paperwork for the warrant requesting Cheryl Callahan's phone records."

I looked down at my watch. 4:38 p.m. The daylight hours were quickly slipping away.

"Thanks, Patrick. Based on what I heard in the interrogation room with Ro . . . Jack Monroe, I think I'll check to see if any complaints of custodial abuse have been filed against Cheryl Callahan. Maybe someone reported the shiner Kimberly got from her mom. Then I'll check in at the Callahan residence and see if Cheryl's coherent enough to talk."

"But then again, maybe she'll be more forthcoming if she's three sheets to the wind," Patrick added in a lighter tone. I knew he couldn't stay angry long. It's not in his nature. I'm the moody, bitter one, not him.

"How about we meet for breakfast tomorrow morning. I'll update you on all my overnight discoveries. My treat. It's the least I can do." For emphasis, I added an exaggerated sad face.

"It's a start . . . I guess."

"What are your thoughts on Jack Monroe?"

"Monroe? He seemed like a nice old guy, a little possessive of her, but at least he gave a damn. It'd be nice if more people took an interest in helping out young kids."

I was dumbfounded. Were we listening to the same interview? But then Patrick didn't know Robert White like I knew him. White—still the master showman. He could make you believe he was a 5'1" oriental woman if he wanted. I simply nodded and kept smiling, afraid my voice would give me away.

"I'll look into Monroe's background later," Patrick said. "See if anything hinky shows up."

The one thing that didn't jive with Robert's story was the Good Samaritan act. When we interviewed Cheryl yesterday, she said her daughter cleaned house for someone in the neighborhood. It didn't sound like Cheryl and Jack had a close relationship. Seemed like a stupid thing to lie about, a detail so easily confirmed or denied. I'd have to find out how close they really were.

Lost in thought about the conversation I needed to have with Cheryl, I didn't see Detective Wozniack barrel around the corner until it was too late. He clipped my shoulder, threw me off balance, and had me spinning into the wall. If Patrick hadn't grabbed my wrist, I would have fallen to the floor.

"Dammit, Wozniack! Watch where you're going. It's not like the Girl Scouts are downstairs," I groused, rubbing my shoulder.

"Right. Good one, Kate." Wozniack chuckled. "I hope I didn't hurt you. You know I've been feeling bad about this ridiculous feud going on between us lately."

*Good one? Kate?* When had Wozniack ever addressed me by my first name? I stood speechless, suspicion masking my face.

"I think I need to go and reflect on the error of my ways." Wozniack gave a snort and continued down the hall.

*Reflect? What the hell did he mean by that?*

## CHAPTER 14

Though the mental box containing my stuffed away emotions was threating to explode, I forced myself to focus. *Concentrate, Springer. Time to put on your detective's hat.* I put a call into the Hillsborough County Sheriff's office to see if they'd investigated a complaint of child abuse on behalf of Kimberly Callahan. They told me a complaint had been filed on May 3, 2010, then rerouted me to Bonita Williams, the Child Protective Investigator in charge of the case.

When I heard Williams' name, I practically broke down crying again. *Finally, a break.* It was almost 5 p.m., but Williams wouldn't hesitate to stay late, helping me with whatever I needed. Last year, I inadvertently ingratiated myself with her after investigating the death of a nine-year-old girl she'd become particularly close with. The two had met after Williams investigated an anonymous call that came into the county's hotline. Williams discovered the little girl was being physically abused by her father. She ended up removing the girl from her home and placing her with foster parents who beat the child to death a few months later. The case really tore Williams up. Nine months we worked together, building an air tight case. Each of the foster parents got twenty-five years to life.

"Kate, dear! Miss me?" Infectious laughter punctuated each sentence. "Are you calling to catch up on old times or ask me out to dinner?" Williams was a gregarious woman with a sense of humor she often used to poke fun at her own ample curves. She radiated a loving warmth that instantly put children at ease. A real asset in her line of work. Just a few minutes in her presence and even the most timid child confessed their deepest secrets.

"You bet. How's next week?" She knew better, but I loved playing along anway.

"Mmm hmm. Don't hold my breath, right? Whatcha need?"

"Oh now, Ms. Bonita, don't be like that. I just got cleared for duty a couple of days ago, and I've got a hot case."

"Aren't they all, sugar?"

"But you know you're the only one who can help me crack it wide open."

"Okay, okay. How can I help?"

"I understand you investigated a complaint filed against a Cheryl Callahan on behalf of her daughter, Kimberly Callahan."

"The name doesn't ring a bell. Let me look it up."

I provided Williams the necessary information, and we continued to chat while her computer searched through its database.

"Finally back to work, huh?" Williams prodded.

"Been quite the whirlwind too."

"I knew you'd be cleared of any wrongdoing. That bastard deserved what he got. All I can say is good shootin' Tex."

"How's your granddaughter doing?" I asked, hoping to change the subject. A couple of months ago Williams took custody of her grandchild when her estranged daughter went to prison for possession with intent to sell.

"Belinda just turned two. She looked so cute in her braids and frilly pink dress at her birthday party. But I can't lie. It's been hard, real hard. I'm too old to start over again. Working all day here, then going home to her, I'm exhausted by the time my head hits the pillow. But what choice do I have? I can't let my only grandbaby get bounced around foster care. I've seen the atrocities that can happen to these kids in the system. No, not my baby. Nothing left to do but keep putting one foot in front of other."

"Sounds like grandma could use a day off. Forget dinner next week, how about I take Belinda to Chuck E. Cheese, and you can stay home and rest?"

"Don't be teasing me now. It's not nice to get an old woman's hopes up then . . . Wait a minute, Kate. I got something here." I could hear the clicking of her long fingernails race across the keyboard. "Now I remember.

Cheryl Callahan."

"Great. What have you got?"

"Looks like a teacher at Buchanan Middle School asked us to open an investigation in regards to Kimberly Callahan. Let me give you the highlights, and after we're done, I'll send you a copy of the full report.

"The teacher, Alice Tanner, noticed a bruise covering Kimberly Callahan's right eye. The extensive black and blue coloring had been somewhat concealed with makeup. The teacher privately confronted the girl about the bruise. Kimberly made the excuse she tripped and fell into her bedroom doorknob. Alice Tanner didn't believe her and when Kimberly got upset and tried to the leave the room, the teacher lightly grabbed Kimberly's shoulder. The girl winced, as if in pain. After further questioning, the girl finally showed an additional bruise covering her right shoulder. When the teacher asked Kimberly if a boyfriend had inflicted the bruises, Kimberly said and I quote, 'No it wasn't a boyfriend or my mom.'

"The teacher believed the mother caused the bruising, but Kimberly wouldn't substantiate the claim. I went to Buchanan Middle School to interview Kimberly. The girl denied her mother gave her the bruises."

"It's a good thing the teacher noticed the marks and cared enough to follow up on it." School was the best place to initially question children, especially if the suspected abuser was a parent. Kids often felt more comfortable and safer disclosing the abuse when not in the company of that parent. Obviously, Kimberly wasn't ready to open up.

"The good ones always do," Williams replied. "I also interviewed Kimberly's doctor. Wanted to find out if there was a history of "accidents". Her medical records were clear. They didn't show any past incidents that could have been a result of abuse. Everyone else I talked to including Kimberly's neighbors, friends, and other teachers all said the same thing. They'd never seen any signs of physical abuse.

"I interviewed Cheryl Callahan at her home. Her place was a mess, a coat of filth covered everything. However, there was adequate food in the refrigerator, and Kimberly's room was spotless. During the parental interview, I noticed Cheryl was intoxicated but coherent enough to converse with. She seemed very up front with me, confiding that she'd been drinking too much lately and experiencing alcohol induced blackouts. Cheryl denied striking Kimberly but demonstrated a willingness to join an outpatient alcohol recovery program. I presented the evidence to the State's Attorney. He declined to prosecute. No further action was taken other than to help Cheryl get into a program."

I wondered how long Cheryl attended the treatment program. Obviously it hadn't worked. "Do you think Cheryl hit her daughter?"

"I do. But the State's Attorney said we didn't have enough evidence to remove Kimberly from her home."

I didn't have the heart to confirm Williams' suspicions and tell her Cheryl had hit Kimberly. "Thanks for staying late, Ms. Bonita. I know you want to get home to your little girl. And don't forget, my next day off it's a date. Chuck E. Cheese, Belinda, me, and all the pizza she can eat. I promise." Closing my phone, I smiled. Bonita Williams had that effect on me.

Cheryl Callahan was next on my list. I wanted to ask about the abuse complaint and if the bruising Kimberly had endured really was a one-time occurrence or a regular thing. I also wanted to find out how long Cheryl stayed in the alcohol rehabilitation program. Originally, I'd planned to serve a warrant to search her place but an erroneous house number voided the document. I'd have to request another tomorrow. Luckily, Patrick noticed the mistake or all evidence seized would have been thrown out of court.

When Patrick and I first interviewed Cheryl, I didn't get the feeling she was involved in her daughter's death. Yet with my own mental state in question these days, I had some doubt as to the accuracy of my ability to read people. On the other hand, I shouldn't be too hard on myself. Patrick didn't suspect the woman either. But now with prior abuse and alcohol induced blackouts thrown into the mix, a whole new dimension was added to the case.

New theories raced through my head. My preference had Cheryl in a drunken stupor, fighting with Kimberly. It escalated, and Cheryl strangled her daughter. When mom finally sobered up, she saw what she'd done, freaked, decided to dump the body, and play dumb. The monkey wrench in that scenario—the semen found on Kimberly's pants. Though she could have gotten it at another time. Maybe one of Kimberly's jelly bracelets got popped at school that day, and she had intimate contact with a boy prior to her murder. Or she threw on a pair of dirty jeans that morning. I'd been guilty of the same offense on more than one occasion.

All this supposition was just that, certainly possible but still only theories. I'd have to bring Cheryl downtown and really grill her. Given enough time and intense questioning, she seemed the type to break. I'd first have to assess the situation once I got to Cheryl's house. Most likely she'd be inebriated, but I didn't know to what extent. Nothing she said while intoxicated could be used against her in court. If she confessed, it would be inadmissible. I'd start with a few probing questions, and if Cheryl was ready to talk, bring her back to the precinct and wait her out. Once she sobered up, I'd crack her like an egg.

I stood at the Callahan's door knocking, realizing I might have to put my plans on hold. The driveway was empty. I pulled out my cell and dialed her number. I could hear the phone ringing through the door but nothing else. No stumbling noises looking for the phone. No voices coming from the television set.

I disconnected when my phone beeped. *Tampa Tribune.* Like I was in the mood to talk to some reporter. I decided to let it dump into voice mail. It was probably some writer behind on a deadline, trying to resurrect the drama surrounding my last case. Those blood suckers really should move on.

Looking down at my map, I realized Jason lived only fifteen minutes from Kimberly's house. Might as well take another crack at locating him while I was nearby. Last Christmas my mother gave me a GPS. I told her I didn't want one, but since I drove all the time, she insisted. The damn thing drove me nuts. This English broad wouldn't shut the hell up. She kept repeating herself. "Turn left," she'd say. Then again, "In half a mile, turn left." And a third time she'd announce, "Turn left here." If I had to listen to her constant yakking every time I drove, I'd need to be committed. The idiot box lasted three days. Then it got regifted. Give me an old reliable street map over one of those techno gadgets any day. At least Patrick liked it.

I pulled up to Jason Reeves' house and another empty driveway stared me in the face. Although, this time when I knocked, I heard rumblings deep within the house. A minute later, curtains fluttered in the window next to the door. Someone was home. Maybe Jason had been hanging around the house while dad worked. When my knock went unanswered, I shouted, "Jason Reeves, I know you're in there." *Damn, what was I in, a bad B movie?*

I could hear the anger simmering in my voice, and I knew I had to check my temper. That's all I needed, the neighbors watching one of Tampa's finest bang down the Reeves' front door. But I couldn't help it, after my brush with Robert White this afternoon, my nerves were frazzled. Screw it. Let his neighbors think they were living next to a teenage killer. Maybe if I embarrassed him enough, Jason would bring his punk ass out here.

"Jason Reeves. This is Detective Kate Springer with the Tampa Police Department. Open up. I'd like to ask you some questions about the murder of Kimberly Callahan."

When he still didn't answer, I left my business card in the door and headed back to the car. I looked back over my shoulder and saw the front room's curtain fall back into place. *Little shit!*

Opening my creaky car door, I commiserated once again on the glamorous life of a detective. Drive, wait, drive, strike out, drive, try again the next day. Out of options, I decided to head home for the evening. I'd taken enough body shots for one day. Time to lick my wounds, heal, and live to fight another day.

# CHAPTER 15

Home, sweet, home. Perched in the bay window, my cat sat licking her right paw. She regarded me with skepticism, probably surprised I was home early. Once I got through the door, she jumped down from her private domain and stalked away giving me the brush off. I didn't take it personally. Hell, I respected the attitude she dished out. I figured I was a cat in a previous life.

I threw my blazer on the worn beige couch and continued towards the kitchen. It was nice to actually walk into a clean house for once. Since I'd been off work for two weeks, I took advantage of the free time and finally attacked the dust bunnies. Well, more like dust dogs. I stored my gun and badge on top of the fridge, vowing to keep the place up this time. Yet even with my next breath, I flipped off my shoes, letting them lie on top of each other in the corner. I headed back to my bedroom as the refrigerator's compressor kicked on with a wheezing sound. That's a new one. Guess I'd have to get George from Home Helpers to come out again.

Time to slip into my pj's. My favorite part of being home—wearing pajamas. They were my one indulgence. I had beautifully tailored silk ones, stacks of cute cotton pairs, even flannels. Although in Florida, the flannels didn't get much wear. I pulled out one of my favorite pair from the clean clothes basket. Silk but still comfy, in the same deep green color as my eyes. Seeing Robert White again . . . I just felt dirty. To combat that feeling, I decided to wrap myself in beauty. I'd always promised myself when I grew up, I'd be one of those women who wore cute pajamas to bed. Even when I didn't have someone sleeping beside me. I'd sleep naked before I ever wore a t-shirt and undies to bed again.

After dressing, I burrowed my way into the bedroom closet, heaving aside tubs of cold weather clothes, boxes of old sheets, and other miscellaneous items that always seemed to add up over the years. I smiled longingly, moving my prized Manolo Blahnik boots out of the way. They were a real extravagance on a cop's salary. I'd saved almost six months to buy them. They were black pull on knee boots made from the softest, richest leather. And they had a stiletto heel so high, they could be considered a deadly weapon. So far, I'd only worn them around the house. I was saving them for a special occasion, maybe a hot date if I ever had one again.

Finally, I reached my intended target, an old yellowed cardboard box containing childhood mementos. I don't know why I kept all these things. Strolling down memory lane only depressed me. But since my head seemed permanently stuck in the past, I wanted to revisit one picture in particular. I found the lone Polaroid sticking out higher than the Kodaks. Me sitting at a table beside a younger version of the Robert I'd seen today. I don't remember who snapped the photo, but we were playing a game of Cribbage. The photographer must have gotten our attention as we both looked up, grinning for the camera. Funny how my smile looked so genuine. I don't know why I kept the picture after all these years. I guess I held on to it as a form of proof. Not for any court of law, just for my own psyche. I could look at the picture and tell myself he was real. The horror I'd lived through really happened.

Looking up from the picture, I noticed a long rectangular piece of paper stuck to the edge of the box. Though it didn't look familiar, intrigued, I pulled it out. A poem.

The distance between us is frightening,
If only on opposite sides of a room.
If you're gone for a minute I'm lonely,
Make it ten and it feels like a tomb.

When you go away I grow colder,
A week? I'm surrounded by ice.
If the question is: do I love you?
My darling, you needn't ask twice.

The ticks of the clock are so dreadful,
For with each one, it weakens my heart.
It symbolizes my time without you,
Death is when we're apart.

You are all that my heart can desire,
All that my mind can envision.
I will be yours til the ending of time,
And for this I need no one's permission.

Love Always,
Robert

I dropped the paper in my lap and rubbed my hands together trying to warm them. Robert had never demonstrated an overly sentimental side, but then I guess the words were anything but romantic. More spooky and controlling. Becoming more melancholy, I grabbed a pen off the bedside table and opened the old journal I'd found in the memento box. To hell with this pity party. I decided to take the doctor's advice and purge these toxic thoughts by putting them down on paper.

September 30, 2010
Here I go again, writing in this stupid journal. Dr. Grace thinks it might be useful. I know I gave her a hard time, but she's right, it helped the first time around. When was that? Looking back through the pages, it seems like I started the journal closer to the end of the abuse, around twelve.
I can't believe I kept this book. It used to be so beautiful. I remember finding it at some local store, Pamida I think. The front cover had pink paisley swirls all over it. It was expensive, but I used my babysitting money to pay for it. At the time, I thought if I wrote down the ugly thoughts in such a beautiful book, the words wouldn't be so repulsive. Looking at the book

now, the cover's torn and a Coke stain marks the upper left corner. Still, I kept it. Through all the moves and all these years. I guess I held on to it as a reminder. Not that I could forget a moment of being raped. But it helped, writing down the words I was too scared and ashamed to speak out loud.

I remember the constant paranoia I felt back then. Had somebody read my journal? Did they know I allowed Robert White to have sex with me? Not abused. I never thought of myself as a sexual abuse victim. But then it was 1985, a time before Oprah was on TV warning us about child molesters.

By the time I fully understood what was happening to me, and I realized my friends weren't experiencing the same nighttime horrors, it was too late. I was in too deep. I felt that since I never told, never did anything to stop Robert, I was responsible. Once the world discovered my secret, they would think I liked it, that I wanted it. I kept going back didn't I? I asked myself that question for years. How did I physically will my feet to leave the warm sunlight of Robert's front steps to enter the cold darkness of his home and heart?

I guess the unknown was scarier than the known. With Robert, with the abuse, I knew what to expect. I'd been dealing with it for years. But once I revealed my secret, who knew what would happen. The thought terrified me. Mostly though, I coasted on auto pilot. Buried all my feelings—shame, fear, disgust, anger, self-loathing—for so long I eventually cut off all emotions. I had to deaden my feelings in order to cope. I know now that's no way to live. I think Kimberly Callahan and I have a lot in common. She's dead like me.

I'm so tired of not feeling. I ache to be fully alive again. But how? Especially after what happened. This afternoon, I came face to face with the monster who stole my childhood. Well, almost. Robert White sat behind a two-way mirror while I stood safely tucked away in another room. He now calls himself Jack Monroe. An odd set of circumstances brought us back together. My partner brought him in for questioning because Kimberly cleaned house for Jack Monroe/Robert White.

I have a horrible feeling Robert was grooming her. I just don't know if he'd made a move on her before she died. He's seventy-five now, and from the looks of him, there's no way he could have physically pulled off murdering her.

Once I solve the Callahan case, I plan on devoting every waking moment to putting the bastard behind bars. Once I start digging, I'm sure I'll find him guilty of some heinous crime. Years ago, I may not have been strong enough to stop him, but I am now. I won't rest until—

Doorbell. Hearing the chime, I stopped writing. I stuck Robert's photograph in the journal, setting it on the floor at the foot of my bed. Probably my next door neighbor needing an egg or cream for her coffee. At eighty-three, she was forever forgetting to pick up some essential ingredient when she went to the grocery store. No matter how many times I told her I didn't drink coffee, she'd forget and ask to borrow some cream. Now I kept a small carton in my refrigerator. It was easier that way.

Looking through the peephole, I saw Lucy James, a big goofy grin on her face. Just the distraction I needed. Lucy always lifted my spirits. When I opened the door, the cat ran to greet the new visitor. She circled in between Lucy's legs, begging for attention. *Traitor.*

"Frank, how's it going?" Lucy asked, bending down to pet the calico.

During the call out to my first murder case, I found Frank walking through her master's blood. The owner had been slain in the hallway and the damn cat made a real mess of the crime scene. Lucy took the extra time to feed Frank and wash her paws—after printing them. Since then, the cat was totally devoted to her. I think it instinctively knew her owner wouldn't be coming back and started angling for a new home.

When Lucy wondered what the cat's name was, I said, "Frankly, I couldn't care less." The name Frank stuck, even after discovering it was female. Unfortunately, Lucy already had three cats at home. Worried she'd become one of those crazy old cat ladies, she asked if I'd take Frank until she found a good home. A few days turned into a few weeks, and well, I never had the heart to make the cat leave.

"Hey, Lucy. What are you doing here?"

"Heard you had a rough day. Thought you might need a friend."

"Let me guess, Patrick?"

Smile widening, Lucy ignored my question. "I brought your favorite."

The smell hit me. Ling's China House. "Did you remember the crab rangoons?"

"Of course."

With a renewed twinkle in my eye, I yanked her through the door. "Then hurry, while it's still hot. Let's be total heathens and eat straight from the cartons." All my close friends knew the way to my heart—food.

"Here. Found this outside your door." Lucy handed me a box after I placed the takeout on top of the kitchen counter.

I groaned when I saw the writing on the box. QVC. "Mom strikes again."

"Oh no. Not something else for your kitchen."

Lucy knew my mother was notorious for buying new gadgets from QVC. Hell, she often benefited from the many gifts that came my way. Mom knew I could barely make a peanut butter sandwich so why I kept getting all these "modern kitchen marvels" had me stumped. Rarely did a couple weeks go by that I didn't find a box waiting for me on my front porch. Many of the items were still sealed in their plastic bags sitting in a high cabinet over my refrigerator. Once or twice a year mom would visit, unpack them all, and give me a quick tutorial on each piece. She missed her calling as a TV hostess.

I couldn't help but roll my eyes. "I swear if there was a twelve step program for QVCaholics, I'd set up an intervention and fly my mom to a recovery center myself." When I reminded myself it was just her way of showing her love, my annoyance quickly melted into a smile.

"I'll open it later." I threw the box on the counter with the other two packages. The Pasta Express and the Debbie Meyer Stay Fresh Green Bags.

Lucy filled Frank's dinner bowl with the cat food she found in the pantry. "I heard Russo processed Tommy Lynch's house. Sounded like a real house of horrors. How'd he do?"

"You know, green."

"Weren't we all at one time?"

"Not me." Though we both knew that was a big fat lie.

"You heard the story about Detective Wozniack back when he was a rookie, right?"

"No! How did I miss that juicy tale?" I pulled open the closest Chinese carton and wrinkled my nose. Lucy grabbed her dinner from my grasp and sat. She handed me a pair of chopsticks which I impatiently waved, trying to get her to refocus on the story. Only when she started talking again did I attack my Lo Mein.

"Well . . . Wozniack being Wozniack was as cocky back when he joined the force as he is now. Late one night, he and his Field Training Officer got called out to do some follow-up interviews for one of the homicide detectives. Down in the projects, corner of Lake and Central. Anyway, Wozniack thought he was hot shit so the FTO told him he could take the call himself. His superior hung back, and when he saw Wozniack leave the squad car's engine running and the doors unlocked, the training officer decided to teach him a lesson. He moved the car blocks away, waiting to watch the fallout.

"From what I heard, Wozniack got back to the street and practically crapped his pants thinking his squad car got pinched. He totally freaked out. The FTO could hear him cursing all the way down the street. Wozniack ended up hoofing it back to the station because he didn't want to call it in and hear the ribbing he'd take from dispatch. Took him almost forty-five minutes. When he got back, Wozniack thought he would get suspended or at least put on desk duty. But he figured it out real quick when all the guys were laughing their asses off."

By the end of the story, I was doubled over howling with laughter. I had to wipe away the tears streaming down my face before I could talk again. "I would have given my pension to see that," I finally managed.

No matter how hard I tried, I couldn't get the picture of that fat ass of his rocking back and forth jogging all the way back to Franklin Street.

When I described the visual to Lucy, she let out one of her pig stiletto laughs, spewing fried rice all over the table. This started the hysterics all over again. After a day like today, I never would have imagined it ending in peals of laughter.

"Sorry," I said, finally calming down. "What were we talking about? Oh, I know, Tommy Lynch. He's definitely a scumbag, but he's not Kimberly Callahan's killer. Nothing like a time stamped porn video to provide an alibi."

"Still, great job nailing him. At least he'll be off the streets. Who are you looking at now?"

"It's a close tie. The boyfriend, Jason Reeves, has motive, but I have no idea if he has an alibi. Hell, I can't even track him down. Supposedly, no one's seen him in two days. I stopped by his house on the way home. He's there but not answering. Looks like Kimberly's mom is also a suspect."

I filled her in on the child abuse complaint. "The perp definitely knew Kimberly. Most likely the killer planned to bury the girl behind the old Lynch house, but the dogs' barking spooked him off. Or *her*. So backup plan—lay the body out and cover it up."

I took my last bite of crab rangoon, savoring the richness of the bite. Ling's made the best in town. Lots of cream cheese and no green onions.

"What happened back at the station to make Patrick so worried?"

Averting Lucy's curious gaze, I felt a twinge of guilt because I didn't want to tell her the truth. Good sign though. Usually I could tell a lie without batting an eye. "He didn't tell you?"

"No. I guess he figured you would . . . so?"

When I didn't respond immediately, a hurt look crept over Lucy's face.

"It's no big deal, really. I just felt guilty I hadn't been completely honest with Patrick. At the Callahan crime scene, remember when I looked upset? It was because the dead girl looked like me at the age of thirteen."

Lucy's mouth dropped open. After a moment's thought, her face wrinkled in confusion. "Why didn't you say something then?"

"Surprise. Shock. Take your pick. I really didn't know what to make of it. I kept playing it over and over in my mind. First I thought it was a coincidence. Then when it looked like Tommy Lynch had killed Kimberly, I convinced myself I imagined the resemblance. Now . . . well I couldn't keep it from Patrick any longer. It felt wrong. Like I said, I felt guilty. Guess I'll be eating humble pie for awhile."

Lucy pushed her glasses farther up on the bridge of her nose. "How fitting. The phrase 'eating humble pie' dates back to the Middle Ages. After a hunt, the lord of the manor would eat the finest cuts of meat during a feast. People in the lower classes would be served a pie consisting of the innards and entrails which was known as 'umbles'. Back then finding yourself seated at the wrong end of the table being served 'umble pie' was humiliating."

"Where do you get this stuff?" I unsuccessfully tried to stifle a laugh. I was happy she'd come by tonight. A little levity was definitely what I needed. Especially after—. *No. Don't go there, Springer.*

"Albert Jack." Lucy actually beamed. Probably excited she got to share some of her archaic knowledge. But I shrugged my shoulders as I still had no idea who she was talking about.

"Albert Jack," she repeated. "He's an author who among other things writes about the origin of well-known sayings in the English language. I love his blog."

"Alrighty, then. Hey, I know." I snapped my fingers twice. "Let's bust out the blender. It's margarita time!"

"Oh no you don't. Last time you mixed drinks, I ended up sleeping it off in your spare bedroom."

"Was that so bad? You said it yourself, Frank makes a great snuggle buddy. Of course, I'll have to take your word on that. But come on, Lucy. This is one day I could really toast an end to."

With a pained look, she sighed. "Just promise we'll stop after the first pitcher."

# THURSDAY

# CHAPTER 16

Jolted awake, disoriented, I felt my heart thump as fast as a pack of greyhounds chasing a rabbit around a track. The numbers on the alarm clock read 6:20 a.m. Dammit! I hated when my last few minutes of sleep were stolen. It didn't matter if it was one minute or ten, I felt totally robbed. Ouch. Head pounding, too many margaritas. Make that too many pitchers of margaritas.

Then it hit me, my dream. Jerked awake because of a nightmare about Robert White. The heavy feeling of terror still weighed down on me. It was like waking up to find Hulk Hogan droppin' the big leg on your chest. Not the best way to wake up. Even though Robert hadn't stalked my dreams in years, there was a time in my life I was plagued by nightmares. The combination of counseling and discovering the devil in my own backyard caused a chain reaction. One doozy of a nightmare.

I slammed the off button on the alarm clock, and dragged myself into a sitting position. Taking stock of the last forty-eight hours, I realized I had to stop feeling sorry for myself. A quick pep talk and I was ready to tackle the day with a good attitude. No matter what happened.

<>

Before heading out the door, I checked in on Lucy who lay in a coma-like sleep in the spare bedroom. I snapped a picture of her with my cell phone. If I could pull it off later, I'd load it as a screen saver on her work computer. The drool pooling on the pillow combined with the cat's tail lying across her forehead was sure to get a good laugh.

I gently shook Lucy's shoulder, but she was slow coming to. If she didn't have to be at work in a couple of hours, I'd let the poor girl sleep. Once she opened her eyes, her headache would make her wish she'd kept them shut. Lucy never could hold her liquor. Guess we should have taken her advice and stopped after the first pitcher. Or even the second.

My cell phone rang, and Lucy cried out. Hurrying out of the bedroom, I heard her muffled grumbling as she jammed the pillow over her head.

"Hello, Detective Jessup. How are you this fine morning?"

"Did I get the wrong number? Is this Detective Kate Springer?"

"Ha, ha. Yes, it's me. I'm wearing my happy hat today. What can I do for you?"

"O . . . kay . . . We need to meet before work. It's important. Sally's Diner. You can buy me the steak and eggs."

"Yeah, right. Your wife would kill me."

"Then you order them, and I'll sample some of yours."

"Thanks for sending Lucy over last—"

"See you in a bit." Patrick hung up, completely cutting me off. Maybe he was still angry.

I walked out to my car, opened the door, and noticed a single white daisy on the windshield. Odd, but I guess with a windy morning like this one, not unusual. Maybe the rainstorm the weatherman kept promising would happen after all. I snatched it off my window and threw it to the ground. I hated white daisies. Robert always had them in vases around his house.

<>

When I opened the door to the diner, I was hit by the smell of bacon frying and a symphony of clanging dishes. Mornings were always hopping at Sally's. Patrick sat in the back, lucky enough to garner a corner booth. Most days I was stuck sitting at the counter balancing precariously on one of their wobbly, red plastic cushioned stools. I swear if I could channel Bob Villa, I'd bring in my ratchet set and fix the damn things myself. *Ratchet set? Is that even the right tool?*

The grim look on Patrick's face made my happy hat slide a little, but I steeled my resolve and kept going, sliding into the seat across from him. He pulled a copy of this morning's *Tampa Tribune* out from underneath the table, placing it in front of me.

Without looking at it, I set the newspaper aside. "Thanks, but let's order first. Tell you what, since you've been so understanding lately, I'll let you order the steak—"

"No. Read the paper first," he said sternly, putting it in front of me again. I had to grab it before it fell into my lap. Kind of pushy, but since he insisted.

"Son of a . . . how in the hell did the Tribune find this out?" So much for keeping a good attitude.

On the front page of one of the local newspapers, a paper read by over 600,000 Floridians, was my eighth grade school picture side by side with Kimberly Callahan's school picture. Our facial features were near identical. The headline read *Tampa Detective Spitting Image of Murder Victim.* The paper also included a smaller photo of me taken in my police blues. Anger radiated through my entire body. Unclenching my tight-fisted fingers, I had to smooth out the wrinkles I'd made in the paper just to read the article.

TAMPA - On Tuesday, September 28 at 7:30 a.m. Tampa Homicide Detective Kate Springer responded to what she thought would be a routine murder investigation. In an odd twist of events, the murder victim, thirteen-year-old Kimberly Callahan of Tampa, closely resembled Detective Springer when she too was that age. A coincidence? A crucial detail related to the murder? A source close to the investigation reported Detective Springer is stumped. There are no suspects in the case at this time.

Kimberly Callahan was strangled and dumped behind a vacant house on Morris Bridge Road, her body covered in dead leaves and scrub brush. The victim's hand, sticking out from underneath the leaf pile, wore bite marks made from the neighbor's dog. Neighbor Eric Steele commented, "I was walking my dogs like I do every morning when Bruno rushed over to a pile of leaves. Thought he'd found something dead. Turns out he did. But it wasn't no squirrel."

Callahan, an eighth grader at Buchanan Middle School, is survived by her mother, Cheryl Callahan. A memorial will be held in Kimberly Callahan's honor in the school gymnasium on Thursday, September 30 at 3 p.m. The public is welcome to attend. Becky Granger, Kimberly's guidance counselor, had this to say. "All of us are surprised and saddened by the loss of one of our dearest students. She attended Buchanan for the past three years, and I've had the pleasure of watching her grow and mature into a lovely young lady. I can't believe she's gone." Grief counseling will be provided to any student wishing to participate.

Detective Kate Springer, born in Elgin, Illinois in 1973, was also in eighth grade in the picture shown above. Springer transferred to the Tampa Police Department in 2001 where she worked as a patrol officer. In 2008, she was promoted to Homicide Detective. Detective Springer has been unavailable for comment.

carlosgarcia@tampatrib.com

"A source close to the investigation," I said, repeating the quote from the newspaper. "What a crock! I'd bet my pension Wozniack leaked this information. That little piss ant probably stood right around the corner yesterday listening the entire time. I'm going to get him if—"

"Kate, you have bigger problems than plotting revenge on Wozniack. Have you thought about Sergeant Kray and the shit storm that is about to befall you?"

Laying my head in my hands I groaned, wondering where it all went wrong. The one thing the Sergeant said was "don't get in the papers," and here I was front and center on the first page. I was screwed.

"Let's get out of here, Patrick. I better bite the bullet and make sure I'm sitting in front of Kray's office before he has to be the one to call me in."

A waitress shuffled over, asking for our order.

"Do you want something for the road, Kate?" Patrick stretched his leg out into the aisle, rubbing his knee. His old football injury was more reliable than the six o'clock weather report.

"No." The smell of grease saturated the diner's air, making my already queasy stomach churn. "I don't have much of an appetite anymore." Guess there was a first time for everything.

## CHAPTER 17

Sitting across from Sergeant Kray, the florescent lights reflected off his dark bald head. Hesitantly, I laid the paper in front of him and braced for the coming explosion. He took his time reading the article, and I thought he might have read it twice considering how long it took before he spoke.

"Please tell me how this happened," Kray began in a very measured tone. "Tell me how one of my detectives made this morning's front page."

"The only time I openly discussed the fact I resembled Kimberly Callahan was outside the interrogation room up on eight." The homicide detectives were housed on the eighth floor as well as Sex Crimes, the Criminal Tracking Unit, the Crime Analysis Unit, and the Economic Crimes Unit. "Detective Jessup and I were discussing this facet of the case. Someone must have overheard our conversation and leaked it to the press."

Ratting out Detective Wozniack wasn't an option. Since I didn't have definitive proof, it would only enrage Sergeant Kray. He didn't look kindly on unsubstantiated claims against one of his detectives. Anyway, I would deal with Wozniack on my own.

"Are you saying one of my detectives talked to the press about an open case?"

I kept my mouth shut and waited in my chair. Kray didn't really want an answer. The less I talked the better.

"Have you made any comments or had any interaction with the reporter who wrote the story? This Carlos Diaz?"

"No sir. I got a phone call from *The Tampa Tribune* yesterday at 6:40 p.m., but I didn't answer it. Figured it was a reporter fishing for a quote about the Kline kidnapping."

"Good. Under no circumstances are you to talk to this reporter. From now on, there will be a complete communications blackout from this department. I'll make sure of it. Our Public Information Officer will hold a press conference later this morning and work to diffuse the situation. Shit, Springer! The lieutenant is gonna to have my ass. And the chief, you don't want to know what she'll have to say." Kray was trying to keep his emotions in check, but I could tell they were brewing right below the surface. Hopefully, I wouldn't get burnt from the boil over.

"I want to know every scrap of information you've unearthed," he added. "No detail is too insignificant."

I recounted all the particulars for Sergeant Kray. All but one. I took a huge risk not informing him Jack Monroe was really Robert White, but by now I already knew it would end badly. I was gambling White wasn't involved in Kimberly's murder, thus my connection to him would be inconsequential and stay buried. Once I solved this case, I wanted a chance to nail the son of a bitch, and I couldn't do that with the TPD knowing our shared background and breathing down my neck.

"You may not have a definite suspect in the Callahan case *yet*," Sergeant Kray said, "but I'll have our PIO highlight the fact that during the course of this investigation, you and Detective Jessup busted a child pornographer trolling our middle schools. I'll get an update from the Sex Crimes Unit to make sure the Lynch case is solid. Hopefully, this will help keep the media and the bosses at bay. But you'd better watch it, Springer. If some sensationalist newscaster shows up on my front step, you're gonna wish you never transferred to this town. I'll demote your ass so far down the food chain, you'll think meter maid is a glamorous job. From this moment on, both you and Jessup eat, sleep, and breathe this case and this case only. On second thought, there will be no sleeping until this thing is solved. And I want updates every two hours. Do you understand me? Every two hours. Now send in your partner."

Patrick and I switched places so he could hear the same speech. My meeting with Sergeant Kray went far better than expected. I still had my badge, and I was still assigned to the case. Time to beat the pavement and see if I could get something to stick to Jason Reeves or Cheryl Callahan. I didn't want to waste time behind the wheel, so I pulled out my phone and dialed the Reeves' residence. No answer.

Just as I closed the phone, it rang. I looked at the incoming caller's name and sighed. Dr. Grace. I knew I should answer, she was only checking in on me, but too much had happened since I'd seen her yesterday. I didn't have the time or energy to explain, and I couldn't afford to get side tracked from the case again. It was hard enough to maintain focus and not fall apart.

"Why don't we split up? Make the most of the day," Patrick suggested after leaving Kray's office.

"Definitely. You want to head over to Al's Auto Body and take a crack at Harold Reeves?" I pushed the elevators down button.

"Sure. We need to get Jason in an interview room. Today. If he really is innocent, maybe he'll consent to a lie detector test. Not that it's admissible in court, but if he passes, we could rule him out as a suspect."

"Then we could stop wasting time chasing our tails and instead concentrate on finding the real killer."

The elevator doors opened. We walked in, and Patrick pushed the G button, taking us down to the garage.

"After I work my magic on Harold Reeves," Patrick said, "I'll check in with the Criminal Intelligence Bureau. They're setting up surveillance at Buchanan Middle School for Kimberly's memorial."

"I plan on focusing all my attention on Cheryl." Although even if she consented to a lie detector test, I wouldn't be able to hook her up to one. Any controlled substance in the body, whether it was drugs or alcohol, skewed the results.

Once in the parking garage, Patrick and I headed in different directions. I walked to my car, thinking about Cheryl's increased consumption of alcohol, the blackouts, and the suggestion of child abuse. Added together, it was very damning evidence, but did it add up to murder? I passed by a couple of guys from Vice, and we exchanged some friendly insults. With all the commotion, I didn't hear the footsteps behind me.

"Detective Kate Springer," a voice announced. Instinctively, my hand went to my gun as I spun around. "Sorry, detective. I didn't mean to startle you."

"You didn't."

The smirk on his face suggested he didn't believe me.

"Who are you?" I barked. "Don't you know this area is restricted? Police personnel only. Show me some identification, or I'll have to escort you off the premises immediately."

"I only need a minute of your time." The man was a little taller than me, maybe 5'11". Clearly of Latino decent, he gave off a kind of Ricky Martin vibe.

"Great, we'll talk on the way out." I grabbed his elbow, and we started walking towards the exit.

At the stairway, he stopped and jerked his arm away from me. "I'd like to talk to you about the Kimberly Callahan murder."

Maybe this guy had a good tip. I'd give him five minutes. "How can I help you Mr.—?"

"Diaz. Carlos Diaz."

"What? Wait a minute. You're the asshole reporter who splashed my picture all over the *Tampa Tribune's* front page. Where the hell did you get your information?"

"I'm sorry, Detective. I can't divulge a source." Diaz looked almost apologetic.

"Whatever. Don't bother. I already know who called you. You really threw a wrench into my case, I hope you know that. You might have jeopardized the whole damn thing. Now because of you, a mother may never know who killed her only daughter." A slight exaggeration, but I was pissed. "What are you some newbie reporter?" I could see by the way he shifted his weight from one foot to the other, I'd hit a nerve. "This isn't the way we do things around here. Your name is now mud. You'll never get an exclusive, a lead, hell, you'll be lucky to get a 'No Comment."

"I'm only doing my job. I got a lucky tip and ran with it. This story could make my career, and I won't apologize for it."

Then it hit me. I shouldn't even be seen talking to this guy.

Fortunately, there was no one in the stairwell, but that could change any minute. If Sergeant Kray heard I talked to the very reporter who created this whole fiasco, I could kiss my pension goodbye.

"Blood sucker."

I turned and flew through the door, headed back to my car. Diaz followed but wasn't quick enough. I revved my engine, drowning out his incessant questions. *Persistent little shit.*

## CHAPTER 18

The sight of media vans blocking both sides of the road greeted me when I turned my car onto Cheryl Callahan's street.

"Dammit!" I shouted, hitting the steering wheel in frustration. In only forty-eight hours, this case had turned into a real freak show. Neighbors congregated together on their dilapidated porches watching the spectacle. Some were even standing in their front yards being interviewed by local TV stations. Only 10 a.m.—obviously these people had no day jobs. In this neighborhood, I'd be surprised if they even knew the Callahan's. But then what did it matter. They were ready to get their fifteen minutes any way they could. At least the cable news stations hadn't shown up. Yet.

I parked one street over and broke into a light jog, steeling myself for what I knew was coming. One house away, I heard a gasp and the words, "There she is."

All at once, a throng of reporters encircled me. I stopped dead in my tracks, unable to break free from the mob. Cameras and microphones were shoved in my face. The roar of the reporter's questions was deafening.

"Detective, what's it like—"

"—a few questions,"

"What's your involvement with the victim?"

"—help us out here,"

Again and again, questions were hurled at me. I kept my mouth shut and head down. The crowd parted for a split second, all I needed to shoulder my way through. I ran to the door and started pounding, hollering for Cheryl to let me in. The reporters stood behind me still shouting over each other. Luckily, Cheryl had been peeking through the curtains at the mob scene in her front yard. She opened the door just as the reporters started pushing their way up the steps. Once inside, I slumped back against the closed door, trying to catch my breath.

Livid, Cheryl began tearing into to me. "Do you see what I've had to put up with around here? They won't stop knockin'. They won't stop callin'. They're drivin' me crazy!"

She was spitting mad, but it was hard to take seriously as each of her words slurred from too much drinking. Looking more to vent than get any real answers, Cheryl crushed her cigarette in an ashtray and headed towards the kitchen. I followed close behind. At one point, I grabbed Cheryl's elbow to steady her after she ran into a chair. Unfazed, she started slamming cabinet doors, obviously looking for a bottle of something. Finding none, her mood took a nose dive. She completely broke down, falling to the floor sobbing.

I stepped away to call Sergeant Kray, updating him on the circus outside and requesting backup. After I hung up, I walked over to Cheryl, gently taking her hand. I guided her to a standing position so she'd come with me to the living room couch. After a few stumbles, she finally sat. I looked around for some tissues.

"Don't bother." Cheryl pulled the bottom of her shirt up, using it to rub the tears and snot away.

I couldn't help wrinkling my nose. "Why didn't you call me? I would have sent an officer to help with crowd control."

"I didn't know what the hell was goin' on. First thing this mornin' some stupid TV broad knocks on my door and shoves a camera in my face. She asks a question about my feelin's on my daughter lookin' like the case detective. What the hell was she talkin' about?"

"On the front page of today's newspaper is a picture of Kimberly alongside my eighth grade school picture. We look a lot alike. Someone overheard me telling this fact to my partner, Detective Jessup. They must have leaked the story to the press. I'm sorry you had to go through all this."

Cheryl hung her head. Her anger having now dissipated. Waves of despair rolled off her like a tsunami crashing towards land. "What does this have to do with my daughter's murder?" she murmured.

"I don't know yet. But I promise you, I'll find out what happened to

Kimberly. I will find her killer. Do you think you're up for answering a few questions?"

Cheryl nodded. I exhaled a slow breath and pushed the record button on my digital voice recorder. I knew these were going to be difficult questions, considering Cheryl's emotional and physical state. But when I thought of Kimberly and her lifeless body dumped behind that vacant house, I knew I needed to find out who'd killed her. Even if it turned out to be her own mother.

"Cheryl?" Slowly, she raised her head. I hoped for her sake, her eyes felt better than they looked. Bloodshot and red rimmed, they were working overtime trying to blink away her last set of tears. "I have some questions I need answered, and I know they might be hard. But you really need to talk to me, to tell me the truth. Can you do that?"

Cheryl nodded.

"Great. Do you remember back in May when you got a visit from a Child Protective Investigator?" Cheryl's eyes grew large. "A teacher at Buchanan Middle School saw Kimberly with a black eye and a large bruise on her shoulder. Kimberly told the investigator you didn't make those marks, but Kimberly's teacher believes otherwise. Do you remember your daughter showing you those bruises?" Cheryl bit her bottom lip and turned her head to the side, new tears rolled down her cheeks.

"I need you to talk to me about this, Cheryl." Hoping she would fill the awkward silence, I stopped speaking.

After a couple minutes, thinking I'd have to prod more, Cheryl finally started muttering. "I swear I don't remember hurtin' her, but then, I don't remember much about the mornin' she said she got those bruises. I only remember the pain. Felt like my head had gone through a meat grinder. It'd been a rough couple of days."

Cheryl's sadness turned to anger. "I caught my boyfriend slammin' some skank. I was pretty busted up. Went on a real bender. The whole weekend's kind of a blur. Then on Monday mornin' I saw Kimberly's eye. Got real upset thinkin' some boy been pushin' her around. When she told me I did it . . . well, I didn't believe her. I couldn't do somethin' like that to my own daughter. But she was cryin' and tellin' me it was so."

Cheryl finished with a shrug. I guess if she didn't remember hitting her daughter, she wasn't going to take personal responsibility for it.

"Kimberly made me feel, like . . . all guilty and shit. So I went out and had a few." Again that damn, nonchalant shoulder shrug. "When I got home, I found some cop sittin' in my livin' room. Little miss high and mighty lookin' down her nose at me. Said she looked around my house— my house—and didn't think it was a . . . what did she say? Oh yeah, 'a proper environment for a thirteen-year-old girl.'"

"Did you tell the investigator about your blackouts?"

"Yeah," she leaned over, grabbing her pack of smokes. "I talked way too much. But I was scared she'd take Kimberly away. She's all I got. All I had anyway." Cheryl lit a cigarette and took a long drag.

"When did you start having these blackouts?"

"I don't know, maybe around Christmas last year. I'd wake up feelin' like hell and my friends would tell me about the weird shit I'd done the night before. At first I thought they were makin' it up, havin' a little fun with me, you know?"

"Are you still experiencing the blackouts?"

Averting her eyes, Cheryl mumbled, "Yeah."

"As I understand, you voluntarily attended an outpatient alcohol recovery program. Outpatient because there was no one to take care of Kimberly."

Cheryl snorted a quick laugh. "Voluntarily, right. I could see the writing on the wall. Start a program or lose my daughter. That place was a joke. They couldn't help me."

That was the problem with being pushed into quitting. No one could successfully graduate from a program they weren't a hundred percent committed to. A drunk had to hit rock bottom and really want to change their life before they actually could.

"Come on, Cheryl. At least be honest. What you really meant to say was you didn't want help. You weren't ready to climb out of the bottle yet."

"Don't you dare judge me! You don't know me." Hands shaking, Cheryl ground her cigarette out and immediately lit another.

"Trust me, I know your kind. You're a drunk. You're drowning in so much self-pity you can barely keep your head afloat. Well, boo hoo. Why don't you try thinking of someone other than yourself for a change? Try thinking of your poor dead daughter who at this very minute is lying on a slab in the morgue's freezer. So cut the crap and help me out here." Giving Cheryl the visual of her daughter seemed to help squelch the attitude. Though her white pasty skin turned a shade whiter.

"Have you ever been on Morris Bridge Road south of Cross Creek Boulevard?"

"That's where you found Kimberly's body, right?" When I nodded, she told me she hadn't. "It's way the hell up north. Why would I ever go there? Anyway, my car's a piece of crap. I'm lucky to get to the store and back." *Yeah, the liquor store.*

Cheryl sounded truthful. But if she really did kill Kimberly, who knows how much she committed while in an alcohol induced blackout. I made a mental note to check into this condition. Find out what one could accomplish and not remember.

"Has Jack Monroe looked in on you since Kimberly's body was discovered?"

"Jack who? Oh, right. No. Why would he come over here?"

That gave me the answer I needed, so I shrugged off the question. "Can you tell me more about Monroe?

"He's an okay guy, I guess. Kimberly met him riding her bike around the block like she used to do when she was younger. One day she came home tellin' me about this guy she helped. He'd fallen in his yard or somethin'. Anyway, when she got a little older, I said she could start cleaning his house to make some extra money. Could always use more cash around here."

"Besides cleaning house, did Kimberly spend much time at Monroe's house?"

"A little. I think she missed her dad bein' around. Normally, I'd worry the man wanted a little more than just help cleanin' his toilet, if you know what I mean. When I talked to Kimberly about it, she laughed and said he was too old to get it up."

It would be nice if that were true, but I knew better. Pedophiles never got too old to abuse children. Even if their plumbing no longer worked, they were a creative bunch. So either Robert hadn't made a play for Kimberly yet, or she lied to her mother about it. Although, the ME had reported Kimberly was menstruating at the time of her death, and I knew from personal experience Robert preferred prepubescent girls.

"Did Kimberly own a cell phone?" I knew Cheryl's daughter contacted Jason Reeves somehow. Because of the frequency, I doubted she'd been using a friend's phone.

"Didn't you hear me? I don't have that kind of money. I'm lucky to keep my own phone from gettin' disconnected each month. But now you mention it . . . Kimberly did start showin' up with a bunch of other pricey stuff. I thought maybe she was taking advantage of the five-finger discount. Come to find out Monroe gave her presents to say thank you for helping out around his house. But I never saw a phone."

I found it interesting Cheryl never asked about any suspects in her daughter's death. I didn't know if it was the alcohol clouding her judgment or the fact she already knew who had committed the crime. Greasy hair, filthy shirt, stained pajama pants—Cheryl looked like she'd been drinking nonstop since Tuesday afternoon.

"The first time I visited your house, I asked if Kimberly had a boyfriend. You told me no." Cheryl looked away. "You sticking to that story?"

"Hey, I didn't mean nothin' by it. I just didn't want you thinkin' my girl was a tramp. She was a good girl."

"Right. That's what you keep saying. But I think Kimberly used to be a good girl. Then something happened. She changed. Hell, you obviously didn't even notice. Guess it's kind of hard when you're smashed all the time. Everyone Detective Jessup and I talked to gushed over how sweet Kimberly used to be. How she always got good grades. Until this past summer. What happened, Cheryl? What happened to turn your happy-go-lucky daughter into a moody adolescent who started wearing all black, even dying her hair black? From what I hear, Kimberly started providing sexual favors to the boys at school. She began a sexual relationship with a seventeen-year-old and even stalked him when he tried to end it. So what happened? Did she get tired of cleaning up your vomit after a weekend binge? Did she get sick of—"

"Stop it! Stop it!" Cheryl screamed. "I can't help it if my daughter turned into a whore. It's not my fault. I can't watch her every minute. She came wantin' to cry on my shoulder after some stupid boy broke her heart. I told her she shouldn't have been puttin' out for him in the first place. Trust me, I know. Once you drop your pants for a man, you ain't gonna get no respect." Cheryl stood abruptly. "Whatever, I gotta piss."

I sat, stunned, thinking about everything Cheryl had said. She obviously knew her daughter was having sex, and it pissed her off. I could tell Cheryl was the type of mother who harped on her daughter, telling her not to make the same mistakes she did. I envisioned Cheryl even telling Kimberly how she regretted having sex early because she got pregnant and ended up in this hell hole. Nothing like a guilt trip about your being alive to make you feel wanted.

Cheryl had no alibi. She told me the first time we spoke she'd started drinking after her job interview Monday morning. She could have easily gone into an alcohol induced blackout. Maybe that evening Cheryl fought with Kimberly, lost her temper, and strangled her daughter. My gut said the killer knew Kimberly, and the statistics backed me up. Almost seventy-five percent of homicides are committed by someone known to the victim. That means three out of four times, the victim knows their murderer. Made me want to keep a closer eye on all my friends.

Strangulation is such an intimate act, not sexual, but intimate. To strangle Kimberly, the killer had to look her directly in the eyes. While exerting an enormous amount of pressure on her windpipe, the killer literally watched the life drain out of the girl's body.

Cheryl kept saying she loved her daughter, but her body language told another story. All of the shoulder shrugs and facial expressions suggested indifference. Alcohol was the only love of Cheryl's life. She was too self-absorbed to know what was going on with Kimberly or for that matter, care.

Decision made. Once Cheryl finished in the bathroom, I'd escort her to the precinct where we'd continue this interrogation. I'd been taping the interview, but when Cheryl sobered up, I'd ask everything again to see if I got the same answers. If Cheryl lied too many times, it'd be difficult to keep everything straight. I'd challenge her with the same questions over and over, hoping she'd entangle herself in a web of her own lies.

I leaned over, crushing the cigarette burning in the ashtray and stood up. Though it was a myth coffee sobered up a drunk, it wouldn't hurt to get a to-go cup ready. Coffee was still a stimulant, and the caffeine would help clear the cobwebs away quicker. Even so, I knew I was in it for the long haul. I'd be waiting several hours babysitting Cheryl before she sobered up enough to answer questions on videotape.

At the kitchen's threshold, I stopped. Seemed like Cheryl had been in the restroom a long time. The coffee could wait. I walked to the bathroom door and knocked. When I didn't hear anything, I rapped harder—a thump, a groan.

"Cheryl?" I rattled the doorknob. Locked. I thought about busting through the glorified plywood door but realized I should first check above the door frame. Bingo! Just like at my place, a skeleton key. I popped the lock and found Cheryl slumped over on the floor between the toilet and bathtub.

Dropping to my knees, I heard her mumbling. It sounded like she was repeating the same phrase. Something like, "I didn't mean to hurt her." I checked Cheryl's pulse and found it dangerously slow.

"Wake up, Cheryl. Wake up!" I clapped my hands in front of her face, trying to get her to open her eyes and focus on me. "Cheryl, are you saying you didn't mean to kill Kimberly or you didn't mean to hit her?" Again, another clap. "Cheryl, tell me what you mean!"

No use. She kept repeating the same phrase, but the words were getting more unintelligible. I looked around the bathroom to see if she'd ingested something. Adding a large dose of alcohol to pills or some other controlled substance could be a lethal combination. I found an orange prescription bottle in the trashcan. Thirty Xanax prescribed to Cheryl R. Callahan. That's all an addictive person needed, an excuse to get a script for anxiety and depression brought on by a family member's death.

The bottle was empty. I had no way of knowing how many she'd ingested. Cheryl had the prescription filled yesterday. The day after Kimberly's body was discovered. The directions explained Cheryl could take three pills a day. If she actually took the prescribed amount, there would be twenty-five pills left. Twenty-five pills she may have just swallowed. Was it a suicide attempt? Did Cheryl feel guilty for killing her daughter? Or did the bottle have fewer pills because she'd been popping them like candy?

Cheryl stopped mumbling. I looked over and saw she'd passed out. I pulled out my cell phone and dialed 911. "This is Detective Kate Springer from the Tampa Police Department. I have a Caucasian woman in her thirties who may have ingested a lethal dose of Xanax and alcohol. Her pulse is slowed, and she's fallen unconscious. I need a bus to 14006 Wedgewood Dr. in Tampa. Be advised media vehicles are blocking the street."

While I waited for the EMT's to arrive, I called Sergeant Kray. I updated him on the situation and asked for additional backup. One officer trying to hold back a pack of blood thirsty reporters who'd caught the scent of a developing story was like keeping Wozniack away from an all-you-can-eat smorgasbord at the local steakhouse. Kray said he'd call the officer standing guard outside the Callahan residence so he'd be aware of the ambulance en route. My next call was to Patrick. He didn't answer, but I left a fifteen second message asking him to meet me at University Community Hospital. Less than two miles away, UCH had the closest emergency room.

I looked through the sheer curtains, waiting for the cavalry to arrive. The sound of sirens grew nearer, and I was thankful the additional police officers and ambulance arrived together. The reporters also heard the sirens. A buzz started to build. They were practically foaming at the mouth, hoping for a new lead. Two EMT's were escorted to Cheryl's front door as four police officers blocked the hungry mob of reporters. I opened and closed the door as quickly as possible. Chunks of shouted questions rushed in. The police officers remained outside the house acting as a barrier between the door and the reporters.

I led the way to the bathroom, providing details about the suspected overdose. One EMT checked Cheryl's vitals and started an I.V. Because of the tight quarters, I stood in the hallway with the other paramedic. Cheryl was gently maneuvered onto the backboard and hoisted into the air. She remained unresponsive through the entire process. When they reached the front door, I knocked letting the police officers outside know we were ready. The reporters were pushed back from the sidewalk, allowing us space to head towards the ambulance.

The trip seemed like something out of a dream. The ambulance was only a couple hundred yards away, but the more we walked, the further away it seemed. Questions were being hurled at us, but no one said a word. Though even if we had, our answers would have been gobbled by the deafening roar.

The paramedics loaded Cheryl into the ambulance, and I jogged the rest of the way to my car. I pulled away from the curb, planning to follow them to the hospital. In my rear view mirror, standing in the middle of the road was Carlos Diaz, feverishly writing notes in his steno pad. He must have felt my eyes boring into him as he looked up and stared directly at me. At least he had the decency not to smirk.

## CHAPTER 19

A thorough search of the Callahan residence could wait. Cheryl wouldn't be released from the hospital anytime soon. If this was a suicide attempt, she'd be put on a seventy-two hour psychiatric hold for her own safety. Forced to dry out, maybe she'd finally start giving some truthful answers. Especially if hooked up to a lie detector machine.

Patrick showed up in the hospital waiting room only minutes after me. He looked well pressed and chipper. A stark contradiction to my own rumpled attire and attitude. Before noon and already I looked like I'd lost a three round bout to Evander Holyfield. The ER team was working on Cheryl. It would be awhile before we received an update on her status. I suggested heading to the cafeteria. I'd kill for a Coke.

Patrick headed towards a back table for added privacy. We didn't want any more prying ears. Before sitting, I made a quick detour. Even after all I'd been through this morning, my stomach rumbled. Not surprising since after I saw the morning paper, I'd skipped breakfast. Hospital food could be hazardous to your health, so I played it safe and picked a prepackaged blueberry muffin for a quick snack. I didn't have to worry about settling for a fountain drink. I already had my Coke. Rule number one—always know where the vending machines are.

I headed towards the table with the can squeezed under my arm, my muffin in one hand, and a coffee for Patrick in the other. I held the coffee cup as far away from my nose as I could possibly manage. With every whiff, the pungent aroma transported me back to my childhood. The taste didn't bother me. I'd never gotten over the smell long enough to even try a sip. What really pushed me over the edge was coffee breath. I remembered having to kiss Robert White. As if the mere fact of being forced to kiss a man more than seven times my age wasn't bad enough, to endure it through coffee breath was even worse. To this day, I was adamant about any man I dated having fresh breath. Not that I was a big fan of kissing anyway.

Patrick was also a coffee breath offender before I properly trained him. When we were first partnered together, I'd offer him mints following his morning coffee. After a few weeks, he caught on that his breath was less than desirable. Now he just stashed packs of white Tic Tacs in his desk.

"Here's your cup of Joe." I handed Patrick the paper cup. "Where'd they come up with that saying anyway?" Cup of Joe?"

"I don't know. Text Lucy."

A snort escaped my pursed lips. "You're bad." I sat across from Patrick, grabbed my Coke and popped the top, enjoying the fizzing sound.

He talked while I ate. "Obviously your morning has been a lot more exciting. I'll go ahead and get my update out of the way. As we speak, the Criminal Intelligence Bureau is setting up surveillance equipment at Buchanan Middle School for Kimberly's memorial. It's amazing how a little face time on the news will get your request to the top of the pile. Anyway, they'll have the gymnasium wired for video and sound by the time it starts."

"Maybe someone will show up that hasn't made a blip on our radar yet." Some killers couldn't resist watching the grieving family. Videotaping a victim's service provided photographic evidence of everyone in attendance.

Patrick nodded and blew into his coffee cup. "In my search for Jason Reeves, I discovered he's still MIA at Chamberlain High School. So I visited Harold Reeves at work. He wasn't real pleased to see me. Told me his boss would fire him if cops kept showing up. I told Harold we'd disappear as soon as he brought Jason in for an interview. And you know me, being my ever charming self, I told him I understood the long hours he worked and that you and I would be happy to meet with him any time, day or night."

"Always thinking of others, aren't you?"

Patrick gave me a wink. "Anyway the short version is Harold Reeves finally understands the importance of bringing his son into the precinct. However, dear old dad still hasn't seen Jason since Monday before school.

Harold did admit Jason was home yesterday while he worked. Most of the clothes from the clean laundry basket were missing. He said his son never puts anything away, especially laundry. Harold figured Jason took them when he left."

"I knew the little punk was home yesterday."

Even though Cheryl hovered near the top of my suspect list, I couldn't rule out Jason. I felt like staking out his house so I could nab him once he left and haul him downtown. Unfortunately, it infringed upon Jason's right against search and seizure. In order to compel Jason to talk to us, I'd have to take him into police custody where he'd then have to waive his Miranda rights prior to making a statement. I had to follow procedure, or anything he said would be thrown out of court. And I couldn't take Jason into custody since I didn't have enough probable cause to obtain a warrant for his arrest. I had nothing to tie him to the crime. Another Catch-22. *Damn constitution.*

"We still need to find out if Jason has any connection to the body's dump site." I plopped the last bite of muffin into my mouth.

"That kind of in-depth computer search is going to take more time than we have right now. I'll talk to the Crime Analysis Unit. It shouldn't be a problem getting their assistance. If there's a connection between Reeves and the old Lynch place, they'll find it. So tell me about your morning. Looks like it went from bad to worse. If that's even possible."

I gave the play-by-play starting with the media frenzy outside Cheryl's house ending with the paramedics taking her to the hospital. "I know I couldn't have prevented Cheryl's overdose, but I still feel a little guilty. Maybe I squeezed too hard. If she didn't kill Kimberly, I'm going to feel like a shit for putting her through the ringer." I toyed with a leftover muffin crumb, sitting on the table.

"Don't beat yourself up, Kate. It's the job."

"Yeah. We'll see if you're still singing the same tune when tomorrow's headline reads *Detective Interrogates Grieving Mom, Pushes Her to Overdose.*"

"Don't even kid. Sergeant Kray would kill you."

"Who knows? Maybe this will be the final push Cheryl needs to get sober."

"A couple of days in the hospital will dry her out. Maybe it'll stick."

We both knew better, but one could only hope.

"What should we do about the memorial Buchanan is holding for Kimberly?" I glanced at my watch. "It's scheduled for 3 p.m."

"That's a tough one. There's no way Cheryl will be released in time to attend, even if she convinces the doctors she didn't overdose on purpose." Patrick grabbed a napkin from the dispenser on the table and used it to clean up the muffin crumbs littering his side of the table. "Should we call the principal and ask them to reschedule?"

"I know I'm being selfish, but I'd like the memorial to go forward as planned. I'm hoping Jason Reeves is dumb enough to show up. And you never know what kind of information you can glean from the people who speak." Last year we had a case where a father spoke at his son's funeral. Overcome by grief and guilt, he'd disclosed details of his son's death no one but the killer knew. We nailed him with that one slip up.

"Maybe one of the Buchanan Boneheads will be so overcome with grief," I added, "that they'll finally start talking."

Patrick cringed when I said "Buchanan Boneheads". I made a mental note to watch my choice of words.

Hoping to break the uncomfortable lull in the conversation, I went to stand in line for some more food. From across the room, I watched Patrick rub his temples. Probably remembering his three hours spent in Purgatory. I came back with a second cup of coffee for him and a cheeseburger and fries for me. I knew I was taking my life in my hands, but one little muffin wasn't doing it for me. Anyway, how do you screw up a burger?

"Speaking of Sergeant Kray," I said. "What are you going to tell him at the next update?"

Patrick caught the *you* in that sentence and raised a questioning eyebrow. Teasingly, I smiled. I knew I was stuck with the updates for the duration of the investigation. Only fair since it was my face in the paper.

"We haven't been able to find Kimberly's cell phone," Patrick said, obviously ignoring me. "And there's no listing for a cell under Kimberly or Cheryl's name. Either someone purchased the phone for Kimberly and they're paying the monthly bill, or she owns a throwaway phone."

The market was flooded with untraceable disposable cell phones. Criminals loved them. Though regular folks used them too. They could purchase a prepaid calling plan, only buying the minutes they needed instead of being stuck with a lengthy contract. It was affordable if you didn't use it much—emergencies mainly. Yet, it didn't make sense for a teenager who made numerous calls and texts each month.

"Maybe Jack Monroe is paying the bill," I interjected. "Sounds like he helped her out quite a bit. You want to check with him?"

"Sure. I'll also talk to one of her friends, try and get Kimberly's cell phone number that way. Until we have a number, we can't subpoena her texting records from the phone company. And time is ticking."

Phone companies only stored the last seven to fourteen days of a customer's past text records. Every day that passed critical information would be lost.

"What happened with doing a reverse search on the incoming numbers on Jason Reeves' cell phone?" I asked. "We figured if Kimberly stalked Jason, there would be one number standing out from the rest."

"The ASA couldn't get us a warrant. Not enough probable cause."

"Wonderful. Now back to the subject of the memorial. As much as I want it to proceed, I really think we should let Cheryl make the decision."

Patrick agreed and looked down at his watch. "It's almost 12:30 p.m. I think it's time we track down Cheryl's doctor."

"Might as well." I threw my cheeseburger down in disgust. *Should have trusted my instincts.*

# CHAPTER 20

"Thanks for giving us a moment of your time, Doc. We know you're busy today," I said, shaking hands with the emergency room physician who'd worked on Cheryl.

"Sure, no problem." Though he was clearly distracted by all the chaos happening around us. I suggested we go behind one of the empty curtained exam areas.

"Can you give us an update on Cheryl Callahan?" Patrick asked.

The doctor's eyes narrowed in confusion.

I jumped in. "The patient who took a handful of Xanax after she already had enough alcohol in her system to kill a horse." ER docs—they annoyed the hell out of me. They never knew the patients' names. Just treat 'em and street 'em.

Finally, the memory caught up to the doctor's brain. "Oh, yes. When the patient arrived, she was unresponsive. Her pulse was slow, in the low 50's, and she had a respiratory rate of 8. The EMT's gave her fluids and started her on oxygen en route, but once she got to UCH, we had to intubate her. We checked the patient's urine to see what drugs were in her system. She had a level of 300 mg/dl of alcohol as well as benzodiazepine."

I was amazed Cheryl's alcohol level tested so high. She didn't seem that inebriated when I interviewed her. 300 mg/dl equaled a .3 blood alcohol level on a breathalyzer test. To get a DUI in Florida, you only had to blow a .08. Cheryl's blood alcohol level reached almost four times as much. The benzodiazepine didn't surprise me because of the empty Xanax bottle found in Cheryl's trashcan.

"When can we talk to Ms. Callahan?" Patrick asked the doctor. "Is her breathing tube still in?"

"Her breathing's better. I took out the tube right before you showed up. But the patient's still out of it. Might be for quite awhile. We'll set her up in a room and keep her under close observation. Check with the nurses in about an hour."

"Do you think Cheryl overdosed on purpose, Doc?"

"I couldn't say. We'll have psych come down and talk to her, see what's going on."

"Things might be tough for her these next couple of days," Patrick said. "She's an alcoholic."

"Thanks, we'll take care of her." The P.A. announced the doctor's name, and he turned his head, listening to the request. "I have to go, but you can get updates from the nurse once the patient's been moved to her room." The doctor left before we could respond.

"Patrick, I've been thinking. Would it be alright if I talk to Cheryl alone? She's been through a lot today. Hell, this whole week's been no picnic. If we both go in, it might be too much. She might lawyer up."

"Sure. I can keep working on Kimberly's cell number. Just get back to me about the memorial."

"Will do. I'm also going to check in with a nurse that works here. I'll ask her about alcohol induced blackouts. I want to see if Cheryl really could be capable of murdering and dumping her daughter and not remember it."

Before Patrick left, he reminded me to update Sergeant Kray. Always the Boy Scout. Then again, I was sure his motives were somewhat selfish. He didn't want me kicked out of homicide, or he'd have to start all over with a new partner. Ask any detective, the first year was like living as a newlywed couple. You were on your best behavior. You acted interested in the other person's stories. Even let them choose where to eat. It could be exhausting. Now in our third year together, Patrick and I were totally comfortable with each other's investigative style as well as little idiosyncrasies. Hell, we were finally at the point where we could pee in front of each other. Metaphorically speaking, of course.

I walked out to the ER admitting desk, showed my badge, and asked to speak with Tracy LaCroix. Not impressed, the nurse told me to take a seat while I waited. A seat, right, like that would happen. I'd rather pace. I hated hospitals, especially emergency rooms. I didn't know what was more overwhelming—the smell of piss and vomit or the overpowering cleaning agent used to mask the odors. I'd never been wheeled through those double doors, and I planned on keeping it that way.

Almost a half hour later, finished with Kray's update and tired of cooling my heels, I was ready to throw my weight around at the front desk. Impatience wasn't the only problem. I couldn't stand watching people in obvious misery waiting their turn to find relief. Another reason I preferred working with dead victims instead of live ones.

One guy in the corner was bent in half, cradling his stomach. I estimated two minutes before he ran for the bathroom. A couple seats down, a mother held a striped dish towel over her young son's hand. The fabric grew redder by the minute. I don't know how she could sit, waiting so calmly. A dozen other people stood or sat, all in obvious pain of some kind. I was contemplating who I had to hurt to get them shepherded through faster when I saw Tracy rushing towards me.

She didn't look like your stereotypical RN. Tracy had a flaming red pixie cut, a tiny metal bar pierced through her right eyebrow, and the tail of a dragon tattoo peeking out from beneath her blue scrubs top. With the nursing shortage, hospitals had finally started judging applicants more on their knowledge and less on their physical appearance. If I were ever rushed to UCH, I'd want Tracy at my bedside, ink and all.

Tracy talked fast and walked even faster. "Sorry about the wait. We just finished with a multicar auto fatality."

"Must be why they're backed up in the waiting room."

"Stupid drivers and their cell phones."

Guilty as everyone else, I stayed quiet while we power walked towards the vending machines.

"Got about ten minutes to spare. Whatcha' need?"

"Thanks, Tracy. I'm working on a case and wondered if you could tell me about alcoholic induced blackouts." I slid a dollar bill into the machine. The least I could do for monopolizing her break.

"Sure. The blackouts are like amnesia, but it's due to drugs or alcohol, not a traumatic event. During the blackout, a person's consciousness remains, but they can't recall their actions during that time. Even with friends telling them some of the crazy stories the next day. What the person did during the blackout is never imprinted on the brain, so it can't be recalled."

Tracy made her selection from the vending machine and immediately opened the pop can. The fizzing sound caused a Pavlov reaction in me, and I inserted another dollar, buying a Coke for myself.

"There are two types of alcohol induced blackouts," Tracy continued. "The first, fragmentary or partial blackout isn't that severe. A person has a few drinks and only a low-level of alcohol builds up in their system. With this type, the person may forget names or what they're saying mid-sentence, but with some prodding they can be reminded of what happened while drinking. The second type is complete or en block blackouts. Here a person is mentally and physically able to perform actions, but they may not be their usual self. During this type of blackout, the person won't remember what they did no matter how much prompting."

"How much alcohol would a person need to ingest before they blacked out?"

Tracy finished a hit of Mountain Dew. "Depends. It usually happens with binge drinking. If someone drinks an excessive amount of liquor in a very short period of time, they can suffer from a partial or complete blackout. Let me ask you, are the blackouts happening to a male or female?"

"A female. Why? Is that important?"

"Females black out easier than males because of the difference in how they metabolize alcohol."

"Isn't a 300 mg/dl blood alcohol level abnormally high?"

"Not if the person's a functioning alcoholic. They'll have a higher level in their system, hovering between 100 to 200 at all times. Then if they binge drink, it could easily go up another hundred. Where a level of 300 would kill us, it's not unheard of in an alcoholic."

"One more thing, Tracy. Can alcohol induced blackouts change your normal behavior?"

"Oh, sure. While in a blackout state, many people have reported engaging in high-risk activities they wouldn't normally. Like unprotected sex, driving while intoxicated. The problem is during a blackout state a person has impaired judgment and virtually no control over their impulses."

"So theoretically someone could commit murder while in a blackout state and never remember it?"

"Definitely. As a police officer, I'm sure you've had plenty of experience with mean drunks. Sometimes alcohol makes people giddy, kind of like me," Tracy said smiling. "Other times it brings forth the rage brewing just below the surface. While sober, the person's able to tamp down those feelings. Add large quantities alcohol into the mix, and it's like striking a match to a stick of dynamite."

"Boom," I murmured. I thanked Tracy for her time and went in search of Cheryl Callahan's room.

Had Cheryl attempted suicide? Were the feelings over her daughter's death too overwhelming to deal with? I wasn't standing in judgment. Hell, I could empathize with her. I knew what it felt like to be at the end of your rope. Feeling like death was the only escape from painful emotions. Before all this, Cheryl obviously hurt enough that she'd already chosen to kill herself. Just at a much slower rate. One drink at a time. Maybe Kimberly's murder and the ensuing media circus had finally sped up the inevitable.

I was ten when I first tried to kill myself. Admittedly, a pretty weak attempt, but when I heard a girl in my class had "accidentally" strangled herself, I thought it sounded like one of the least painful ways to greet the afterlife. Just tie my bathrobe belt around my neck tight enough to pass out. Eventually from a lack of oxygen, I'd never wake up again.

I remember the morning I made the attempt. Predawn. The darkness still held firm. Holding my breath, I snuck out of Robert's bed and tiptoed into my bedroom. Well, the room posing as mine—Robert had to keep up appearances. I never actually slept through the night there. Tears streamed down my face as I lightly touched the desk, realizing I'd never play school again. I placed my favorite tattered koala bear in my lap and pulled the robe's belt out from its loops. Twice, I wrapped it around my neck. The tighter I pulled, the faster tears streamed down my face.

Nothing happened. Deep down I knew I couldn't take my own life. After all, hadn't the priest at last Sunday's sermon said it was a mortal sin? Who wanted to escape one hell only to be thrust into an eternal one full of fire and damnation?

I found Cheryl in a room on the third floor. The drop in room temperature caused a shiver to climb up my spine. She shared the space with a lady who looked even more comatose than she did. I shook Cheryl trying to get her to wake up. No response.

I didn't have all day to wait around for sleeping beauty to gradually awake from her slumber. My first loyalty was to Kimberly. I had a duty to find her killer. No matter who that might be. I hefted the yellow pages I found in the bedside drawer and let it drop to the floor. It hit with a whack that echoed off the walls. In the silence of the room, it sounded like an aluminum bat cracking a home run ball.

The roommate didn't stir, but Cheryl's eyelids fluttered. I closed the curtain between the two hospital beds so Cheryl would feel like she had more privacy than we really did. I bent over close to her ear and started whispering. Though I wanted her awake, I didn't want her frightened and in need of sedation. I couldn't imagine how disconcerting it would be to close your eyes in your own bathroom, only to wake up under the harsh fluorescents of a sterile hospital room. Especially with padded wrist straps holding your arms down.

"Where . . . what . . .?" Cheryl croaked.

"Don't worry, Cheryl. You're fine. You took a few too many Xanax, and now you're in the hospital. Cheryl? Cheryl?" More fluttering, then her eyelids finally stayed open. I could see she had difficulty adjusting her vision. Who knows how long she'd be awake to answer questions? Most likely, she'd be in and out of consciousness throughout the day.

"Cheryl. In your bathroom this morning, you said 'I'm sorry I hurt her'. What did you mean?"

"Kimberly . . . why did she have to die?" Cheryl closed her eyes again.

"Cheryl, did you kill your daughter?" When I didn't get a response, I thought she had slipped under again. In this state, I knew there would be no confession. I skipped ahead to the most immediate question.

"Cheryl!" With great effort, her eyes finally opened. "This afternoon Buchanan Middle School is memorializing Kimberly. Can I get your blessing to go ahead with the tribute?" The only answer was a silent stare.

"I know you'd like to attend, but I have a feeling this room will be home for awhile. I know it would mean a lot to Kimberly's friends to publically remember her." Tears leaked from the corners of Cheryl's eyes. They trailed down her cheeks, staining her hospital gown. Still no answer.

"Cheryl, how about this? We're videotaping the memorial. How about I set it up so you can watch it live on TV here in your room? Would you like that?"

"Yes," Cheryl muttered, nodding her head slightly. I doubted she'd be coherent enough to watch, but at least I got my yes. That's what mattered. And it's not like I'm totally heartless. I'd make sure she received a DVD copy of the recorded service.

"Thank you, Cheryl. Why don't you go ahead and get some . . ." But she was out before I even finished my sentence. I know it wasn't exactly ethical, phrasing the questions the way I did, but when you're trying to catch a killer sometimes the line is blurred.

I took out my phone and dialed Patrick. "I got the go ahead from Cheryl for the memorial."

"How's she doing?"

"Pretty out of it. I could barely get her to stay awake long enough to get permission. I doubt I'll get anything else out of her today. It's a waste of time to stick around here. Where are you?"

"I'm still over at Buchanan Middle School. I wanted to make sure all the audio and video equipment is in place. We're all set. It's a good thing you got the green light for the memorial or these intel guys would be seriously pissed. Oh, and guess what? When Jack Monroe didn't have Kimberly's cell phone number, I had an epiphany. I knew Kimberly's new friends would rather spit on me than give me the time of day, so I checked the emergency contact cards the school keeps on file for each student. Guess whose number was listed in the cell phone category?"

"Kimberly Callahan's? Sweet. Nice work, Jessup. I'm impressed."

"Thank you. Thank you very much," he mimicked, using his best Elvis Presley impersonation. Not a bad imitation of The King, I had to admit.

"My next move," Patrick said, "is to furnish the cell phone company with a warrant. They'll provide me with a printout of all Kimberly's texts as well as a copy of the incoming and outgoing phone numbers. When the information arrives later tonight, we'll grab an armload of snacks and put on our wading boots."

"Sounds good. I can't wait to find out who Kimberly spoke to last and exactly when it happened. Kids these days are always on their phones either talking or texting. This could really help us pinpoint her whereabouts in the hours leading up to her death. By the way, are any of the guys from the surveillance unit still at the school?"

"Sure, they only finished up a few minutes ago. One of the techs is going to stay and run the equipment, but the other is leaving now. Why?"

"Can you ask him to come over to UCH before heading back to the precinct? I need him to figure out a way to broadcast the memorial onto the TV in Cheryl's hospital room?"

Patrick groaned.

"I know, but it's the only way she'd agree."

"Okay, but we're seriously going to owe these guys. They've really hustled to put this all together for us, and very last minute."

"Yeah, I know. Find out if they need any new kitchen gadgets?"

"What?"

"Never mind. I'll take care of it. Can you talk to the principal and update her on Cheryl? Give her the bare bones and ask if she'll say something on behalf of Kimberly's mother."

"Nice touch. Sure, I can do that. Did you get a chance to talk to your nurse friend?"

"Yeah. Tracy gave me the low down on alcohol induced blackouts. Guess it's not just a bunch of hippy crap defense lawyers use to get their clients off. It really is a medical condition. Looks like Cheryl could have blacked out, yet still been lucid enough to go into a rage, murder her daughter, dump the body, and never remember a thing."

"If that truly is the case, we can forget a confession. How's she going to admit to a crime she doesn't remember committing?"

"A lie detector test won't help either," I said.

"Looks like we're going to have to get some hard evidence if we're going to prove mom's a killer."

"Maybe the lab can match soil samples from her shoes to the crime scene."

"We should be so lucky," Patrick said. "Who knows what we're going to find searching the Callahan house? Going to be tough, considering there's no blood evidence."

"I know you wanted help wading through the Callahan's list of phone numbers, but I really should execute the search warrant on Cheryl's house tonight. The warrant's only valid for today. I'd hate to go back to the judge a third time."

"You suck, Springer. You know that, right?"

"Stuff a sock in it, Jessup. It's not like I hand-picked the cherry project. Who knows what kind of disgusting specimens I'm going to find in the Callahan's house? You've seen it. That woman hasn't picked up a cleaning rag in years. It's going to be a collection nightmare. Good thing I'll be wearing gloves."

"Point taken. Don't be late for school."

<>

Less than two hours until the memorial, time to head over to Buchanan. Preoccupied with my call into the boss, I hadn't noticed the media congregating near the hospital's sliding glass doors. I took my first gulp of fresh air and cameras started clicking. Thankfully, the number of reporters had dwindled considerably compared to those at Cheryl's house. The vultures must be circling the school staking out the best plot of grass to get their next sound bite.

Across the street, I caught a glimpse of a familiar looking gray haired man. Goose bumps broke out over my forearms. I stretched up on my toes to see over the crowd's head, but the busy intersection now stood empty. Ignoring the reporter's questions, I headed towards my car.

For a moment, I really thought it was Robert White. I must be losing it. Though in my mind's defense, it was quite a distance. Almost a hundred feet across eight lanes of traffic. My imagination must be running in overdrive. Robert doesn't even know I'm working the case. Hell, he doesn't even know I live in Tampa. The surprise on his face would make busting him taste that much sweeter. Still, I scolded myself for not being more attentive. No cop could afford dull senses.

"Detective Springer?"

*Great, I knew that voice.* I turned around, hands on my hips. "What do you want now?"

Carlos Diaz easily caught up, matching my purposeful long stride. "Detective, how is Cheryl Callahan? The hospital won't talk." As he spoke, he softly ran his fingers down my arm. Probably hoping to get me to stop walking. Again with the damn goose bumps. Though this time for a completely different reason.

I jerked my arm away and increased my pace.

"And what? You think I'm going to look into those baby browns and simply spill my guts? It might work with the other girls, Diaz, but not with me. You screwed me once, it won't happen again."

"Whoa, Detective! I don't know why you're pissed. It was only one story. Wait a minute. Did you forget to mention to your superiors you resembled your own murder victim?"

Unable to stop myself, I shot him a vicious look. *Dammit, how far away did I park?*

"They didn't know, did they? Hey, it's not my fault. You can't blame me for squealing on something you should have already disclosed."

I kept my mouth shut, concentrating on putting one foot in front of the other. It took all my strength, but I knew if I took the bait, I'd regret it. Diaz could print anything I said, and I really hated to think of what I'd look like in a meter maid uniform.

Diaz stopped following me, but as I got into my car, I could still hear him shout. "Get used to it, Detective. I'm not going anywhere. Until this case is solved, consider me your shadow."

## **CHAPTER 21**

The middle school's gymnasium, the meeting place for all of Buchanan's assemblies and pep rallies, was the place to be this afternoon. A buzz filled the air. You could feel the nervous energy which only added to my already well caffeinated mood. The bleachers were pulled out and hundreds of students crammed in elbow to elbow. The gym would heat up rapidly with this many bodies crammed in. Fortunately, I'd be in a nearby room monitoring the surveillance equipment.

I told Patrick I wanted to watch the faces of the students listening to the speeches. That way I could get a read on who should be singled out for further one-on-one interviews. This was true, but I also had an ulterior motive for staying out of sight. If Robert White showed up, I didn't want him to see me. Patrick would stay in the gym and keep a look out for Jason Reeves. If he showed, Patrick would grab him or anyone else looking suspicious.

The surveillance room had a bank of four small TV's lined up on top of a brown cafeteria table. One camera located on the west side of the gym would capture kids entering and exiting from that entrance. It could also pan halfway through the crowd. A second camera picked up where the other left off. It would monitor the east side of the room and its exit. Patrick stood on that side already tugging at his constricting tie. The third camera, aimed at the speaker's podium, would be piped into Cheryl Callahan's hospital room. The fourth captured the outside of the gym. Probably not much to see, but just in case, it was there.

The surveillance tech provided a quick tutorial on the equipment. As I tested the joystick, zooming out to pan the crowd, I saw Robert White enter the gym from the west side entrance. He must suffer from the same problem Patrick did with impending rain. Robert's limp was much more pronounced today. He was really favoring his hurt left leg. *Damn shame.*

Robert took a seat up front, one cordoned off for family and friends of Kimberly Callahan. Sadly, he was the only one sitting in that section. When the school's principal started speaking, I turned my attention to the third television screen.

"Thank you everyone for coming today." *As if the kids had a choice.* The principal coughed, trying to clear her throat. She looked uncomfortable standing next to a blown up school picture of Kimberly. The photograph, the same used in today's newspaper, sat on a sturdy easel and had a wreath of white flowers surrounding it.

"Today we want to celebrate the life of Kimberly Callahan, a life extinguished much too early. Kimberly was a bright, outgoing girl who attended Buchanan Middle School for the past two years. A gifted writer, she was active in the yearbook club and the school newspaper. I know she'll be missed by many. Unfortunately, her mother couldn't be here today because she was admitted to the hospital earlier this morning." The hum in the room grew louder.

Trying to regain control of the crowd, the principal continued in a commanding voice until everyone settled down. "But I was informed Ms. Callahan will be watching today's memorial from her hospital bed. All of us at Buchanan know this is an extremely difficult time for Kimberly's mother and wish her a speedy recovery. Now I'd like to introduce Ms. Blake, Kimberly's homeroom teacher."

A woman, arriving in a rush, sat down in the front row of the reserved section. She left two empty seats between her and Robert. I didn't recognize her from any pictures I'd seen at the Callahan house. Her bone structure and body type didn't suggest she was a relative. Maybe a friend of the family.

I spoke into a microphone that sent my voice to a receiver in Patrick's ear.

"Patrick." When I said his name, he looked up at the east side camera. "A plump red head just dashed into the gym. She's sitting in the reserved section near Jack Monroe. She's wearing too much makeup, in a black polka dotted dress. I'm thinking she could be a family friend. After the memorial, can you ask her to come back to the surveillance room?"

Patrick nodded.

As Kimberly's teacher spoke at the podium, I panned the camera, scanning faces in the crowd. Many had checked out, now wearing bored expressions. They were getting a jump start on their homework, listening to music, and texting friends who were probably sitting right beside them.

Ms. Blake's words were heartfelt, showing how much she really cared for her departed student. She fought to keep her emotions from overtaking her. I switched gears and started searching for the kids actually paying attention to the teacher's words. The pictures Kimberly had taken were displayed on the table before me. Patrick had already given me names to match the faces. He'd identified her old friends and the Buchanan Boneheads from his original interviews at the school.

Alice Tanner was the second teacher to eulogize Kimberly. When she introduced herself, I realized she was the teacher who had contacted the sheriff's office on Kimberly's behalf. With ears tuned into the speech and eyes on the crowd, I found Junie Foster about half way up in the middle of the bleachers. She dabbed at her eyes with a pink tissue. Patrick had told me how Junie was upset when Kimberly blew her off last summer. Even so, it looked like she still missed her old friend.

A group of the Buchanan Boneheads huddled together near the top of the bleachers. Four of them had starred in Kimberly's YouTube video. The girls were writing on a piece of paper they passed back and forth to each other. Old school texting. One sat a little apart from the group. When I zoomed in on the girl on the fringe, I could see her eyes brimmed with unshed tears. She chanced a quick glance at her friends, then quickly swiped at her eyes, trying to erase the evidence she had a heart. I searched through the photographs in front of me and found the girl's name. Samantha Richter. She had a jet black bob, and skin so white she looked more like a resident of Alaska, rather than the sunshine state. Samantha definitely nailed the whole Goth look, even down to the black fingernails.

"Patrick. Look up on your side of the bleachers, near the top.

Kimberly's new group of friends is up there. One girl, Samantha Richter, is kind of sitting apart from the others." After I described her, he nodded. "Though she's trying to hide it, it looks like she's getting pretty emotional. When this is over, can you discreetly grab her and bring her into the surveillance room? Maybe she's ready to talk."

After a few more of the faculty spoke, the principal returned to the lectern. "I know many of Kimberly's friends wanted to say a few words about what she meant to them. If you'd like to come up, now's the time."

Quite a few of the boys and girls filed down the bleachers. They took their turns standing at the microphone, stumbling through half-hearted platitudes. I wondered how many of them had actually been friends of Kimberly's and how many spoke just to feel a part of the event. Sadly, the kids probably thought this was the most exciting thing to ever happen at Buchanan. Fortunately, the principal banned the media from attending, or it would have been mayhem. While the students were expressing how much they missed Kimberly, I searched for Jason Reeves. I'd hoped to see him tucked in the crowd, trying to look inconspicuous. No luck. And the only person outside the gym was a woman sneaking a quick smoke.

I directed the camera towards Robert White, surprised he hadn't made his way up to the podium. He sat rigidly in his chair, face set like a stone. Misery and pain filled the room, yet he looked unaffected by it all. Robert was either doing a hell of a job keeping his emotions in check, or he had none to feel. Quite a contrast to the woman sitting two seats over. By now most of her makeup dripped downwards, tears having washed the color out of place. She looked like a maniacal clown in a horror show fun house.

Movement at the east side bleachers caught my attention. I panned the camera to see which student suddenly decided to get in line to add their two cents. Instead of walking towards the podium, a girl was trying to duck out of the gymnasium.

"Patrick! Samantha Richter is headed your way. Grab her. She's trying to skate out early."

Through the video feed, I saw him intercept the crying girl and whisper something into her ear. Patrick escorted her out the gym. A minute later, the door to the surveillance room opened. I gathered Kimberly's photos and turned them over.

Patrick led the defiant girl to a seat I'd moved so she'd be facing me, with the television monitors at her back. Then he quietly slipped out of the room to finish monitoring the end of the memorial. The surveillance tech discreetly plugged earphones into his monitoring equipment, quieting the feed from the podium.

I introduced myself and handed the girl a fresh tissue. School was almost over for the day. It was more important to talk to the girl than finish watching the service. "Samantha Richter, right?"

"Sammy," she corrected, slumping theatrically into the chair.

I could tell by her demeanor, she'd need some coaxing to open up. "I know you and Kimberly Callahan were tight these past couple of months. I can only imagine the pain you're feeling right now."

The water works started up again. Sammy reached for the box of tissues and put them in her lap.

"If Kimberly meant as much to you as I think she did, she could really use your help." Sammy lifted her head, a frown on her face. "I know she's gone, but that doesn't mean you can't help me understand what she'd been going through."

Sammy lowered her head, pulled out another tissue, and blew her nose. The girl extended the silence as long as possible, continuing to dab her now dry face. What could I say to get her to open up? If she'd only start talking, I knew I could keep her going.

"Ha!" I exclaimed a little too loudly in the over packed room. Sammy's head snapped up. "What a best friend you are. Loyal? Right. What a joke. So loyal your silence will help Kimberly's killer walk. You really think she'd want that? You don't like talking to cops, I get it. But you know what, sweetie? This ain't about you. This is about your friend, Kimberly. This is about you telling me what I need to know so maybe I can figure out who took her away from you. Do right by your best friend. This one last time."

"What . . . how . . ." Sammy stammered, flabbergasted at the way I spoke to her. She hung her head in defeat. "Whadya wanna to know?"

"When did you and Kimberly meet?"

"The first day of eighth grade. Scored too high on a math test last year, so they moved me up to an advanced class. It totally sucked cause I wasn't with any of my girls. Teacher made us pair up to do some stupid math exercise. Kimberly sat next to me."

Sammy pulled her leg up and rested her shoe on the chair, playing with the tied laces until they came undone. Then she made a show of tying them again. Slowly.

"And?"

Sammy let out an overly exaggerated sigh. "Come to find out, she wasn't so bad. Kimberly knew I wasn't the advanced class type, but she didn't try to make me feel like an idiot. After about a week, I invited her to go shopping with me after school. Like, I had to make her over if I planned on introducing her to my buds. The next day, Kimberly really rocked the look I picked out for her. She fit right in. Seems like she was looking for a change, and we were it."

"Why do you think Kimberly wanted to make a change?"

"Have you seen the girls she used to hang around with? Whatever."

Sammy's attitude began to rear its ugly head. Time to switch it up. "I know Kimberly had it pretty rough at home. Did she ever talk about her mom?"

"Once in awhile. Kimberly's mom drank like a fish. I only went over to their house once. I don't think Kimberly expected her mom to come home early. When Ms. Callahan showed up, stumbling, and totally drunk, I thought it was kind of funny. Kimberly was totally embarrassed though. We hung out in Kimberly's room until her mom started screaming about having no food in the house. We decided to jet back to my place. Before we could sneak out, Ms. Callahan got in Kimberly's face and started yelling. She was totally slurring her words. I couldn't even understand her. When she shoved Kimberly into the wall, I grabbed Kimberly's hand, and we ran. Her mom's a real peach." Sammy finished with an ever popular teenage eye roll.

"How much abuse did Kimberly suffer at the hands of her mother?"

Wrinkling up her face, Sammy looked at me like I was the biggest moron she'd ever met. "I don't know? She told me about some cop coming over to her place, snooping around. Mostly though, she didn't like talking about her mom. It always made her sad, so I never brought it up."

"Did Kimberly talk much about the guy she cleaned house for? Jack Monroe?"

"Yep. She totally had the old fool wrapped around her little finger. She always got free stuff from him. Sweet deal, if you ask me. I was wishin' I could get me somethin' like that hooked up."

I was in wonderment at how easily Sammy could slip in an out of ghetto slang. She was a real oxymoron. One minute she was showing off her vocabulary skills, the next she was using improper English.

"Do you think Jack Monroe ever made an advance towards Kimberly?"

"Nah, she would have told me."

"What kind of stuff did Monroe give her?"

"Clothes, gift cards, minutes for her phone, even a sweet digital camera. We had so much fun taking pictures of each other." This must have triggered a memory as tears gathered in the corners of Sammy's eyes.

"Did Kimberly always have her cell with her? We've yet to locate it."

"She didn't go nowhere without it. It was one of those pay by the minute phones. I told her she'd save money by switching over to a monthly service, but she couldn't risk her mom beating her to the mailbox and seeing the bill. We were constantly texting back and forth. My mom's always bitchin' at me for texting at the dinner table."

"Sammy, this is very important. We haven't been able to pin down Kimberly's whereabouts from Monday after school until her death that night. Can you tell me if you two talked or texted?"

Sammy chewed her pinkie cuticle, eyes averted towards the ceiling, thinking.

When she didn't answer, I suggested, "If it would help, maybe you could check the call history on your phone."

"Good one." Sammy pulled out a cell phone from her backpack. "We're not supposed to have these in class, but whatever. I have to stay in contact with my peeps." Her fingers flew across the tiny buttons at warp speed. "I have it here. We take different buses home, and as usual Monday we were texting the whole way. Just your basic chit-chat. Later in the afternoon, I called her. I had racked my brain for almost an hour trying to figure out how to do this stupid math question. You see, it asked for the hypotenuse of the—"

"Sammy," I interrupted before my head exploded. Eighth grade geometry had that effect on me. "Just tell me what time you last talked to Kimberly."

"Let's see . . . 4:47 p.m. Anyway, we worked on homework over the phone, and I remember asking her what she was gonna do later. You know, not much good on TV Monday nights. Unless you want to watch over the hill wannabees dancing around in circles. She told me she wanted to leave the house. Her mom was at home hitting the booze pretty heavily. Kimberly said Jim Beam brought out the worst in Ms. Callahan, and Kimberly wanted to leave before it got ugly. She could have come over to my house if it wasn't for my little brat of a brother having a karate thing. He tested for some new belt. You know, family unity and all that crap. Suggested she tag along, but Kimberly said she'd call Justine or Lexie and see if she could crash at one of their places. After Kimberly's . . . well you know . . . death, I asked the girls if she stayed with one of them. They hadn't even heard from her."

"Had she—"

"Wait a minute!" Sammy interrupted. She'd been looking down at her phone while talking but now stared directly at me, eyes wide. "I don't know how I forgot about this. I've been so upset since I found out about Kimberly. Then with the memorial—."

"Sammy," I said exasperated. I rubbed my forehead trying to keep the exhaustion at bay. More mental and emotional, but another forty-eight hours into this investigation, and I'm sure I'd be able to add physical exhaustion to the list.

"Right, sorry. At 6:24 p.m. Kimberly texted me. She was super stoked because Jason Reeves had finally answered her. She'd been calling and texting him like crazy. She . . ."

Sammy put the brakes on her train of thought and stopped talking.

"It's okay. I know about Kimberly and Jason. They had a sexual relationship. Her first as I understand it." When Sammy nodded slightly, I took it as a good sign. "Then Jason broke it off with Kimberly. Is that right?" Again a nod. "Kimberly wasn't too happy with Jason. She kept trying to get him to talk to her, right?"

"Bastard! He only wanted to get in her pants. I told Kimberly he was no good, but she kept going on and on about how he really loved her. Yeah, right. There's only one reason a seventeen-year-old boy is paying attention to a thirteen-year-old girl. I felt sorry for her. Kimberly just wanted someone to love her. He exploited that and if I ever see him again, I'm going to cut off his—"

"Sammy!" I stopped her before she could finish the threat. I was a police officer after all. "You said Kimberly's excited, she's finally getting her chance to see Jason. Did she say anything else?"

"Kimberly told me Jason planned on picking her up at her place around 7 p.m. That's the last I heard from her. I don't know if he actually showed up or not. Wait a minute! Do you think he killed Kimberly? Because if he d—"

"Calm down. There's no evidence he was involved."

Lost in thought, Sammy played with the jelly bracelets on her arm.

"I couldn't help but notice your bracelets." A blush spread across the girl's cheeks. "Orange, yellow, pink, gold. Glad to see you're only wearing those colors."

Sammy's choices told the world she liked kissing, hugging, holding hands, and making out. Considering what the other colors represented, I was glad she hadn't crossed over to performing sexual acts yet.

"I noticed Kimberly owned all the colors. It would really help, if you could tell me which ones she regularly wore to school."

Silence crowded the room.

"Please?"

Sammy hesitated a moment, then let out a soft sigh. "Kimberly wore the same colors as me . . . until a few days before she went to the party where she met Jason. Said she was bored and wanted a little excitement. She switched her colors and started wearing blue and black." Those two colors represented oral sex and intercourse.

"I don't want to lecture you but—"

"Then don't, Detective." Sammy's body language read impenetrable fortress. I knew a hopeless cause when I saw one.

"Thanks for talking to me, Sammy. Before you leave, can I ask one more thing? Please don't talk to the media about anything you told me here today. It could damage the case."

"No problem. The last thing I need is *my* face all over the paper." Sammy's eyebrows darted up and down in a knowing gesture. "You sure did look like Kimberly when you were her age. Does it have anything to do with her being murdered?"

"That is yet to be determined. But I guess it's a good thing someone your age actually reads the newspaper."

"Whatever. Like, it was splashed all over the web this morning. You're hot news, Detective."

*Great.* I now have notoriety with the thirteen to seventeen-year-old demographic.

"Can I go now? I'm going to miss my bus?"

"Sure. Thanks again." When Sammy stood up, I remembered to ask about Kimberly's social networking accounts. "Real quick. Do you happen to know Kimberly's passwords for Facebook and MySpace?"

"MySpace is so last week. As far as Facebook goes, I don't need to know her password. We're friends. I can read everything on her page."

When Sammy saw my eyes light up, she quickly back pedaled. "No way. Don't go thinking you're going to befriend me just to navigate onto her page. That's all I need, some cop reading me and my friend's posts."

"Once Facebook complies with my warrant, I'll read everything anyway. It would be helpful if I could get the information a little quicker."

"Fine. I'll email you her notes pages and profile posts."

I could live with that. Still, once the warrant came through, I'd check out Kimberly's page for myself. I didn't want Sammy self-editing some key piece of information out of misplaced loyalty for her dead best friend.

"It's been one shitty week." Sammy exhaled slowly. "First Kimberly, then Tessa."

When I didn't comment, Patrick, who had silently slipped into the room a few minutes earlier, jumped in for me. "Yes. It was through the course of investigating Kimberly's death that Detective Springer and I discovered Tommy Lynch videotaped girls at Buchanan. We're sorry your friend was involved."

"He did a real number on her. I had no idea. I wish she would have said something. Me and my posse would have—"

"Right," I interrupted. "You don't have to worry about Tommy Lynch anymore. He couldn't make bail. He's in prison awaiting trial."

I gave Sammy my card which had my email address and phone number. I told her to call me if she thought of anything else that might help the investigation, and to email me the Facebook information. In turn, she made me promise not to tell her peeps she'd blabbed.

When Sammy finally left, the surveillance technician started packing up the equipment. I'd stolen a few peeks over the girl's shoulder and knew the memorial ended halfway through the interview. I asked the tech if he could get me two copies of the taping by the end of the day.

"Why aren't you with the woman who sat in the reserved section?" I barked at Patrick.

"Well, hello to you too."

"Sorry. Antsy to get this case solved."

"I'm with you there, partner. The woman's name is Janet Moore. Once upon a time she and Cheryl Callahan were best friends." Getting ready to interrupt, Patrick held up his index finger, indicating I should be patient. Not one of my virtues.

"Janet Moore told me she had a babysitter watching her two-year-old. She couldn't afford to stay and talk to us now. I told her we'd be happy to come over to her house tonight and talk there. She suggested 6 p.m., her son's dinner time. Moore thinks we'll actually be able to hold a conversation if he's stuffing his mouth full of food." A smile broke across Patrick's face and he sighed. "I remember those days."

"Speaking of food . . . ."

# CHAPTER 22

Patrick and I met at a deli that had recently opened up not too far from the middle school. I waited beside his car while he finished up a phone call. From the one-sided conversation, it was clear he was on with his wife Alina.

"I know. I know," Patrick said into the phone. "I can't. Sergeant Kray will be all over my ass if I do . . . Tell Lanie I'm sorry I have to miss her recital. . . It's not like she doesn't have one every month. . . I know. I know. . . Tape it, and I'll be home when I can."

"Sounds like you'll be sleeping on the couch tonight."

"Like we're going to be allowed to sleep until this damn case is solved."

"Guess it's a good thing we're taking time out for a pit stop. Gotta build up those reserves for the long night ahead. I haven't seen one of these restaurant chains since I moved to Tampa. When I lived in Illinois, I used to grab the Toasted Turkey at least once a week. It's the best sandwich on the menu." The growling of my stomach seconded the statement, making Patrick grin.

"I can't believe you allow the alfalfa sprouts to lie on your sandwich. You do know they're green, right?"

"More white than green. But I'm good now. I've had my vegetable for the week."

Patrick decided on some ham and salami concoction, and we both sat down at a booth in the back of the warm building. The smell of baking bread had me salivating. I couldn't tear into the paper wrapper fast enough.

After we inhaled our sandwiches, I pointed towards the corner of Patrick's mouth. He touched his face and came away with a finger full of mayonnaise.

"Wasn't I right about this place?"

"Definitely a new favorite." Patrick used his napkin to finish the cleaning job.

"Oh yeah, and thanks for paying."

After an exaggerated eye roll, Patrick couldn't help but fall prey to my goading. He wore a determined look when he shot me a new trivia question. "What's the only X-rated film to win an Academy Award for Best Picture?"

Ah, page twenty-six. "The Midnight Cowboy." I decided not to push it by telling him the movie won the award back in 1969. Might tip my hand.

While Patrick finished his last few chips, I contemplated getting a second sub to keep in my car for later. Luckily, common sense overruled my stomach. Mayo and September heat didn't mix very well. Still pouting over his inability to stump me, I decided to fill Patrick in on the interview with Sammy. I wasn't sure which parts he'd heard.

"Sounds like either Cheryl Callahan *or* Jason Reeves could be our killer," Patrick said when I'd finished my report. "With Cheryl drinking all day, she could have blacked out and killed her daughter. We just don't know if Kimberly left the house at 7 p.m. to meet Jason or if he stood her up, and she stayed home."

"If Jason pulled a no-show, Kimberly would have been in a sour mood."

"Could have made her more prone to lock horns with her mother."

"Definitely," I agreed. "On the way over, I called the hospital and got an update on Cheryl's status. She's been put on a seventy-two hour psych hold. We won't be able to talk to her until next week at the earliest."

"Wonderful."

"At least she'll be sober," I added optimistically.

"She'll probably lawyer up. This could be a long drawn out case."

"Just what the Sergeant doesn't want."

"Speaking of which, have you updated Kray lately?"

"Yeah, in the car on the way over. Since Cheryl's out of commission, we need to keep working the Jason Reeves angle. What time did Harold

Reeves get off work Monday night? I forgot to ask him when we talked."

Patrick consulted his notebook. "He worked 11 a.m. - 7 p.m. on Monday and 7 a.m. - 7 p.m. both Tuesday and Wednesday."

"Where the hell is Jason sleeping?"

"After the pressure I put on Harold Reeves, I believe him when he says Jason hasn't been crashing at home."

"When we're done here," I said collecting my trash, "I'll call in a BOLO on Jason."

Short for *be on the lookout*, these bulletins were disseminated to Tampa police officers at roll call and through email. If a patrol officer recognized Jason, he'd call me and hopefully I'd make it to their location in time. Not much else could be done since we couldn't lawfully detain Jason. He was only a person of interest.

"Good idea. You know what?" A smile broke out on Patrick's face. "You said Kyle Winters received a text from Jason where Jason threatened Kimberly. Add that to what Samantha Richter said about Jason meeting Kimberly at 7 p.m. the night of the murder, and I bet we have enough to justify a warrant for Jason's phone records."

"Those records could really help fill in the missing pieces. We could figure out if Jason actually showed up that night. If he blew Kimberly off, she'd be pissed and texting him like crazy."

"Or maybe we'll get lucky and find out that after Jason killed Kimberly, he freaked and sent a very telling text to one of his buddies." Patrick crumpled his empty wrappers and headed towards the trashcan.

"Yeah, right. Only happens on TV." Still, I hoped for that very thing.

Patrick held the door open for me. I stopped midway through. "Flowers," I said.

"Flowers? Sorry, I didn't quite catch the train on that one."

"Your earlier conversation." I held my fingers to my ear, mimicking a phone conversation. "You need to bring flowers home tonight."

"My wife doesn't need flowers. She wasn't *that* mad."

"No goof, for your daughter, Lanie. Daddy missing any recital is a big deal to an eight-year-old. Buy a cute vase full of wildflowers, and all will be forgiven."

"Thanks." Patrick brightened at the suggestion. "Don't know why I didn't think of it? Growing up, there was always a fresh bouquet of flowers sitting on the dinner table. With eight mouths to feed, Dad put in crazy hours at the store. He was always missing a school play or some other important event. But when he came home with flowers, all would be forgiven."

"Glad I could help. Meet you at Janet Moore's house."

Patrick pulled out his cell phone while walking over to his car. I was happy to see a lift in his spirits. Now if I could only work on mine.

Something from Kimberly's memorial service had nagged at me all through dinner. I couldn't quite put my finger on it. It flirted right there at the periphery, and I couldn't grab onto it. Something I'd seen wasn't quite right. Damn, it was frustrating. Guess I'd have to let it brew in my subconscious for a while. My mind was like that. It would work over a problem for a couple of weeks, then BAM, it would come to me. I only hoped it wouldn't take that long.

With food in my belly, I felt reenergized as I pulled my old Porsche out of the parking lot. I glanced in my rear view mirror and saw Carlos Diaz smiling at me. He drove the maroon Honda Civic behind me. *Relentless.* I only hope he didn't misquote me and report I ate the Total Porker. I hated that sandwich.

A Buick idled behind Diaz. Just another customer or another reporter? At this point, did it really matter? It only caught my attention because a cigarette butt flew out the driver's side window. People who thought the world was their ashtray really pissed me off. I wish I could pull the inconsiderate asshole over to see the look on his face when I handed him a ticket. Technically, the litter bug could be fined up to one hundred dollars, but it wasn't worth the paperwork or the ribbing I'd take back at the precinct. If the guys discovered it was one of my hot buttons, they'd be ruthless. I could see it now. Walking down the hallway having butts flicked at me or even better, I'd open my desk drawer to find it overflowing with half-smoked cigarettes. Funny as hell as long as you weren't on the wrong end of the joke.

# <u>CHAPTER 23</u>

I pulled up in front of Janet Moore's ranch home, parking behind Patrick's car. Before I got out, I texted Lucy James. I wanted to see if she'd be able to finagle the search assignment at Cheryl Callahan's house. A few minutes later Lucy replied. WSH COULD. STUCK IN CRACK HOUSE. NTHG MORE FUN THAN PRNTING CRACK VILES. SAW MRNING PAPR. BEEN SWAMPD. CALL U SOON. CHIN UP. So I put a call into the precinct requesting a crime scene technician arrive at Cheryl's house at 7:30 p.m. Should be enough time to finish the interview and get back.

From the look of things, the Moore's had fared far better than the Callahan's. Definitely your average middle-class neighborhood. Nice place to raise 2.2 kids. The area was a mixture of professionals and blue collar families. The blue collars got here by buying a more expensive mortgage than they could afford, the white collars stayed because they couldn't afford to move somewhere better.

Patrick knocked on the door, and I heard a shriek that instantly put me on edge. I was ready to bust through the door when Patrick waved me away. "It's only Moore's toddler." He shook his head. "You seriously need to spend more time around kids."

I quickly stuck my tongue back in my mouth as Janet Moore opened the door. She'd reapplied a fresh coat of makeup and changed into a velour jogging suit. I never understood dressy jogging suits. I mean, make up your mind. Either throw on some comfy sweats or wear a nice outfit.

Over Janet's shoulder, I could see a little boy running in circles, screaming. I still couldn't tell if it was angry squeals or little boy laughter. It all sounded like noise to me.

"Hello again, Detective Jessup." Janet shook Patrick's hand, then extended a hand to me.

"This is my partner, Detective Kate Springer."

"Thanks for letting us come by," I said. "We really appreciate it."

"Don't know how much help I'll be, but come in, have a seat." Janet headed towards the kitchen and swooped up her son along the way. "Time for dinner, you little gremlin." She plopped him down in his high chair and told him to say hello.

"Haalo," Jacob dutifully replied. He pulled at the bib his mother draped around his neck. All the fussing in the world wouldn't help his chubby fingers maneuver the snap.

"Mrs. Moore, can you tell me about your relationship with Cheryl Callahan?" Patrick asked, joining me at the table.

Janet stood at the kitchen counter cutting fruit. "I've known Cheryl since we were in high school. Seems like we've been best friends forever. I moved down to Tampa from the northeast when I was fifteen. Been here ever since."

I could still hear a bit of the Maine accent she hadn't completely lost. "Do you work outside the home?"

"Not anymore. I used to be a dental hygienist but once I had Jacob, I decided to stay home full-time. He's our miracle baby." Janet must have read the uncertainty in my expression because she continued. "My husband Roy and I got married when we were twenty. We had a lot of trouble conceiving. Finally one of the invetro procedures worked." Janet looked at Jacob, beaming. I could tell she felt blessed to have her son. He was oblivious, more interested in mashing his hands through a pile of buttered elbow macaroni.

"You knew Cheryl's husband, Russell Callahan?" Patrick asked.

"Great guy. The four of us would play cards, have barbeques, you name it. We were inseparable. When Kimberly came along, we mostly hung out at their house. It was easier since we didn't have a baby then. You wouldn't believe how much stuff you have to cart around to spend an afternoon somewhere. The toys, diapers—"

I wanted to halt the mommy tangent, so I quickly interrupted. "What we really need to know is how things have changed at the Callahan's since Russell died."

Janet looked away from her son and gazed pensively out the kitchen window. "Right. Before the accident, things were fantastic. Cheryl was happy. She finally had the family she always wanted. Growing up an only child with uninvolved parents . . . well, Cheryl always seemed to have an aura of loneliness around her. Things changed when she met Russell. He was able to fill the emptiness. But when he died, a light went out inside her. Cheryl seemed to fold inward. In the months after the crash, I stayed at her house a lot. She could barely get out of bed. So I helped as much as I could with Kimberly. Sweet little Kimmie, only eight at the time. She took it real hard. Even harder when her mom closed herself off. The girl tried to stay strong, helping her mom, trying to ease her burden."

Janet looked back at me. Unshed tears glistened in her eyes. "Once the insurance money ran out, Cheryl finally pulled herself together. She got another job, and it looked like things were getting better. But it was all smoke and mirrors. One day I checked in on the two of them. I was helping out in the kitchen and found bottles of alcohol stashed all over the place. When I confronted Cheryl about it, well . . . she blew it off. She always did like to party. Cheryl seemed fine when we were talking, definitely not wasted."

"She was a functioning alcoholic," Patrick said.

Janet nodded. "I know that now, but back then, well . . . Then she found Harley."

"Harley?" I asked.

"Oh, right. His real name is Willy Davidson. Everyone called him Harley. You know—Harley Davidson."

*Real original.*

"Do you remember when they started dating?" Patrick had to raise his voice to be heard over the constant babbling of the little boy. How he could make so much noise while eating was beyond me. Although Jacob seemed more interested in throwing the apples and macaroni on the floor than putting them in his mouth.

"I believe she met him early June of last year. Harley thinks he's this bad A—S—S biker dude, all tatted up, hanging down at the local motorcycle bar."

*How cute, Janet spells the bad words.*

"When they first got together, my family and I went over to Cheryl's house one afternoon for a cookout. Now being a good Christian, I try not to judge a book by its cover. But Harley was disgusting. All through lunch, he could barely keep his hands off Cheryl. I mean come on, PDA, and in front of Kimmie. Totally inappropriate."

Racking my brain, I finally remembered PDA stood for Public Display of Affection.

"After Cheryl and Harley hooked up, I stopped hanging out at her place. Kimmie would still have sleepovers at my house though. I was like the aunt she never had. Cheryl didn't have any siblings. Anyway, the complaints about Harley seemed to multiply every time Kimmie stayed over. He wasn't mean or anything. She just thought he was gross and a bad influence on her mother. Kimmie said if anything, Harley didn't want her around." Janet wrinkled her nose every time she said Davidson's name. Either she completely detested the man, or Jacob had a stinky diaper.

"Cheryl told us she caught her boyfriend cheating on her. Was that boyfriend Harley?" Patrick asked.

"Yes. I say good riddance, but Cheryl took it hard. I heard she went on a real bender that weekend. She called me in tears later in the week saying a teacher accused her of hitting Kimmie. Cheryl was worried the state would take her daughter away. I was shocked but thought the scare might help sober her up, especially when she started the treatment program. It didn't. Cheryl wasn't ready to quit."

"Did you know Cheryl was having alcohol induced blackouts?" I asked.

"No. What are they?"

"When someone drinks large quantities of alcohol quickly, they black out but are still up moving around. The next day, they don't remember their actions while they were in this blackout state."

"How do you know someone's in it then?"

"It can be difficult. Mostly it's their demeanor. They may not act like themselves. For example, they might go into a rage over what you and I would deem inconsequential. Someone experiencing an alcohol induced blackout has lower impulse control. Because their inhibitions are lowered, they may participate in riskier behaviors."

"Did you ever see any of that with Cheryl?" Patrick asked Janet.

"One time over at Cheryl's house, Kimmie sat in her bedroom sobbing. When I finally got the poor girl to tell me what was wrong, she said her mom was always drunk, and she'd had enough. She told me Cheryl would fly into fits of rage for no apparent reason. Kimmie had given up pleading with her mom to stop drinking. She knew it would never happen."

"Sorry, when was this?" Patrick's pen was poised over his steno pad.

"After Cheryl's breakup with Harley, around May of this year. Kimmie told me she didn't care anymore that her mom left the house every night. I was shocked. Kimmie was only thirteen, at a critical point in her development. I tried spending extra time with her. Not only to give her the support she obviously needed, but to see with my own eyes what was going on around the house. Kimmie was right. Cheryl would sleep all day while Kimmie went to school, then go out in the evening and be out all night. At least Cheryl had the decency not to bring strange men home while Kimberly slept."

*Real considerate.*

Janet leaned over, grabbing a few apple pieces littering the floor. "I confronted Cheryl. She was livid. She screamed it was none of my business and to get the H—E—L—L out of her house. I'd never seen her lose her temper like that. Finally, when Cheryl threatened my son, I got really scared. I tried to do my best for Kimmie. She was like my own daughter. But I knew I had to break off the relationship. You can't help someone who doesn't want to be helped. Cheryl made it clear I was to stay away from Kimberly. Unfortunately, I did and look what happened. If only I would have . . ."

There went the mascara. Had to give the woman credit. She'd kept it together until now. With all the tears Janet had shed today, you'd think she'd consider switching to a waterproof formula.

Patrick handed Janet the towel sitting on the table between us. "There's no use in playing the what-if game, Janet. Don't feel guilty. If anything, you were the only one in Kimberly's life who gave a damn."

"How did Cheryl threaten your son?" I asked. Cheryl had already demonstrated she was capable of verbal and physical abuse. Was it such a stretch to think she was capable of murder?

"Cheryl said if I ever stepped foot in her house again, she'd choke the life right out of my son."

I shot Patrick a look and saw we were on the same page.

"After hearing something like that, I can understand why you cut ties with the family," I said.

Janet finally pulled herself together. She started wiping off Jacob's hands and mouth with the same black streaked towel. "At the memorial, they said Cheryl had been admitted into the hospital. What happened?" Janet pulled her son out of the highchair and into her arms. He sighed contentedly, snuggling into her shoulder.

What I wouldn't give to experience a moment of that all-encompassing peace. The kind you can only achieve as a child in the arms of a protective mother. Lost in the moment, I didn't speak.

Patrick answered for me. "She combined alcohol with too much Xanax. Cheryl's been put on a psychiatric hold for seventy-two hours. I don't know what's going to happen to her afterwards, but it sounds like you and Cheryl were close once. Maybe you can talk her into giving a recovery program another go."

Janet nodded, but I didn't know if she'd be able to give Cheryl a second chance. You didn't threaten a mother's child and expect absolution easily.

"Do you know where we can find this Harley Davidson?" Patrick barely contained his grin when he used Willy's nickname.

"He used to hang out at The Rusty Bolt. Don't know if he still does."

Patrick and I thanked Janet for her time and honesty. I couldn't help but add that if she was interested, Janet could find Cheryl at University Community Hospital.

Once outside, Patrick told me he was heading back to the precinct to start scouring the Callahan's phone records. "I'll also talk to the State's Attorney's office and get the warrant started for Jason Reeves' phone records?"

"Great. Maybe we'll finally get some answers to our ever growing list of questions. I'm heading over to Cheryl's house to start the search. I'll call if I find anything or should I say catch anything."

# CHAPTER 24

When I pulled into Cheryl's neighborhood, I realized I had a few minutes before the crime scene tech was scheduled to arrive. I couldn't help myself. Instead of going straight at the stop sign, I turned left and took another right. Robert White's street. I purposefully hadn't driven past his house yet. Afraid I'd do something rash. But now, as if a sailor succumbing to a siren's song, I was lured towards Robert's house. I parked a few houses past his and looked through my back windshield at his place.

He'd kept it in better shape than most of his neighbors. The streetlights showed off a well-manicured lawn. A real feat, considering Florida's grass behaved more like a weed. Two large oaks stood like bookends on either side of the dark colored house. Well-kept bushes lined the front of the house with the top of the hedge sitting right below the large picture window. The garage was closed, all the lights off. Nothing moved outside. The house didn't feel threatening. Maybe because it stood empty. Did Robert have to be home for me to feel the same sense of foreboding I'd felt outside his home as a kid?

A beep indicating an incoming text pulled my attention away from the house. The tech had arrived at Cheryl's place. I indulged in one last day dream of clicking the handcuffs around Robert's wrist, tightening them until his skin paled. Then I forced myself to pull the car away from the curb.

All of the reporters had thankfully packed up and left the Callahan's front lawn. When Cheryl went to UCH, the story had moved with her. Well, all the reporters except one. When I pulled to a stop, I had enough of a head start that I made it inside before Carlos Diaz could ask any more of his never-ending questions.

Frankie Russo, the crime scene tech, was waiting for me at the door. Since I had Cheryl's keys, gaining entry wasn't a problem. The ER staff had bagged Cheryl's belongings after admitting her. Besides the keys, her shoes were the only other item of interest. The lab would compare the shoe's treads with the samples collected at the crime scene.

I wasn't too optimistic about this search. Not like I would find a murder weapon or even trace amounts of blood. With strangulation, there wasn't much evidence to find. And since it was Kimberly's house, I'd find her fingerprints, hair samples, and all the DNA evidence I could ask for. Cheryl's car was another matter. The one thing I wouldn't expect to find is Kimberly's DNA in the trunk of her mom's car. The vehicle would be towed to our garage later.

I gave Russo a list of items he should print in the house. "Also make sure you dust the wall over the john."

Russo raised an eyebrow. I took a deep breath and reminded myself he was a newbie. He'd done well on the last couple of searches we worked together, so I decided to use this as a teaching moment instead of a browbeating one. Plus he had two of my favorite qualities in a man—didn't talk much and took orders.

"Men sometimes rest a palm against the wall when they lean over the toilet to take a piss."

The prints could tell us if Jason Reeves had definitely been in the house. Also Cheryl and Harley broke up three months before Kimberly died. That was plenty of time to parade a whole collection of men through the front door. Any of whom could have taken an unhealthy interest in Kimberly. Maybe some of the prints would match ex-cons in the area. Lucy had already dusted Kimberly's room so Russo only had to work on the living room, kitchen, bathroom, and Cheryl's bedroom. We were fortunate Cheryl wasn't much of a housekeeper. There would be a variety of prints.

The house reeked of stale cigarette smoke. Both times I'd been here, Cheryl, a chronic chain smoker, constantly puffed one cigarette after another. And even though the house sat empty, the stench continued to saturate the air. I ran a finger over the dark wallpaper. A black residue stained my clear latex glove. It was the smoke emitted from cigarettes that had polluted the air and stuck to the walls. Years of buildup had stained them and left an actual residue behind.

After looking through end table drawers and miscellaneous stacks of paper, I headed to the kitchen. I left the new search warrant Russo had delivered from the ASA on the counter next to Cheryl's collection of empty bottles. Looked like Jim Beam was Cheryl's drink of choice, but I found plenty of cheaper brands in the trashcan. In a bad economy, she probably settled for whatever she could afford. More overflowing ashtrays were littered around the kitchen. The contents of Cheryl's refrigerator were even more depressing than mine—a few condiments, a carton of leftover Chinese, and a case of Miller Lite.

That always griped my soul. Parents had enough money for smokes and alcohol but not enough cash to keep their fridge stocked with food for their kids. Over the years, I'd witnessed too much neglect and abuse of children. If I ever stopped long enough to take it all in, the emotions would be overpowering. When you see so much ugliness in the world, it's hard to believe there's enough good left to combat it. Just another reason why I put my badge on every morning. I knew firsthand the evil that was out there, lurking in the shadows. And as they say, evil thrives when good men do nothing. Good women too.

I checked Cheryl's medicine cabinet, usually a very telling location during a search. A second full container of Xanax sat on the bottom shelf. The label showed a different prescribing doctor and pharmacy than the bottle Cheryl had used overdosing. Not surprising, considering Florida was known as the pill capital of the U.S. Later, I would confiscate it. Not so much for evidence but simply to remove it from the house. After all, the prescription was legal, but Cheryl didn't need that kind of temptation facing her when she came home.

At the end of the hall, I found the master bedroom. When I opened the door, my nose was assaulted by the stench of a honky tonk at closing time. To call this place a pigsty would be an insult to pigs everywhere. Even they wouldn't sleep in a dump like this. Mounds of dirty clothes were piled high in a corner. Ashes stained the sheets on Cheryl's unmade bed. No wonder Kimberly's room was in such pristine condition.

It made me wonder how Kimberly would have turned out if she'd lived. Probably didn't have a chance in hell. Already headed down the wrong path, it was only a matter of time before she started swiping a few pills from her mom's Xanax bottles and sneaking some beers out to share with friends.

Kimberly needed a consistent role model in her life. At one time, Janet Moore filled that position, but Cheryl had put a stop to that relationship. If Janet had been a constant figure in Kimberly's life, the girl could have looked to her and said *yes, my life sucks now, but here's an example of how it can be done right*. If a child doesn't have that example growing up, they don't know how good things can be in their future.

For me, that example was my aunt and uncle. My mom got married and divorced multiple times, two of which were to abusive husbands. That added to the abuse I'd suffered from Robert White, and I could have easily turned into an addict. I didn't. A major reason—my family. Every weekend, mom would drive an hour to grandma's house. All the aunts, uncles, and cousins would congregate. It was the highlight of my week. It made such an impact on my life, watching what it was like when a mom and dad loved each other. To see how a healthy family unit operated.

I found a cheap scrapbook inside Cheryl's nightstand. A visual diary of happier times, starting with Cheryl and Russell Callahan's courtship. There were snapshots of them enjoying a picnic lunch in a field of wildflowers, blowing out birthday candles around a faded old dinette set, snuggling under a blanket on the bleachers at a baseball game.

Thinking back on the information gathered about the Callahan family, I remembered the two of them married when Russell was 23 and she only 20. I figured Cheryl would have gotten knocked up and married young, but I was guilty of judging Cheryl based on what I knew of her today. A completely different woman smiled up from the glossy 4x6's in Cheryl's album. Here her hair was dyed a beautiful golden blond, nails neatly polished, skin wrinkle free. Cheryl's husband was a clean-cut guy. He had a hairstyle that screamed military, though I don't know if he ever served.

By the various backgrounds of the pictures, I got the impression the Callahan's didn't have much money. Russell was a bricklayer, and Cheryl worked for a dry cleaners. Two years after they married, Kimberly came along. Their daughter resembled dad more than mom. They both had the same little dip on the upper edge of their earlobes. From the looks of these pages, Kimberly's parents doted on her. Past Christmases, pictures with the Easter Bunny, all the major holidays were photographed and cataloged. Even a Mother's Day card stuffed in between the pages. Drawn in the hand of a preschooler, it said *Happy Mothrs Day! I luv you!! Luv Kimberly.*

The last page of the scrapbook was very telling. A short obituary was pasted in the center of a striped page. I already knew the story based on a few newspaper articles I'd read. On the evening of February 4, 2006, Russell drove home after a long day at work. A drunk driver swerved into Russell's lane and hit his car head on. The driver died instantly, but Russell stayed in a coma for almost two weeks before the family discontinued life support. I can only imagine how hard it was for Cheryl to make the decision to pull the plug on her husband who lay brain-dead in the ICU. According to Janet Moore, this event was the jumping off point for Cheryl's alcohol addiction. I'm sure it was equally difficult for Kimberly. Not only did she lose her father in a car accident, but she lost her mother to an addiction. *Such a waste.*

Though loathe to do it, I knew it was time. Time to look through the mound of dirty clothes. I only hoped a rat wouldn't scamper out. Near the bottom of the pile, I lifted up a holey pair of acid washed jeans. A balled up piece of notebook paper fell to the floor. I called Russo in to photograph the evidence. Then I slowly spread the piece of paper out, trying to flatten the wrinkles. Short and to the point, the one paragraph was written in a girl's flowery handwriting. It had no signature at the end, though later I would compare it to papers found in Kimberly's room to see if the handwriting matched. For the time being, I was pretty certain Kimberly had authored the letter since it began with the words *Dear Mom.*

Dear Mom,

I've tried talking to you, but you won't listen. I'm hoping you find this letter in a rare moment of sobriety. Your blackouts scare me. It's not just the bruises you've given me. It's—I don't know, hard to explain. When you drink all day, you withdraw to this dark place. You used to be a sad drunk, but lately you go into these horrible rages. The stupidest things set you off, so I try and stay out of your way. I know you'll never really hurt me, but I'm still afraid. Not of you but for you. I'm worried one morning I'll wake up and find you dead on the couch. Now that Daddy's gone, you're all I have. I only wish I was enough for you. Important enough that you'd quit drinking. After you read this, please come find me and tell me you'll go back into treatment. I know they can help if you try. Please. For me.

The nerve Kimberly had to lay it all out like that, leaving herself exposed. It was admirable. Then to have her mother crumple up her heartfelt words and toss them aside like they were a piece of trash. Who knew when Kimberly wrote the letter? It could have been months old or the spark setting Cheryl off Monday night. What I did know was that after her mother's repeated rejections, Kimberly hardened, eventually leading her to transform her appearance. With Kimberly's new Goth look, her outside became as black as her insides probably felt.

Russo bagged the letter. He'd check for prints back at the lab. While he packed his equipment, I gave Patrick a call and filled him in on the items I'd found.

"Sounds like Kimberly was frightened of her mother," Patrick said. "We need to personally escort Cheryl downtown after she's released from the hospital. While she's still sober."

"Might be tough if she gets transferred into an alcohol treatment center."

"That will push Sergeant Kray right over the edge."

"Yeah, I think I'll wait and see if it happens before I mention it. My ass is still sore from the chewing it got this morning." I absently rubbed my bottom, remembering the conversation. I stopped when Russo looked at me strangely. "Have you found anything in the phone records?"

"Only got through Cheryl's numbers so far." The sound of papers rustled in the background. "Nothing unexpected there. I found Cheryl's ex-boyfriend, Willy Davidson's phone number. They started talking at the beginning of June 2009. This went on for almost a year until May of this year, which is consistent with what Janet Moore told us. Then there's miscellaneous numbers all leading back to various men. We can start tracking down all of these guys in the next couple of days. I'm checking to see if any have records. Maybe one of them was more interested in Kimberly than her mother."

I looked down at my watch. A little after 9 p.m. "I'm going to check out The Rusty Bolt. See if Harley still hangs out there."

"Want me to meet you there?"

"No thanks, Dad. I don't need a chaperone."

"Heck, I know you don't. I thought Harley might."

"Whatever could you mean?" I asked in my most innocent voice.

"Play nice, Springer."

"Gotta go, Dad. I'm already past my deadline with Sergeant Kray. Do you think he'll want another update come midnight? He did say every two hours. I'd hate to ruin his beauty sleep. You know, I bet he sleeps with a cap on? Has to maintain a high glossy shine on that bald head of his."

Russo laughed as he followed me to the front door.

"Goodbye, Kate!" Patrick said clearly exasperated.

# CHAPTER 25

The Rusty Bolt was a dive biker bar. This was going to be fun. I walked to the back of my car, dug around in the trunk, and yanked out a blazer from my extra clothes stash. A little wrinkled, but it would work. I wanted something to cover the gun on my belt, and I'd only worn a short sleeve shirt to work today. At least my black pants matched. Too bad I didn't have my cowboy boots. I really would have blended in with the natives.

I tugged the ponytail holder out of my hair. As the strands fell loose around my shoulders, I ran my fingers through my hair, fluffing it slightly. Mama always said you could catch more flies with honey than vinegar. I chuckled thinking if Lucy were here, she could tell me the origin of that stupid saying.

Looked like Friday night at The Rusty Bolt was the place to be. I wondered if I had enough tattoos to gain entrance. Probably a two tatt minimum. That's okay, a winning smile could go a long way. I weaved around the motorcycles packed into the parking lot and followed an overweight biker couple into the bar. With both of their hairstyles long and braided down the back, I found it difficult to tell which was male and which was female.

The place might have been short on ambiance, but the music pumping through the speakers more than made up for it. David Allan Coe belted out a song about the day his mom got out of prison. I hadn't heard this tune in a long time. After the day I had, I was half tempted to saddle up to the bar and order a shot. Or three. But I had to remember why I came, so I walked past the one empty stool to the end of the bar. Each step made a popping noise. Finally there, calf muscles sore, I gave a sweet nod to lure the bartender down my way. He was every bit the stereotypical biker bartender.

The man was built like a tank and wore a permanent scowl.

"I haven't seen Harley around tonight? Is he here yet?" The line was so sticky sweet, I thought the big guy might actually see through my act. But no, he was too busy staring at my chest to notice. I actually had to bend down slightly to break his trance. "Harley. Is he here?"

"Davidson?"

Either there were quite a few Harley's in the bar tonight, which wasn't out of the realm of possibility, or the big lug couldn't believe I'd be interested in a guy like Davidson. I'd take the compliment and believe the second scenario true. If everything I'd heard about Davidson was accurate, I knew after tonight's performance, I would deserve an Oscar. I couldn't parade in here as myself, some ball busting chic detective. No way would Davidson talk to me in front of his buddies, and I didn't have time for some macho bravado bullshit. It was vital I play this charade if I wanted information.

"The one and only. Is he here?"

The bartender motioned towards the back of the bar. Through the haze of cigarette smoke, I saw a small billiards room. The neon lights from the beer signs illuminated the way. Patrick had emailed me Davidson's DMV photo. I scanned the crowd, looking for anyone matching his description.

At the far table, Davidson was bent over, stick in hand, taking a shot at the nine ball. He was a large guy, not fat, just built. His driver's license reported a height of 6'2". When he stood up after making his winning shot, I could see it was a slight exaggeration. Davidson had wiry, dishwater brown hair and an unkempt goatee. As I strutted my way across the room, I noticed he was dressed for a night out. He wore a dirty Beavis and Butt-head shirt circa 1993. I didn't think they even made those anymore. Though considering the condition it was in, it might have been an original. A black leather vest covered the shirt—probably his lame attempt to dress up the look. No wonder the bartender was shocked when I asked about this loser.

I took advantage of the game ending and placed a five dollar bill on the table.

"Bet you can't do that twice," I said in a seductive tone.

A lecherous smile broke out across Davidson's face.

"Beat it, Jim," Davidson said to the guy he'd just whipped. The man looked like an accountant playing dress up on the weekend.

"Sorry, Jim." I said, adding a playful wave.

"Your money's no good here, babe. If you're gonna play at this table, there's stakes to be made. What do I get when I win?"

"Cocky. I like it. If you win, I leave here with you."

Davidson's eyebrows practically disappeared under his hairline. "And if you win?"

"I leave here with you."

"Well then," he said, licking his lips. "How about we cut out the middle man and leave now?"

I can't believe that worked. Cheryl Callahan must have been seriously smashed to date this idiot for a year. Her late husband and this guy were nothing alike. I can only imagine what Kimberly felt when her mom brought Davidson home. I grabbed a beefy hand and led him out the front door. He followed me down the steps and around the back of the building.

"Kinky." He laughed at his seemingly good fortune.

In one swift move, I spun Davidson around pushing the front side of his body into the wall. I heard an *oomph* when I moved my hand down to his right wrist and yanked his arm up between his shoulder blades. I had his left arm trapped horizontally across his back. As Davidson struggled to break free, I jerked harder on the arm facing upwards. If he didn't stop, I'd pop his shoulder out of the socket. He cried out, struggled another second, but quickly realized the futility of his effort.

"What the hell's ya problem, bitch!" He spat into the stonework.

"Watch the mouth, asshole!" I jabbed my right elbow into his spine.

The scuffle caused a dime sized baggie to fall from the inside of his leather vest. *Now I've got you.* The parking lot lights illuminated the packet of tiny white crystals. Meth. I'd bet my badge on it.

"Harley, Harley, Harley. You're in a world of hurt now. Let me introduce myself. I'm Detective You're Screwed with the Tampa Police

Department." I could feel him inwardly groan. "But I'll make you a deal. Tell me what I want to hear, and I'll forget about the drugs."

I let him consider his options. When he took a little too long, I gave his arm another tug. "How about it?"

"Fine. Fine. Just stop."

"Now, I'm sure this is slightly uncomfortable. Tell you what I'm gonna do. I'll remove my hands from your arms, and you'll slowly turn. Then I want you to sit on the ground. Don't get any bright ideas. My partner's right around the front. Don't give me a reason to haul your ass in for possession." In one fluid movement, I released his arms, pushed him deeper into the wall, and took two giant steps backwards.

Davidson rubbed his arms as he turned, sliding down the wall. The look on his face almost made me feel sorry for him. A few minutes ago, he planned on getting lucky. Now he faced drug charges.

"What do ya want to know?" He stuck his chin in the air, putting on a defiant air. His ego refused to declare defeat.

"Cheryl Callahan."

"What about her? I haven't seen that head case in months."

"Tell me about her?"

"Is this about her dead kid?"

"Real compassionate, asshole. Yeah, it's about her daughter, Kimberly, who was found strangled earlier this week. Now that you bring it up, where were you on Monday?"

"Hey, don't go pinnin' nothing on me." Davidson started getting antsy and looked like he was about to shoot up from the ground. One intense look settled him down.

"Tell me where you were."

"Monday I worked the eleven to seven shift. I drive a forklift for Buckley's down on Adamo Drive. After I took my girl to a movie, she came home and crashed at my place."

"Must be a real serious relationship if you were so willing to leave with me."

Davidson answered with a noncommittal shrug.

I wrote down his girlfriend's phone number which I would use to check his alibi immediately after I finished here. The jury was still out on whether I'd rat him out.

"What movie did you see?"

"I don't know. Some stupid chic flick. I hate those damn movies, but if I let Darlene drag me to 'em, she more than makes up for it later."

*Disgusting visual.*

"So there's no way I could have killed Cheryl's kid."

"Her name is Kimberly." This jerk weed was really starting to piss me off. "Tell me about Cheryl and Kimberly's relationship."

"I don't know. The kid always scrammed when I came around. Good thing to. I'm not looking to be no one's daddy."

I took a deep breath, trying to calm my emotions. "Did Cheryl ever tell you she and her daughter fought?"

"Cheryl didn't talk much about her kid. She knew I could care less. This one time though, guess it was closer to when we broke up, I went over to her place. The two of them were screaming so loud, I could hear 'em outside. Thought about turning around and going home, but then I decided it might be a good show. Had nothing better to do. Kimberly yelled at Cheryl about being a drunk and not giving a crap about her. Cheryl gave it back saying the girl was a no good, spoiled brat. They were all up in each other's faces. Very Jerry Springer. Ended pretty quick though. Cheryl shoved her kid in the chest and made her fall on her ass. Kid ran out the door, didn't show up again until the next morning. Worked for us, had the house to ourselves."

"You and Cheryl broke up in May. Tell me about her behavior right before you two split."

"That last month, something was up with her. She turned into a sloppy drunk. Not a real turn on. And she was constantly on my ass about something, yelling all the time, acting real paranoid. That's what finally did it for me. Always saying I was screwing some other chic. We'd go out and even if I looked someone else's way, she'd freak. Whatever. I don't take no shit from no—"

"So you broke it off?"

Davidson nodded.

"How did Cheryl take it?"

"Hell if I know. I never talked to the crazy bitch again."

"I plan on checking your alibi. You think I'm a pain in the ass now, Davidson. You'd better not be lying to me, or I'll have to show up at your job and really rain some shit down on your head."

"I'm not lying. Darlene'll tell ya."

Threateningly, I moved towards Davidson. In one swift move, I bent down and grabbed the baggie sitting beside him on the pavement.

"Remember what President Bush said about drugs."

Davidson gave me a vacant look.

"Just say no." I'd dispose of the meth back at the precinct. This asshole wasn't keeping it. "Now get the hell out of here."

Davidson hesitantly stood, then high tailed it around the building. Probably going back inside the bar to lick his wounded ego. Once he disappeared, I heard a clapping noise carrying towards me on the night breeze. I pocketed the drugs just as Carlos Diaz stepped out from behind the dumpster near the far corner of the building.

*You've got to be kidding me.* I hit him with my best you-are-scum look. "If you print anything you heard, so help me . . . so help me, there is nothing I won't do to completely ruin your career."

His hands flew up in a defensive gesture. "How about a peace offering, Detective? I realize how much my article hurt you, hurt your investigation. For now, I won't print anything I heard. On one condition."

"And for a moment there, I thought you'd grown a conscience. What is it, Diaz?"

"Promise me an exclusive."

I threw my hands in the air, wondering why me, and headed off in search of my car. Diaz matched my stride.

"It's either provide me with an exclusive once you've solved this case, or tomorrow's headline will read, *Detective Ignores Meth Possession in Exchange for Details on Callahan Murder Case.*"

Still walking, I clamped my fists together tightly, trying to keep myself from decking the man. Before I slammed the car door, I managed to get two words out. "Fine. Deal."

Diaz had the grace and good sense to back off. Who knows if he'd continue to play follow the leader, but for now, at least he was gone. I sat in my car fuming until finally I exploded. I let out a rage-filled holler, pounding my hands on the steering wheel.

Eventually, the pain in my palms halted the tantrum. I couldn't wait to solve this case. Get back to the punching bag at the gym. I seriously needed a release. Or maybe I'd pick up some guy and work out my frustration on him.

Once I'd gotten myself under control, I dialed Patrick to see if he'd discovered anything in Kimberly Callahan's cell phone records. When he answered, I told him I was leaving The Rusty Bolt. "Just got done with Harley Davidson. He's a real piece of work."

I heard my phone beep. "Wait a minute, Patrick. I got another call. You know what? I'm headed downtown now. I'll bring snacks, and we can update each other when I get back."

"Okay . . . good talking to you," Patrick said, ending the conversation before it had even started.

The phone's display read *Caller Unknown*. I switched over to see who wanted me at 10:17 p.m. It wasn't Lucy, her number would have shown up.

"Detective Springer."

Dead air. I really hoped it wasn't another politician begging for my vote. My answering machine was tired of being accosted by the yahoos running in November's election. The pollsters hadn't discovered my cell number yet, but I thought that might have just changed.

"Hello? Say something . . . or I'm hanging up."

About ready to disconnect, I heard a male voice hurriedly respond. "Wait a minute, don't hang up. It's Jason Reeves." Bingo! I felt the clouds part and the angels smile down on me.

"What time do you want to meet at the precinct?" I asked. "We need to talk."

"That's why I'm calling. But if you want to hear my side of the story, I won't do it at the police station. No way. We're gonna meet on my terms. And I'll only talk to you. I don't want that jerk-off partner of yours there. My dad says if that guy shows up at his work one more time, he's gonna get fired. He needs his job. You guys gotta stop."

Score one for Patrick. He must have really rattled Harold Reeve's cage during yesterday's visit.

"So you *have* seen your dad?"

"No," Jason answered, a heaviness in his voice. "He left an ugly message on my cell phone. He's seriously pissed. Told me to take care of this mess right away. Dad's pulling an extra shift tonight to try and smooth things over with the boss. I'll meet if you promise to stop harassing him at work. My dad has nothing to do with this."

A dilemma. I had to talk to Jason Reeves right away. He offered to meet me, but was adamant it happen tonight, without his dad or Patrick, somewhere of his choosing. Nothing Jason said would be admissible in court, but I had to know if he killed Kimberly. Or could give me information implicating Cheryl. I made up my mind to meet with him alone and talk. If he had something important to say, I would pick up his father at work and drag both their asses downtown. Threaten dad, and Jason would eventually fold, giving me a statement.

"Fine, Jason. Name the place."

"University Mall. Thirty minutes from now. I'll be waiting on the sidewalk out in front of the food court. Where we're sure to be seen."

What was this, some bad spy movie? Did Jason think I'd throw him in the back of an unmarked white van? Tie him up inside a dark windowless room and pull out my rubber hose? I could see it now. Me standing there rubbing my hands together maniacally cackling *we have ways of making you talk*. Of course in my head, I had a Russian accent and a kick ass long black trench coat. Jason obviously watched too much TV, but I'd humor him. Hell, I'd stand on one leg and squawk like a cockatoo if it made him talk.

"I'll be there."

No time to waste. I pointed my car towards Fowler Avenue and took off. I didn't want Carlos Diaz following me, so I took the long way there, looping through back streets and running all the yellow traffic lights. When I couldn't see him in my rear view mirror any longer, I headed towards the mall. Now that Jason Reeves was finally willing to talk, even the man upstairs couldn't keep me away.

# CHAPTER 26

Even though it was late, kids swarmed the mall. They buzzed in groups from one place to the next smoking, skateboarding, and in general making a public nuisance of themselves. I found an empty parking spot halfway between the road and the shopping center. It wasn't long before I spied a lanky boy walking briskly up the sidewalk to the right of the food court. The skittish teenager nervously checked over his left shoulder every few seconds. At this distance, I couldn't make a positive ID. I hopped out of my car to get a better look. When the kid stepped into the halogen lighting, I could see it was a punk, just not my punk.

A Buick pulled in a couple of spaces down from my car, the lights temporarily blinding me. To escape the brightness, I rested my head on top of my hands and leaned the weight of my body into the car. *Damn, I'm tired.* This is one day I'd like to mark off my calendar. It seemed I racked up a lot of those lately. I couldn't wait to get into my pj's and jump into bed. Maybe I'd wear the pale green softies tonight. A cool breeze ran across my neck, and I thought of how nice it'd feel snuggled up in something cozy and plush.

I groaned when my cell phone chirped, alerting me to a new email. *Now what?* The mother of all surprises. Sammy Richter emailed me Kimberly's Facebook notes pages. As I scrolled through the message, I wiped away a few sprinkles dotting the face of the phone. The beginning of that rain storm Patrick's knee promised.

I noticed Sammy only included the notes, not the recent posts. I knew from my own dabbling in the Facebook arena the notes pages allowed users to journal electronically. Want to list your favorite top ten bands of all time or create a poll for your high school buddies, simply create a new notes page. By not copying the regular posts, it told me Sammy's cooperation only went so far. Probably afraid to give me access on anything that might incriminate her or her friends. No matter. Once the social networking company complied with our warrant, I'd check out Kimberly's account myself.

A sudden loud thunder crash made me jump. Soon I'd have to take cover but for now I waited, leaning against the car. One more glance around for Jason Reeves. No luck, so I continued scanning Sammy's email. Most of the pages were ramblings of a teenage mind, but one note in particular, entitled *Obsession*, caught my eye. Not only did the title speak to me, but it was the last one written before Kimberly's death, dated September 3, 2010.

A man lives his life obsessed. Obsessed with fitness, obsessed with order, obsessed with the girl living in his neighborhood. Two of the three obsessions lead to a healthy life, a fit body, a regimented mind. Where does the third lead? His downfall. Or hers.

How did it all start? Innocently enough. A brush of a hand against a cheek, the resting of fingers on a backside. Her comfort level grows, so does his. Advancing to kneading out a kinked shoulder, stroking a sore calf.

What girl doesn't love presents? It's only a phone, it's only a camera. Or is it?

No. Stop. Please don't. How could you?

Life's all a matter of perception. Who will believe if you tell? A struggle ensues. Internal within myself, choices to be made. External with him, should I stay, no must go. His obsession pulls me back, I'm losing myself.

Poignant. It's a shame Kimberly never grew up to try her hand as a professional writer. The note read like a fictional short story written for a class assignment, but I knew better. It was about Jack Monroe, a.k.a Robert

White.

Wait a minute. Obsessed with fitness? The memorial. BAM! Just like that, it hit me. I finally realized what my subconscious knew all along. When Robert left the interrogation room yesterday, he dragged his right leg. At Kimberly's memorial, he dragged his left. He's been playing us. Robert hadn't turned into a decrepit old man. He wore the loose clothes as a smoke screen, playing the part. I'd bet at seventy-five, he was still as active and in shape as ever. I had to call my partner right away and—

A crackling sound behind me interrupted my train of thought. I'd heard it before, like amped up static electricity. Turning around, I realized too late the only time I'd ever heard that exact noise was in the police academy during the taser—

# FRIDAY... MAYBE

## <u>CHAPTER 27</u>

Sleepy . . . groggy . . . trying to break free from the blackness. Pain . . . splitting through my head . . . throbbing in my lower back. My mouth's pried open. I can't stick my tongue out, something's blocking it. Panic wells up like a bubble in a hot spring. My hands and feet won't move. They're stuck, tied down. I'm afraid to open my eyes, scared at what I'll see when I do. So I keep them closed, listening. But I hear nothing. There has to be some sound. I strain harder hoping to hear something. Anything. Breathing, water dripping, a clock ticking, a bird chirping?

Nothing.

Finally, the fuzziness in my head cleared, and my senses told me I was alone in the room. I cracked my eyelids, barely able to register a faint light. Little by little, I continued to open my eyes. Blurry, they struggled to adjust. I looked down and saw rope bound my wrists to the arm rests of a chair. What looked to be an antique dental chair. I tried to think of some bad dentist joke, but my mind couldn't attempt even that little bit of levity. The rope was large in diameter. The stray pieces itched my arms.

The scant padded seating was a drab institutional green color, and from what I could see of the rest of the chair, it was silver metal. My ankles were bound together with the same rope which was then secured to the bottom footrest. I was seated in an upright position.

If the chair truly was an antique, maybe I could pull hard enough to break the damn thing apart. I struggled against the restraints, squirming, trying to lift my arms and legs. I only got rope burn for my efforts. The chair was a beast. I forced myself to stop before my mind snapped, and I lost what was left of my calm. I was almost glad a gag blocked my mouth. If I were able to scream, I don't think I'd ever stop.

A puzzle, that's it. I had to look at this like a puzzle. I couldn't allow myself the emotion, or I'd never get out of here. The feel of my midsection was lighter. My belt holding my gun, cell phone, and other essentials had disappeared. It was almost like losing a leg, the phantom pain. I'd carried a gun for so many years, I could still feel the weight of it resting against my hip. I knew my mind was playing tricks on me, but I couldn't help checking one more time.

A light source emanated from the middle of the room. On a small square card table sat a battery-powered light like the ones campers used. I had a similar model at home in my emergency hurricane supply kit. The dim light illuminated the small space just enough that I could see all four walls draped in heavy black fabric hung from the edge of the ceiling down to the thick tan carpeting. The drapery was too long, about an inch and half of extra material gathered on the floor. Above me, I saw egg crate foam stapled to the ceiling. There were no windows, no doors. Heavy fabric, foam, plush carpeting. It all added up to one thing. A poor man's soundproofed room. What the hell was going to happen to me in here? No. I wouldn't go there. I couldn't.

This room could be anywhere—a house, storage locker, warehouse, but probably not a basement. You didn't find many in Florida. The entire state's built on sand. Then it struck me, I may not be in Florida anymore. But who has me? Unable to stop this new wave of panic, my chest began rising and falling more rapidly. I couldn't get enough air. I felt like I was choking on the gag stuffed in my mouth. I tried to stave off the tears that threatened. Getting snotty from crying would only make it harder to breathe. Dammit! I told myself I would never be at someone's mercy again. I refuse to be a victim. No matter what happened to me in here, I wouldn't let it break me. That's better. Anger. A familiar emotion. One I could channel and use.

I thought back to my last memory, waiting at the mall for Jason Reeves. He was running late, so I stood resting my head against the car. Then I got a message containing Kimberly's Facebook notes pages. Her writing about Jack Monroe made me think more about Robert White, and that's when my subconscious threw his limping ruse to the forefront of my conscious mind. Right when I'd made the connection, some asshole blitz attacked me with a taser gun. Damn that hurt.

I'd been tasered once before back in the police academy. The instructors thought students should feel what it was like. That way when we were out on the street, we'd only use force as a last resort. We were told it would teach us empathy. Bullshit! The instructors got their rocks off tasering us.

The shot affected everyone differently. The lucky ones said it felt like a pulsing sensation throughout their entire body. Others cried out and collapsed. One guy completely fell over. It was like one of those old cartoons where something heavy fell from the sky. The cat got bonked on the head, falling backwards straight like an ironing board.

I remembered what it was like when I stood on the mat, waiting my turn. Knowing I was about to get hit with up to 50,000 volts of electricity was like stepping off the curb knowing a twelve ton bus barreled towards me. Once the barbs struck, it felt like the bus made contact. Being attacked earlier at the mall was just like in the academy. As soon as the barbs went into my back, all my muscles locked up at once, and I could feel the electricity coursing through my body. Afterwards, I went limp.

I fell back into someone's arms, heard words whispered into my ear. I remember the voice was male, but don't recall what he said because as he spoke, the man placed a moist cloth over my nose and mouth. Chloroform. It put me right out. Depending on the concentration, it could have rendered me unconscious for fifteen minutes or a couple of hours.

What time is it? I could feel the weight of my watch still on my wrist, but my blazer covered it. Useless. My cell phone. I could only hope it sat in one piece powered up somewhere near here. If so, Patrick could trace my location using its internal GPS feature.

Patrick. Maybe the cavalry would be here soon. I vowed to do everything I could to make sure I stayed alive until he got here. If he got here. No, I wouldn't think like that. Patrick was the best damn detective I'd ever known. He wouldn't sleep until he found me. But would he be searching yet? When would the alarm be raised? He expected me back at the precinct after I left The Rusty Bolt. After an hour, if I didn't answer my cell, Patrick would worry. Not checking in with Sergeant Kray would be the icing on the cake.

My initial jolt of adrenaline began to wane, my eyes grew heavy. I didn't know how I could possibly sleep at a time like this, but who knew the side effects of the chloroform. I really should reserve my energy. I might need it later. I promised myself I'd only rest my eyes for a few seconds, then get back to solving the puzzle. A few sec . . .

# CHAPTER 28

"Katie. Katie, wake up."

Not another nightmare. I'm so tired of Robert White haunting my dreams. What will it take to exorcise him once and for all?

"Katie, it's time to get up." A chuckle. I could feel breath tickle my face. I didn't want to open my eyes. This time I knew what I'd see if I did. But when a finger gently caressed my cheek, my eyes popped open of their own volition. Not a dream, but still a nightmare. Robert White. An older version of the man I escaped from twenty-four years ago, but still the same monster.

"Katie, I'm glad to see you're awake now. I was afraid I'd used too much chloroform. You've been out for so long."

Katie. Nobody had called me by that name since I was thirteen. The familiarity Robert had when he spoke those two syllables made my skin crawl. I felt like I'd stepped through a portal back to 1986. The only other time Robert had restrained me. It neared the end of the abuse when he was getting bolder and crueler. Using his neckties, he bound me to the bed. I remember lying there looking at the Santa tie he'd wrapped tightly around my wrist. I didn't understand how he could hurt me so badly using a present I'd bought him for Christmas.

I tried to remind myself I wasn't that scared little girl anymore, tried to concentrate on Robert's words.

". . . look at you, all grown up. Can you keep a secret?" he asked, raising a finger to his lips.

"Of course you can." He laughed at his own joke pointing to my gag. "I've been watching you for years."

Surprised, a garbled sound escaped through the saliva drenched cloth.

"Do you have something to say? Hmm? If I take this gag off, will you promise not to yell? Probably not. You always were a lying little bitch, weren't you? Telling your mother I raped you. No, Katie. What we had was love. I loved you, and I showed you that love. I thought you loved me? You always told me you loved me."

Infuriated, I started speaking right through the restraint. I knew everything I said was unintelligible, but I didn't care. What he said was crap! Robert trained me, rather harshly I might add, to always repeat the words *I love you* back to him. I had no choice. To this day, I refused to utter that overused phrase to anyone.

Robert walked over to the card table, grabbed the plastic tray sitting next to the lantern, and brought it over so I could see its contents. A syringe and one individually wrapped alcohol wipe were the only items on the tray.

"In case you get too loud, I've taken precautions." Robert held up the syringe filled with a clear substance.

I lifted my eyebrows in confusion.

"Ketamine."

"Are you serious?" I said, forgetting the gag until I heard the garbled words. The animal tranquilizer doubled as a popular date rape drug. It imitated inebriation, caused spotty memory, and made the victim—person, very pliable. Depending on the dosage, it could knock them out completely.

"Do you promise to act like a proper young lady if I remove the gag? No yelling, no cursing? Then we can have a little talk. I'm sure you're interested in what I've been up to these last few years."

This guy was off his rocker. One second he had impeccable manners, the next he's angry and cursing at me. Now he's acting like we bumped into each other at a coffee shop. Two old friends wanting to catch up after a long separation.

I nodded my head. He walked behind the chair to untie the gag, and I caught a whiff of his signature smell. Pall Mall cigarettes, Baby Powder, with an underlying hint of Irish Spring soap. Once unfettered, I stretched the muscles in my mouth thankful to finally be able to close my lips. However, the cloth had absorbed all the spit in my mouth. Now I found it difficult to speak. I moved my tongue back and forth against the roof of my mouth, trying to generate some saliva.

Robert waited impatiently. Finally, I said thank you because I knew it was expected of me. Scary how easy it was to fall back into the subservient childhood role.

"You said you've been watching me. How long?"

"Twenty-four years."

"What!"

"Katie, you forget. You're mine. You'll always be mine. Just because physical distance separates us, doesn't mean you still don't belong to me. I love you." Robert stood in front of me, waiting for my response. I knew what he wanted, but I couldn't say the words. When I didn't speak, his eyes grew dark. A vein throbbed in his temple.

Again he said, "I love you. . . "

Silence.

Smack!

My head whipped to the right as he backhanded me across the face. Pain ripped through my cheekbone. I could taste the coppery bitterness of my own blood, but I refused to give him the satisfaction of shedding even one tear. Instead, I glared at him.

Robert smiled. "That's what I always liked about you, Katie. Always able to take the pain. You never were a complainer. But I see you've forgotten your manners. Do I need to give you a reminder course?"

Remembering my vow to do whatever it took to leave this room alive, I swallowed my pride. "I . . . I love you too."

"There, that wasn't so hard. Now where were we?" He scratched his temple. "Right. After I left Elgin, I moved south to Joliet. I didn't want your mother changing her mind and sending the cops after me. So I changed my name. It's amazing how little money it takes to create a whole new identity. Viola! Jack Monroe resurrected from the grave. I might have been living in a different city, but I made sure to keep an eye on you. I'd check in, see how you were doing from time to time. I have to say, that boy you went to senior prom with was a cad. You could have done infinitely better."

He's right, Graham Rourke was a heel. When he groped me on the dance floor, I ran to the bathroom and didn't come out until after the king and queen were announced. Still, I was dumbfounded at the thought Robert stalked me for more than two decades. How did I not notice? Some detective I am.

"I liked South Carolina," he said wistfully. "Good choice. I especially enjoyed the fishing. Why a cop though? I thought I taught you better. But then my Katie always did want to save the world. Remember when the little boy down the street pushed Michelle into a mud puddle? You pulled his arms behind his back and walked him over to his mother who was weeding her garden. You recounted the whole story and suggested she punish him by making him go to bed without dinner. Always the do-gooder. What was his name?"

"Jamie. Jamie Robbins."

"Right." Robert laughed, remembering back.

My goal was to keep him talking. Right now he was agreeable enough, but I knew anything could set him off. As a child, I always thought it was something I said or did to make him furious. Seeing Robert now, I realized the switch could flip at any time due to his deranged thought process.

"Why did you move to Tampa, Katie? It's so damn hot down here. As soon as I can make it work, we're going back up north. I miss the seasons, the snow. Although now that I'm older, I'll probably regret living in the cold weather again. The joints aren't what they used to be."

I could tell it was false modesty. Robert seemed exceptionally fit for his age, making him look at least fifteen years younger. His form fitting shirt showed off ripped biceps, though deep red scratches peeked out from underneath the sleeves. Robert also had well-formed pectoral muscles. I'd bet he was deceptively strong. Something I'd have to remember.

It dawned on me his last statement alluded to the fact we were still in Florida. It sounded like he planned on keeping me around. I didn't look forward to the idea of staying with Robert long-term, but it was better than the alternative. If I stayed with him long enough, I was positive at some point, he'd make a mistake. I knew I'd get away. Eventually. I just had to make sure I didn't make him mad enough to regret keeping me alive.

"Why Tampa?" he repeated.

"I wanted to be a detective. The lieutenant in South Carolina didn't think broads could do the job." Funny. I went to emphasize the word "broads" with my fingers, forgetting they were bound. Okay, maybe not funny ha-ha. "I looked around and thought Florida might be nice. I love the beach, and I don't miss the cold. I sent out resumes and Tampa bit."

I knew I shouldn't ask him too many questions. He always liked being in charge, steering the conversation. Yet, I couldn't help myself. "Did you live near me in Myrtle Beach?"

"Katie, Katie." Robert sighed. "What does it matter? We're together again. I'll take care of you now."

"Aren't I a little old for you?"

When the muscles in Robert's mouth twitched slightly, I thought I'd gone too far. I braced for another smack.

"Well, I was going to tell you the good news later, but if you insist. I know you never liked surprises. Every year, after I'd placed your presents underneath the Christmas tree, you'd beg to open them early. You always were very good at begging." A nasty smile spread across his face. I could see his teeth were browned from years of nicotine use. One bottom tooth was missing, making a tiny space in his bridge. Robert had always refused to go to the dentist. Ironic, I was now being held captive in a dental chair.

Noticing he was quiet again, I realized Robert waited for a response. *Right, begging.* "Robert, will you please tell me?"

"Since you asked nicely . . . we're going to be a family again. Isn't that exciting? Though rude, you were right in what you said. You are far too old for me now. But you can be the mommy. Every family needs a mommy, right? And I'll be the daddy. We'll just have to go out and find a little one to round out our new threesome."

I groaned, realizing Robert's plan. Snatch some unsuspecting little girl. I could handle living in captivity, but there was no way in hell I could do it while watching Robert abuse a child. Especially since it was my fault for never having turned him into the police. Knowing the sick, depraved man he was Robert probably planned to have me participate in some way. Despite my best efforts, a single tear escaped.

"Katie. You're overcome with emotion. You must really like my idea. I know you've been lonely all these years, no man to take care of you. But I'm here now."

I couldn't deal with talking about his plan anymore. I tried to think of anything that would get him to change the subject. The topic might be dangerous, but at this point, anything was better. Physical pain I could deal with, emotional pain I could not.

I mustered as much sincerity as possible. "Since you've been so lovingly keeping track of me, did you know I watched your interview yesterday at the precinct?"

"You little scamp. I thought you might be. Of course I knew you and Detective Jessup were partners. When he called and requested I come in for an interview, I was shocked. What are the odds you'd catch Kimberly's case? Like one in ten million? When I dumped the body in Thonotosassa, I had no idea it was still in Tampa's jurisdiction."

*What! Did I hear him right? When he dumped the body? Robert killed Kimberly Callahan.*

Ignoring the shock on my face, Robert continued. "I knew if you were watching the interview. It was only a matter of time before you connected me to the crime. Did you tell Detective Jessup about me? About us?" Again he caressed my cheek. I willed myself not to strain away from the touch of his nicotine stained fingers.

"No. Of course not," he said, answering his own question. "If you told him about me, you'd have to tell him all your dirty little secrets. How much you liked it. How your body would respond to my touch."

Knowing I would regret it but unable to stop myself, I snapped my head away. I spoke in a cold hushed voice. "I remember. I remember how at first, I was upset my body would betray me. I didn't know it was normal to feel pleasure even to unwanted advances. But as I got older, I got smarter. Do you know what I did, Robert? At night in my own bedroom, I'd masturbate to get out all those pleasurable sexual feelings. That way when you carried me to your bedroom in the wee hours of the morning, I'd be able to lay stiff as a board, showing no reaction whatsoever."

I savored the anger flaring up in Robert's eyes. Him trying to get it under control, me knowing he wouldn't be able to. I hoped the punishment he chose wouldn't be too painful, but knowing I'd bested him would help soothe any pain he inflicted. Instead of striking me, Robert took the syringe from the tray and jabbed me in the arm. One last absurd thought ran through my mind. He forgot to use the alcohol swab.

# CHAPTER 29

Nauseous. That's what I felt when I first awakened. I wanted to stay floating in the soothing darkness that surrounded me. Here it was quiet. No pain, no helplessness, no shame. Finally, the churning in my stomach forced me to leave the comfort of unconsciousness, be fully present in the misery swirling inside my body. I wish I could curl up in the fetal position to help ease the worsening cramps. Instead, I was forced to sit straight up in this hard metal chair. To make matters worse, the damn gag was back in my mouth. I tried to concentrate on something other than the pain. I knew if I vomited, I'd aspirate and die.

I wondered how long I'd been out? Depending on the dosage, it could be thirty minutes or twelve hours. It really pissed me off Robert forced a drug like Ketamine into my system. I took pride in the fact I'd never ingested a medication stronger than Nyquil. A real nerd in this age of self-indulgence, but I was too intelligent to ever experiment. With my history of abuse, if I tried drugs, I'd be instantly hooked. How could I not? Something to quiet the thoughts, deaden the pain. That kind of escape was a bliss I never could have turned my back on.

I wondered what Patrick was doing at this very moment. Was he close to breaking down the door? Or throwing his hands in the air at his inability to find me? I knew Patrick would retrace my steps. He'd first check my cell phone records and find out Jason Reeves had called. I almost felt sorry for the poor guy. The boys from the squad would descend upon him like a pack of hungry wolves. No way in hell my partner would believe Jason and I didn't meet up at the mall. Patrick would lose precious time though if he thought Jason kidnapped or killed me.

I wish I hadn't tried so damn hard to lose Carlos Diaz from tailing me.

If he'd continued following me to the mall, he would have witnessed the whole abduction. Harley Davidson would also be in the hot seat. He was one of the last people to see me. All in all, it could be quite awhile before the boys in blue came knocking down the door to rescue me. Guess I'd have to save myself.

Hopefully my survival skills would turn out better than my detective skills. How did I not see this coming? The sighting of Robert outside the hospital, the white daisy on my car, the Buick at the deli behind Carlos Diaz's car, then the same Buick at the mall. I didn't even give it a second thought when the *Tampa Tribune* splashed my picture across the front page. Some detective I am.

My only defense—Robert's return had flipped my whole world upside down. I was overwhelmed by the emotions seeing him again dredged up. The infirmed old guy act had me snowed. When I couldn't find an address for him, I completely shut him out of my mind. To concentrate on the case, I resorted to the same coping mechanisms I always had.

Pain ripped through my stomach again. I had to concentrate on breathing through my nose until the worst of it passed. Why didn't my bladder feel like it was ready to pop? I hadn't gone to the bathroom since I was kidnapped. Maybe if I pissed myself, Robert would untie me to change my clothes. I could overpower him and escape. But no, he was far too smart for that. He'd just shoot me up with more ketamine and then change me. That's the last thing I wanted. My body was obviously doing a poor job of handling all the drugs.

I scooted in my seat, as much as my bindings would allow. I felt a tube resting against my right leg, taped down in four spots. Looking at my feet, I saw the tiny plastic tubing sticking out of my pant leg, snaking back behind the chair. I turned my head to the side and saw the corner of a catheter bag tied up to the back of the dentist chair.

That bastard! After Robert doped me up, he undressed me and inserted a catheter into my bladder. No need for regular bathroom breaks now. He was probably going to feed me an all liquid diet too. The thought of him having touched my naked body made my stomach heave. This time

I had to swallow back the vomit threatening to erupt. An acidic taste burned the back of my throat.

Robert would return soon. I had to come up with a plan. Something more concrete than get the hell out of here. Wishing my situation away wouldn't work. It never had before. Earlier Robert expressed concern about me yelling. Maybe I was being held captive in a small bedroom of a house. People were probably nearby, neighbors or pedestrian traffic. Yet, I had to remind myself this wasn't a TV show. I couldn't count on being saved at the last second. I wasn't a damsel in distress and the hero wouldn't ride to my rescue. If I planned on getting out of this room alive, I had to rely on myself. To do that I had to keep my emotions in check and distance myself from the situation. Treat Robert White like any other perp. Analyze him, figure out how to play him, and get inside his head.

What did I know about Robert? He was a pedophile. He liked little girls' ages seven to puberty. He wasn't interested in intimate adult relationships. However, he fixated on me and continued to love me even though I'd aged. Robert refused to lose something he felt belonged to him. That need trumped the age issue. This fit the criteria for a narcissistic personality. A narcissist is characterized by the need to always be right, which meant everyone else is wrong. They're notorious liars and rarely acknowledge their mistakes. Narcissists also require excessive admiration, have a sense of entitlement, and lack empathy. Robert oozed those qualities.

I also added stalking to the list. Working on previous cases, I'd learned stalkers were jealous, manipulative, needed to control others, and often switched between rage and love quickly. Those characteristics also fit Robert like a glove.

How could this information help me? I'd use it during our next conversation. Robert still professed to love me. Or at least the memory of who I used to be. He also wanted to take care of me. I had to find out how strong those needs were and use them to my advantage.

While I worked on my game plan, I realized the rope binding my left wrist wasn't as tight as before. I couldn't lift it from the padding earlier. Now I had a little give. I painstakingly worked at inching the rope forward closer to the end of the armrest where my palm was. A few times it moved backwards, and I had to start all over again. I was glad for the new distraction though. I barely noticed the stinging in my eye as the sweat breaking out on my brow rolled down my face.

Once the rope was stretched to its limit, I used my index and middle fingers to grip a stray piece of rope that had unraveled from the braiding. Just the tiniest of strands, but it was the only thing I could reach. I was able to pull it hard enough to make the rope move forward. This enabled me to grab more stray strands, and again I moved the rope closer. I felt the knot. My heart skipped a beat. Mistake number one, Robert. The knot should have been tied out of reach. I got more fingers around it, working as fast as I could to loosen it, but it was stubborn. Almost as stubborn as me refusing to admit the sheer impossibility of untying a knot one handed.

In front of me, the fabric slightly rustled as if a door opened, causing air to rush inside the room.

# CHAPTER 30

Robert stepped through the slit in the drapery. Hopefully, he wouldn't notice the rope on my wrist had moved. I immediately spoke so his attention would be drawn to my mouth. Straining to hear the words through my gag, Robert impatiently crossed the room and yanked out the cloth. It fell across my sternum, resting like a loose necklace.

"Thank you for coming back, Robert." I practically choked on the words. I almost added *I missed you,* but didn't want to seem disingenuous. I swear the man could smell insincerity. That was how I became such an accomplished liar. Years of practice.

"What time is it?" I asked.

"Does it really matter? You're not leaving, and it's not like Detective Jessup will ever find you. I smashed your cell phone. There's no way he can trace your location."

Robert thought he'd deflected my question, but I could tell it was a new day by his change of clothes. It must be Saturday, probably sometime in the morning since the scent of his soap was strong. I couldn't smell cigarette smoke. I wondered if he still battled quitting. Robert refused to see himself as weak-minded. Being hooked on nicotine had always infuriated him. All through my childhood, he'd "quit" smoking on a regular basis.

"Sorry I had to inject you with ketamine," Robert continued, the pendulum of his mood now having swung again. "It was for your own good. My temper has a mind of its own sometimes."

"I'm sorry for the way I behaved earlier. I promise it won't happen again. Is that for me?" I nodded at the glass in his hand. "I'm very thirsty? Hungry too."

"It's a little protein shake I whipped up." A mischievous twinkle glimmered in his eye. "Have to keep your strength up."

I thanked him right before he put the straw to my lips, then greedily sucked down the brownish liquid. Once the flavor registered on my taste buds, I coughed, almost causing the shake to shoot out my mouth. It was a concoction of banana and chocolate, though mostly banana. He was testing me. Robert knew I detested the yellow fruit. I couldn't stand its smell, consistency, and especially taste.

"Is there a problem with your drink?"

"No. Sorry. I must have swallowed wrong. May I have some more?" Even though I despised the taste, I knew I had to get something into my stomach. I sucked down half the liquid before taking another breath. In college, I used to do the same thing with beer. I hated the taste, but who could pass up quarter beer night at Stu's. I found if you swallowed it as quickly as possible, half the drink was empty before you actually tasted it.

"You seem to have had a real change in attitude. I knew a little reeducation would help whip you back into shape."

"I've been awake for awhile now, and have had some time to think about your plan for our future. I have to admit, it will be difficult leaving my life behind, leaving my friends. But you were right. It would be nice to have a man around again. Someone I'm comfortable with, someone who knows the real me." I hoped he bought my act. It was literally the performance of a lifetime. "Before I can close the door on my career though, I have to solve this last case. Kimberly's case. Wrap up the details for my own sake. Once I know what happened, I'll be able to start a new chapter in my life. In *our* life. Do you mind talking to me about Kimberly for a few minutes?"

Robert's version of events would be a skewed version of the truth, but I still wanted to hear what he had to say. The wheels turning in his head showed all over his face. He was trying to decide if I was being straightforward. I knew he desperately wanted to believe me. A man doesn't stalk a woman for over two decades and not fantasize about her returning his affections.

Robert abruptly turned, put the cup on the table, and left the room. Damn, I pushed it too far. My acting was spot on. It must have been something I said. Either he didn't want to talk about Kimberly, or he didn't believe I would willingly leave Florida with him.

Again the faint rustle of the drapery announced Robert's return. He carried a brown metal chair which he unfolded near the table. Before he sat, Robert brought me the protein shake so I could finish it. I was right about the all-liquid diet. Too bad it wasn't a Coke.

"You'd like to talk about Kimberly?" Robert asked.

"Yes, when you—"

"Not so fast." Robert wagged his finger as he cut me off mid-sentence. "You want something from me, what do I get in return?"

Why was I not surprised? This was how life with Robert worked. His mantra—you do something for me, I do something for you.

"What would you like?" I asked tentatively. Although, I figured I was safe physically. He'd already expressed his disgust at the thought of having sex with me. Still, I didn't relish the thought of giving him anything he wanted.

"Don't look scared, Katie. It's painless, and more for you than me. After I answer your question, you can delight us with a favorite childhood memory. I really think this will help you remember the good times we shared."

*Yeah right, more for me than him.* Robert wanted his ego stroked. Fine. I could play his game. "Yeah, okay. When you first saw Kimberly riding her bike around the neighborhood, did you plan on grooming her because she was a reminder of me?"

"Yes."

I shot him a hard look. Robert knew if he expected me to talk, he had to give me more than a one-word answer.

"Just kidding," he said and chuckled. He really was enjoying himself. "When I saw Kimberly ride by my window, I thought divine intervention brought her to me. That I'd get a second chance to make up for all the mistakes I'd made with you. The whole falling down thing while I raked leaves—genius wasn't it? It instantly put her at ease, thinking I was a doddering old man. But really, Kimberly's family life made it all too easy. Her mom was a drunk, her dad dead. Kimberly had no one in her life to turn to for support. Until I came along.

"After the hitting incident, Kimberly retreated further away from her mother. Once school let out for the summer, Kimberly isolated herself even more. She'd been cleaning my house for quite some time, trying to earn extra cash. Often, I would invite her over to watch a movie or have dinner. Kimberly didn't care, as long as she wasn't home. You see, Kimberly came willingly. Your turn, Katie."

I felt like I was starring in the movie *The Silence of the Lambs*. I kept expecting to hear Robert say, "Quid pro quo, Katie," adding that awful lilt to his voice. A shiver ran down my spine as I realized how much Robert had grown to resemble a fitter Hannibal Lecter. They both had the same slicked back, gray colored hair.

Trying to shake the coldness settling over me, I remembered how Robert always liked a grateful girl. He couldn't get enough praise over something he'd given or some small kindness he showed. I racked my brain, trying to think of an example. One he would really enjoy, but most importantly, one to keep him talking.

"Do you remember the first time we went to Jamaica?" I asked. When you think of Jamaica, you think of romance. A husband taking his new bride on a honeymoon getaway. It always floored me to think my mother would allow her adolescent daughter to travel abroad without her supervision. Again, one of the many red flags ignored.

"We shared a wonderful trip," Robert boasted. "I really enjoyed showing you the island." He sat there looking extremely relaxed, left elbow propped on top of the card table, head rested against a closed fist.

"We left two weeks before I started sixth grade. It was August, and the island had abnormally high temperatures that summer. I remember walking off the plane straight into a hot wall of air so thick I could barely catch my breath. You laughed, telling me we weren't in Illinois anymore. You said I would get used to it, but I never quite did. This was a time when no one wore sunscreen. Developing skin cancer didn't concern us. The first day I stayed out in the sun too long and got a burn so severe, even the natives offered pitying glances when I hobbled by.

"That night I didn't sleep because I literally couldn't lie down. I sat up dozing in nothing but my underwear. I couldn't stand for the clothing to touch my skin. The burn spray didn't help, nothing relieved my suffering. You went out and talked to some of the island women asking for suggestions.

"Do you remember, Robert? You came back to the hotel with an aloe vera plant, grabbed a knife, and cut one of the stalks in half. This sticky, clear liquid oozed from the chopped plant. I felt squeamish at first. I didn't believe anything could help, but you were so patient and reassuring. I still remember the instant you laid the gooey stalk on my shoulder, how the little circular patch of skin found instant relief. I begged you to rub it all over my body and at the end, we were both in stitches. I was quite a sight. A sticky mess from head to toe. You were my hero that day, my hero for stopping the pain."

Robert's face lit up. He was hooked. With my next story, I would reel him in. Of course this whole last tale I spun was mostly fiction. When I couldn't sleep from the pain and began to cry, Robert told me to shut up, or he'd teach me about real pain. He only picked up the aloe vera plant so I'd heal faster. He said I was ruining his vacation. After Robert put the first dab of aloe on my skin, he said if I wanted more, I had to describe how I'd repay the favor. Burnt from my hairline to the soles of my feet, this back and forth went on for what seemed like an eternity before I completely found relief.

My turn for a question. "When was the first time you made an advance towards Kimberly?"

"Jeal-ous?" Robert drew the two syllables out, trying to taunt me. When I didn't answer, he continued. "Kimberly and I spent almost a year getting to know each other, spending time together. I wanted to take our budding relationship slow. She acted a little skittish, a little untrusting when it came to adults. Understandable. She had it rough with a mom who guzzled every penny she earned. I offered Kimberly a little spending money, but she was too proud. As I said before, I offered her a job cleaning my house. She jumped at the chance. It was just the excuse she needed to spend more time with me.

"When Kimberly's mother started dating that scum Davidson, Kimberly gravitated even closer to me. One afternoon an opportunity presented itself. Kimberly was on her knees scrubbing my bathroom floor when she got a kink in her neck. Being the gentleman I am, I told her I would rub some Icy Hot on it, help relax the muscle. She felt funny about it at first, but I knew she liked it. Afterwards, I found plenty of excuses to put my hands on her. You know, get her used to my touch. At some point, I cupped her breast. It was small but firm, the nipple erect. It felt like yours did at that age. For a brief moment, I had you back."

Robert smiled, a far off dreamy look on his face. An instant later it disappeared, replaced with pursed lips, a narrowing of the eyes.

"Up to that point, the constraint I'd shown amazed even me, but Kimberly got extremely upset. Maybe I pushed too hard, too fast?" Briefly stopping to think about what he'd said, Robert shook his head, changing his mind.

"No. She was probably embarrassed because she liked it so much. She told me it was over, that she didn't want to clean my house anymore. I paid her a visit a couple of days later, apologized, and gave her a digital camera. I explained it all away, saying the touches were purely accidental. It gave her an excuse to come back. And confirmed my suspicions. She wanted me, but was too afraid to admit it.

"The next time Kimberly got all huffy, I gave her a cell phone. This progressed for a while until right before school started this fall. I told Kimberly that by accepting all of my presents and coming back every time, it made her look like she wanted it. If she decided to tell, no one would believe her. After all, I was a feeble old man, and she was the daughter of an alcoholic. A poor girl, trying to extort money and expensive gifts from a man who had shown her nothing but kindness.

"Kimberly started spending less time with me once she went back to school. So I followed her. I was shocked to see her hanging around with all these . . . these weirdos. I won't be cast aside. Who the hell does she think she is, telling me it's over? It's not over until I say it's over. You know what that little bitch did?" He abruptly stood, knocking the chair over onto the carpet.

"Monday evening she came over demanding her last check. Told me I'm some sick pervert, and she wanted nothing to do with me. That's what she thinks? Sick pervert? I showed her pervert. I pushed her to the ground. She was taken off guard, staring up at me with this stupid surprised look on her face. What the hell did she expect, the tease." As Robert relived this memory, the rage in him deepened. I began racking my brain, trying to figure out how I could redirect his anger.

"I pulled off her pants, and she really started to struggle. It was kind of fun watching her futile attempts to break free. Sure she scratched me, but I barely noticed. Once her panties were off, I stuck my fingers inside her, but they were blocked by a tampon. I was absolutely disgusted. She was ruined."

Robert paced like an angry caged leopard. The hardness in his eyes caused me to try and recede farther back into the chair, making myself a smaller target.

"Kimberly had the gall to laugh at me. Can you believe it? I realized I'd waited too long. She was no longer a child. She was no good to me anymore. So I stopped her laughing. Permanently."

# CHAPTER 31

"Robert. Robert! Look at me." I was scared and breathless. "Kimberly didn't deserve you. She wasn't good enough for you. Think about it. If you were with her now, we wouldn't have had this chance to be reunited."

Taking a deep breath, Robert brightened. "You're right, Katie. It all worked out for the best." Just like that, his switch flipped. "Now tell me a story, my dear."

Robert turned to pick up the fallen chair. I took my own deep breath. That was too close.

"Hmm," I said stalling, at a loss for a second narrative. "I'd have to say when I think back at all the wonderful gifts you've surprised me with over the years, my favorite was the bedroom furniture."

"Really? Furniture? Being such a girly girl, I thought the clothes would have brought you more enjoyment. Or even the Polaroid camera." The clothes. I'd forgotten how Robert loved to dress me up in the frilliest little dresses. Some masochistic pedophile designer must have manufactured those treasures. Fine if you're six, not twelve.

"No. Definitely the furniture," I answered a little courser than I'd intended. "I remember the day you told me you had a surprise for me. I was rather young, maybe around eight. You blindfolded me and led me back to the spare bedroom. I was a little scared. Didn't know what to expect. When I opened my eyes, I was amazed at the sight before me. My own beautifully decorated bedroom.

"An eggshell white bed stood against the far wall, a yellow canopy covering it. An intricate swirling design crafted from yellow daffodils adorned the headboard. A plump, yellow comforter covered the bed. It was decorated with the tiniest white flowers. Next to the bed sat a nightstand holding a matching yellow lamp. The mirrored dresser already had all my clothes tucked away inside. My favorite piece was the desk. Remember how I always wanted to be a teacher? I would sit there for hours grading the papers my stuffed animals had worked on during the day. Whenever you couldn't find me, invariably I would be in my room. I felt like a princess surrounded by such beauty. I had never owned anything that precious before."

It was true. That room had always been my escape from reality. Almost magical. Sitting there, I could pretend I was normal, that I wasn't living through my own nightly hell. Unfortunately, I couldn't conjure a magic bubble to protect me from the evil wizard.

"May I ask one last question?"

Robert nodded.

"What made you decide to dump Kimberly's body behind the Lynch's old house?"

"You don't know? Well no, I guess you wouldn't. Everett Lynch and I were old Navy buddies. When we served together, he would tell me stories about his childhood in Tampa. After you and I moved down here, I looked him up. We used to play cards and drink beer over at his house. Until he had a heart attack. Probably couldn't handle life without the old battle axe. Anyway, I knew Everett's place was pretty isolated, but I had no idea about the new neighbors. Just my luck, a damn dog lover moved in next door. I planned on burying Kimberly back in the wooded area behind Lynch's house, but those mutts went crazy. With all the commotion, I worried I'd be discovered, so I left her. I covered her up though. Seemed like the only respectful thing to do."

"Thank you, Robert. Now I think I can finally put all of this all behind me." I pasted on my most innocent smile. "Haven't I been a good girl? Don't you think I deserve some of your homemade chocolate chip waffles? You know how they were always my favorite."

Obviously deciding against the all liquid diet, he said he would go and see what he could rustle up in the kitchen. *That should keep him busy for awhile.* The kitchen, another clue to my whereabouts. Too bad he hadn't stashed me away in some warehouse. He'd be gone longer. Guess I'd have to work faster.

Once Robert left, I worked on maneuvering my fingers to loosen the knot on my right wrist. I tried to concentrate solely on the task at hand, but couldn't help but think about everything I'd heard. It was like one of those horrible late night movies where the bad guy thinks there's no way the hostage will get free, so he reveals all the details of his crime. I planned on staying close to the script by getting out of here as quickly as possible.

Robert was textbook when it came to grooming Kimberly. Child predators start slowly by hugging and tickling, then become more intrusive by trying to kiss or wrestle. They often invade the child's privacy while showering, dressing, or using the bathroom. The adult is always testing the boundaries of the relationship seeing what they can get away with by pushing the limits. When a pedophile violates the physical boundaries like "accidentally" touching the child through her clothes, they're doing it to see what kind of reaction they receive. If the child allows the predator to get away with this, it's an invitation for additional bad behavior.

Once Kimberly had forgiven Robert for such transgressions, she was trapped. At least in her own mind. She knew no one would believe Robert's advances were unwanted because she'd accepted gifts as apologies. After all, she kept going back. She didn't realize adults would have understood. Kimberly was only thirteen, too young to recognize what the gifts she'd received really meant.

I understood the guilt of going back. Growing up, I asked myself plenty of times, *why didn't I just refuse to go to Robert's house?* When I was finally old enough to understand I could make the abuse stop, I was in too deep. Too fully indoctrinated. The level of shame and guilt were like bricks in a wall layered one on top of the other. Eventually, I was surrounded. The wall was too high to see over, much less scale. Another brick was added every time I heard mom say, "Thank goodness for Robert. If it weren't for him, I don't know what we would have eaten tonight," or "That man's an angel. Make sure you thank him for those new school clothes."

Children have no perspective. Tell them their source of food depends on the charity of one person, and they take it to heart. A child's whole life revolves around their household unit. They can't see beyond their four walls. If mom doesn't have enough money to buy school clothes what the child worries about is being teased because last year's jeans have turned into high waters. So what's worse—bearing private humiliation or public embarrassment? Guess I chose the private hell.

Was it my imagination or had the rope inside the knot moved? *Dammit!* I felt the time ticking away. I knew any minute Robert would return with breakfast. I wanted to holler in frustration. I could feel my control slipping. Screams began reverberating off the inside of my head, begging to find their way out. But the gag wasn't in my mouth. If Robert heard me, he'd come running in and shoot me up with more ketamine. I had to remain quiet, but I had to let loose. I began thrashing wildly, as much as my ropes would allow.

A ripping noise. Immediately, I froze. I yanked up hard with my forearms, and this time my right arm raised a fraction of an inch higher. When I moved the ropes forward, I must have inadvertently found a sharp piece of metal sticking out underneath the right arm pad. I vigorously pumped my right forearm up and down trying to finish sawing the rope in half. Adrenaline surged through my body. I felt like I was playing a perverse game of Whack-A-Mole where the stakes of losing could be my life. Finally with a snap, the rope split. A last shake of my arm, and the binding fell to the ground.

I almost whooped with excitement. *Hurry! Hurry! Hurry!* The words circled around in my brain like an out of control carousel. I knew if Robert found me with one arm untied, the next time he bound me, I wouldn't get free. All of the hard work and advances I'd made during our conversation would be undone.

After I freed my left wrist, I bent over working on the knots tied around my ankles. I could almost feel Robert's hand gripping the door knob, tightening as he turned his wrist to open the door. The ropes holding my ankles fell to the floor.

I stood up quickly having forgotten about the catheter. I pulled forward too fast, and the tape ripped from my leg. The catheter came out, and I stifled a cry of pain. The tube slid out from inside my pant leg falling into a heap on the carpet.

The faintest movement of fabric. I didn't know if I heard or saw it first. Was it the whisper of wind when the door opened or the sight of the fabric rippling that marked Robert's return? I sprinted to the left of where he would enter the room. The plush carpet absorbed the sound of my footfalls. I could see a man's outline straining against the fabric. It looked as if Robert carried something. Hands full, he tried to move the heavy drapery aside with a tray. This was my chance.

Robert's arm cleared the fabric, and I swiveled my body towards him, grabbing his other arm still covered by the drapery. I grabbed hold of him and the material tightly. With all my strength, I swung him around and connected my foot to his kneecap. I heard a faint pop before I heard a yowl of surprise, then rage.

Robert fell back into the table, causing it and him to crash to the floor. The tray he held went flying, sending chocolate chip Eggos into the air. I felt an almost maniacal glee watching the imitation breakfast take flight. I knew my grip on reality was slipping, so I opened the mental box containing all the feelings I'd tried so hard to cage. All the fury, hatred, loathing, rage. In that moment, I knew I could hurt him as much as he'd hurt me. I was no longer a woman of the law. I was a renegade ready to exact revenge for the six years of hell I'd endured.

Robert rolled back and forth on the ground gripping his injured knee. I jumped slightly in the air and with all my weight slammed down with my right knee. Pain shot through my kneecap when it collided with the floorboard instead of Robert's stomach.

Crack! A fist hit my left side, like the full force of a sledgehammer pounding into my ribs. I couldn't catch my breath. I couldn't protect myself. Robert easily pushed me over onto my back. I could offer no defense. My hands were splayed palms up high over my head. Crawling on top of my midsection, Robert rested his entire weight on my hips. Pain shot through my battered ribs. He brought his face lower. I could smell the peppermint on his breath.

"You wanted to know how Kimberly died? Let me show you."

Robert grabbed my throat with both hands. He slowly tightened them, a vice like grip. I could no longer even gasp for a breath.

In the far off distance, I heard shouts. "Police. Open up!" The cavalry had finally arrived, but I realized the damsel would be dead before they could save her.

I fought against my own instinct to panic. I knew the effort to claw at Robert's hands was futile. Still, I couldn't stop myself. As I moved my hands forward to try and break Robert's grip, my right pinkie finger brushed up against something sharp on the floor. The needle of the shot. It must have fallen from the table during the scuffle. I tried to fight off the impending darkness threatening to swallow me, but I hadn't the strength anymore.

A loud crash nearby caught Robert's attention. He eased his grip while turning to look behind him. The darkness retreated. I used the diversion to grab the syringe. Robert felt my weight shift beneath him, forcing his attention back to me. But it was too late. Robert's eyes grew wide when he saw the syringe arcing towards his face. I shoved the needle dead center into his eye. When I felt resistance, I pushed harder, depressing the plunger. A few seconds later Robert's dead body slumped to the carpet.

I lay on my back coughing, trying to pull breath into my body. I heard SWAT enter the room and someone shouted, "Clear." The thud of footsteps drew near. Through tear soaked eyes, I saw Patrick's face stare down at me. *Man, I loved that smile.*

"You're ruining my moment, Kate. I'm supposed to be the hero here."

I tried to raise my head and ask him how he found me, but he gently pushed my forehead down. "Shhh, don't try to talk. We're going to get you to the hospital. Do you want me to ride along?"

I nodded as best I could.

My throat burned like fire. I found it difficult to catch my breath. I didn't know if it was from the attempted strangulation or if a broken rib had punctured my lung. But none of that mattered, really. I was alive. And Robert was dead.

# CHAPTER 32

In the ambulance, Patrick sat near my head while an EMT continued monitoring my vitals. Patrick gently swept the hair back from my forehead. Thick stubble had sprouted in patches along his jaw line. If I could talk, I would have teased him about not being able to grow a beard properly.

Patrick looked like he hadn't slept in days. It made me wonder how long I'd been held captive. He still wore the same clothes from the last time I saw him. Now they were rumpled and dirty. A fact I'm sure drove him crazy. Even as terrible as Patrick looked, it seemed he might need to be tethered to the ground to keep him from floating away. His happiness was that evident.

"Kate, I know you're going to hate to hear this, but you have that reporter, Carlos Diaz, to thank for finding you. When you didn't show up back at the precinct, I got worried. I knew something was up when you didn't answer your cell. In our two years together, you've never ignored my calls. When you didn't update Kray, the battle cry went out. Everyone went into full action mode to find you.

"What the hell were you thinking meeting with Jason Reeves alone? No, no, don't try to talk. You'll take your ass chewing and like it. Everyone worked through the night interrogating Reeves and Davidson. Eventually, we figured out neither of them had anything to do with your disappearance. I went to your house. Finally found a use for that spare key you gave me. I saw no sign of a struggle, but in your bedroom I found a picture of you as a kid with Jack Monroe. I was confused until I read your last journal entry."

I looked away, not wanting to see the disgust in Patrick's eyes. He gently touched my chin, turning my head towards him until our eyes met.

"Don't you dare, Kate. You have nothing to be embarrassed about. You were just a kid. I'm sorry for what you had to endure. I really am. I wish you'd told me, but I understand why you didn't. Though I think you're a better cop for having lived through it. You have a rough exterior, but inside is a heart of gold. Not many people get to see that side of you, Kate. I'm glad I'm one of the lucky few."

The water works started again as I realized Patrick had discovered my secret and wasn't repulsed. He wasn't judgmental. Most of all he didn't look at me with pity in his eyes.

Gently, he wiped the tears away with the crook of his finger. "So . . . Jack Monroe was really Robert White. Well, we descended upon his place like the four horseman of the apocalypse. Only we found it empty. I was at my wits end. We had nothing to go on. I went back to the precinct and sat outside at the plaza, trying to clear my head.

"That's when Carlos Diaz showed up. He made a wise ass remark saying you probably hadn't made it into work because of exhaustion from a late night rendezvous. Poor guy. I totally laid into him. Fired so many questions at him, he could barely get a word out. Guess he'd followed your car after you left The Rusty Bolt. Said you tried to lose him on the way to University Mall but couldn't. When I finally got him to shut up about his superb tracking abilities and the exclusive you owed him, he told me he saw you hanging out by your car. A man came up. You turned around and embraced him. Then the guy helped you into his vehicle. Diaz followed you to a house. The house we found you in. He figured you were having a late night tryst so he split. Carlos Diaz led us right here, Kate. Guess you're going to have to give him that exclusive after all."

# WEDNESDAY

## CHAPTER 33

"That's a very harrowing tale, Kate."

I could hear the awe in Dr. Grace's voice as I sat across from her retelling last week's events.

"How are you feeling now?" she asked.

"Two of my ribs are fractured, one broken. At least my lung wasn't punctured." I shrugged and smiled. "I'll heal."

"I didn't mean physically. How are you feeling emotionally?"

I sat for a moment, thinking back on my reunion with Robert. When I explained to Patrick that Robert had murdered Kimberly, Patrick razzed me about the lengths I would go to, to catch a killer. I was just happy he'd forgiven me for all the lies I'd told—Kimberly's resemblance, Jason's request to secretly meet, Jack Monroe and Robert White being the same person. But Patrick's always had my back. This time was no different. Once he read my journal entry and connected the dots, Patrick hid the evidence of my past sexual abuse and the fact I knew the killer. My badge was still intact.

What of Jason Reeves? Patrick told me the little punk had chickened out on our meeting the night I was kidnapped. He pulled a no-show at the mall. Kind of like the night Kimberly was murdered. Jason was supposed to pick her up but changed his mind at the last minute. If he'd had some balls, maybe she'd still be alive today.

I felt sorry for Cheryl Callahan. For what she'd gone through, outliving her entire family. But I was hopeful she could find the strength to heal. Cheryl had voluntarily committed herself to an inpatient rehab center. I planned to visit her on family day and keep tabs once she left. It was the least I could do. I finally got my life back. I wanted to help Cheryl fight for hers.

"Alive," I finally responded to Dr. Grace's question. "For the first time in my life, I feel alive. For years, maybe since the first time I was abused, I felt numb. Dead inside. I held tight to that numbness, afraid of what I'd feel if it ever fell away. Facing death made me realize I want to live again, not just get by. Now that Robert's dead, I can finally shut the door to my past, work on becoming a whole person."

"I'm happy to hear it, Kate. How do you feel about being the one who killed Robert?"

"I know I should feel some sadness at taking a human life, but I don't. Robert was evil and didn't deserve to live. He planned on keeping me captive and kidnapping and abusing a new little girl. I couldn't let another child live through the same nightmare. I'm happy he's gone, gone forever, and I won't apologize for it."

"I'm not asking you to. You've come a long way. I think you'll be fine now."

"I really want to thank you, Dr. Grace. Thank you for everything you've done for me." Holding my side, I slowly rose from the chair.

"Looks to me like you've done it all yourself."

"No. You were there for me when it counted. Always ready with a kind word, an open mind. You listened and didn't judge. It means a lot." I walked towards her desk and laid down my business card. "Call me anytime. Day or night. If you ever need me, I'll be there for you."

"Thank you, Kate. If you need to talk again, I'm always here."

"Thanks, Doc." I turned towards the door. "But I think I'll take it from here." A silly grin spread across my face as I heard the clicking noise from my Manolo Blahnik boots crossing the tile floor. I no longer had to wait for a special occasion. From now on, every day was special.

# THE END

© Black Rose Writing

CPSIA information can be obtained at www.ICGtesting.com
Printed in the USA
BVOW030957120713

325798BV00002B/38/P